the

RULES

UPHELD

by

NO ONE

the

RULES

UPHELD

by

NO ONE

AMIE McNEE

Copyright © 2021 Amie McNee

Published by Amie McNee

www.amiemcnee.com

The moral right of the author has been asserted.

For quantity sales or media enquiries, please contact the publisher at the website address above.

Cataloguing-in-Publication entry is available from the National Library of Australia.

ISBN: 978-0-6451905-0-2 (paperback)

978-0-6451905-1-9 (ebook)

978-0-6451905-2-6 (audiobook)

Book cover design – Lena Yang

This book is a work of fiction. Names, characters, places, and incidents either are products of the author's imagination or are used fictitiously. Any resemblance to actual persons, living or dead, events, or locales is entirely coincidental.

Content warning: Sexual assault

This book is dedicated to the creative community who held me throughout my journey writing this book.

Thank you for seeing me.

PART I

CHAPTER ONE

"It feels like I've pissed myself!" moaned Livia.

"Don't speak like that!" The younger sister shouldn't have to reprimand the elder as often as I did, but I couldn't really blame her for the outburst. I could feel drops of sweat between my legs. Why must we sweat — and there of all places? It was unGodly.

"We will need to cut your hair before you go, Elisabeth. It's far too long." Agnes, my even elder sister, was walking just in front of me.

"Maybe they'll shave it for you when you get there," suggested Livia.

I clutched my long, red waves. No. My hair was staying. I was just weeks away from my removal to a Nunnery, Lacock Abbey. Removal was not quite the right word. I had chosen to go. It suited Mother and Father financially and it suited me, spiritually. I was not destined for marriage like Agnes or Livia. I was for God. It had always been the plan. Mother and Father's plan. My plan and God's plan.

There was an excited hubbub when we reached St Peter's. It

was a modest church in Henley, a half hours carriage ride from home. It had dark stone walls and big stained-glass windows. The only light that entered St Peter's was coloured. I felt a pain as I realised that, come autumn, I would farewell the windows painted bright red, purple, green and gold, the blue of the Virgin's cloak.

There was a commotion around the entrance.

"Go in quickly, Elisa," my mother snapped, putting a firm hand at my back and pushing me towards the large arched doors. But there was no missing the cause of the excitement. I saw Joan — Mistress Wright — immediately. She stood to the right of the door. She wore a white sheet. Just a white sheet. She held it as high as she could, but the material was thin and I could see her bosom.

"Will you forgive me, Lady Knolly?" Joan choked a little as she spoke to my mother but Mama did not reply.

"Get in the Church, Elisa!" She hissed, shoving me in the back.

"Elisabeth?" Joan addressed me by my first name; it was not appropriate. I was the daughter of Lord Knolly, who was personal friend of King Henry. But I stopped, resisting my mother's shoves. This woman needed help. She reached for me. I took her hand. It was shaking. "Forgive me, Elisa."

"Someone stop this!" My mother screeched, snatching at me, grasping my shoulders and pushing me inside.

"What has she done?" I craned my neck to look back at the desperate face. "Where are her clothes?"

"Why did you take her hand?"

"She was asking for forgiveness!"

"You will wash." Mother splashed both my hands in the font by the door, cleansing me from Joan's apparently contagious sins. "She's a Jade." Mama whispered.

I knew what that word meant. My father petted my mother

on the back as we took our seats in the pews. I watched her closely as she regathered herself, her pursed lips and high chin returning to position. My sisters joined us a moment later. They were whispering.

"What has Joan done?" I asked them.

"Do not tell her, Livia." Agnes hissed.

"Mother called her a Jade." I was almost certain someone had made a mistake: Joan and John Wright were a Godly couple. But Livia was nodding.

I shrank back into my dress, my ribs finally unsticking from the front of my corset as I hunched my shoulders in.

"It is worse than this," Livia whispered.

"Worse?"

"The smithy found her with ... three different men ..." my heart sped up "... at the same time."

"No!"

She was speaking out the side of her mouth and the congregation were noisy and unsettled. I had heard wrong.

"Livia!" My mother and Agnes chided her simultaneously: both were red in the face, from embarrassment or anger I could not tell.

I smelt the deep woody incense and heard the gentle swinging of the thurible. Father Nicholas, looking sterner than normal, walked up beside us and took his place at the front. The fragrant air made it hard to inhale. I could hardly get one breath out in time to start the next. I stared up at the dark, vaulted roof and opened myself to the rhythm of the Latin. I let the Lord's words wash over me: they repelled bad thoughts. But the picture of Joan in her bedclothes with three other men was burnt into my mind.

To my left I could see my little brother Edmund clambering over my parents' feet to get to me. He squeezed himself in between Livia and me, slipping a small and sweaty hand into my own. It was not a pleasant feeling but I tolerated it. He reminded me of being young, innocent. When I could not have conceived the demonic actions my sisters had related to me, when nothing like that could distract me from God.

"Elisa!" He hissed. I went to reprimand him, but he was bent on talking. "Samuel told me that when they found Joan she was sitting in front of the fire, knitting —" I squeezed his hand, begging him to stop, shaking my head desperately "— in just an apron!"

There was a tittering of prayers and exclamations from around us.

"Do not speak like that, Eddie!" I hissed. I looked around for Samuel, his tutor, but he would be at the back of the Church. Why in God's name would he have told him that? The Priest spoke louder. His brow furrowed further.

This would be my life soon. Matins, Lauds, Prime, Terce, Sext, None. I would be spending my life swimming in biblical texts. It was so hot in here. Perhaps it would be cooler in the Nunnery. I wondered whether Joan was still outside or if she had been allowed to come within to hear the sermon. It would be so hot out there. So exposed on the street. People would be staring. I began praying. Asking for forgiveness, begging for the thoughts of Joan to be wiped from my mind. But three men? At once? What did they all even do?

Please, Jesus. Please. I do not want to tarnish my mind with such sinful thoughts.

"Put to death your earthly nature: sexual immorality, impurity, lust, evil desires and greed. Because of these things the wrath of God is coming." Father Nicholas's voice echoed loudly. I crossed my legs.

The wrath of God is coming. The wrath of God. I thought of Joan's face. She was so sad, so desperate to be forgiven, but then I thought of her sins. Perhaps she had a demon within

her. The priest should consider that. It might not be her fault
— maybe a snake or a beast or Satan himself had forced her do
the unspeakable things.

I turned to look at Mama. Her eyes were shut and she was
shaking her head. She was disgusted by it all. Disgusted. Just
like I was. But if I was so disgusted by it then why was I
dwelling upon it so? Half my mind was on the Mass but the
other half was filling with questions. Why would she do that?
Had John been one of the men? Did Joan like it? Who were the
other men? Why weren't the men in trouble? Then the question
of how started taking over. From my understanding of ...
marital relations, which admittedly was rather limited, that
shouldn't be possible? Three men? One lady?

I sat Eddie on my lap, bouncing him lightly on my knee.

Joan had once helped Eddie after he had taken a tumble, a
few years ago now. Perhaps in my fifteenth year, when Eddie
was only five or six. He had fallen badly, running away from his
tutor. He had tripped down the road from Church. Joan saw
what had happened before I did. She was so gentle with him.
She had wiped away his tears, hugged him, brushed off the
dirt. There was no brushing off her dirt now.

Communion came. Thank God. Thank God. Perhaps after
eating the body of Christ the thoughts of Joan would go away.
Not that it was the body of Christ any more. I reminded
myself. Merely a symbol, so says the King. I took the symbolic
wafer from the Priest, he looked down at me sternly. He knew
what I was thinking. For the rest of the sermon I focussed on
my favourite passage. It was from Isaiah. 'Though your sins are
like scarlet, they will be as white as snow; though they are red
as crimson, they shall be like wool.' Perhaps someone should
remind Joan of this passage. Should I remind her?

. . .

After the sermon, Father Nicholas approached my father and mother. This was nothing out of the ordinary. I stood behind them quietly, holding tightly onto my brother's squirming hand, incase he escaped and hid up in the bell tower for the third time this month. There was a lot of shaking of heads, and disappointed mumbling. I saw the priest point upwards. He was indicating a gargoyle on top of one of the stone columns. I'd seen her before. It was a carving of a woman, glowing in red light, with wild hair that looked not unlike mine before it had been tamed by my maid. She was naked and tugging violently at her breast, a snake writhed between her legs.

"Woman's desire is insatiable: put it out, it bursts into flame, give it plenty and it is again in need." Nicholas shook his head, his dark eyes not moving from the base depiction of woman. It was an unbecoming speech in front of my mother, a woman of considerable stature and importance in England, but Mama merely nodded.

The Priest's eyes swivelled sideways to look at me. "Happy virgins who know not torment. It is a good thing, Lady Elisabeth, that you are soon to enter the safety of the Nunnery. Protected from yourself."

I bowed my head reverently. "What will happen to Mistress Wright?" I asked quietly.

"Despair is the only cure for lust, my lady, so we shall pray that a darkness settles upon her and cleans away her sins."

I nodded.

Mother hurried me past Joan on the way out, but I still saw her. Her long hair sat lank against her chest. She was crying and I could smell her sweat.

Our carriage had been sent for. No one felt like walking home again. Everyone was quiet but I could tell that Livia had a hundred things to say.

"You will not think about Mistress Wright again," Mother said suddenly. Her jaw was clamped tight and she was looking directly at me. Then she spoke to Agnes. "You will not speak of it near Elisabeth. Her mind must be grounded in the laws of our Lord, and you will not dirty her before she goes to the nunnery." My sisters nodded.

I beat the dust of the road off my skirt, angry. "What about Edmund? Why aren't you telling him not to think about it?"

"Men are not as susceptible to these stories." My father didn't look at me as he spoke.

Edmund by the trousers. He was halfway out the window, like a dog. What a load of rubbish. Eddie would be talking about Joan for weeks. Eddie not susceptible. It was absurd. I'm not susceptible. I'm about to be a Nun. They had all partaken in bed sports, or would. I would never, never ever. I was the pure one.

I was happy to reach home. I jumped out of the carriage before the steps had been put down.

Grey's Court stood above me, huge, magnificent, but familiar. Its mottled red and cream brick and its peaked roofs could always calm my nerves, but I didn't go inside with the others. I didn't want to be near my mother.

Instead, I went into the walled gardens and sat down on a seat. I was vexed. I hated feeling like I was a child. I was a daughter of God. I was eighteen years old and I had chosen to devote my life and my body to Our Lord …

But I hadn't really chosen it. I was the youngest daughter, and whether mother and father wanted to admit it or not, there was only a meagre dowry left for me.

My father took a leaf out of His Majesty's book. They both liked to spend. My parents and sisters were adorned in the latest styles, the most expensive colours and cloth. Grey's Court had servants aplenty, and each room was filled with the latest-fashioned furniture and tapestries, dressed like Henry himself might be dropping in for tea. Even little Eddie was dressed to impress. Our family's fortune, my dowry, had been spent, or was being spent, on keeping up with the Tudors. Keeping up with court. It was important to keep up appearances when one is as important as my father is. But appearances, it seemed, cost more than what we owned and earned. Free flowing pounds and pennies were a thing of the past. I fingered the pearls on my headband. They were glass in clever disguise.

I took a deep breath. The smell of fresh grass, country air and roses calmed me. I am righteous and untouchable. God has chosen me. I am pure. I watched a robin nesting in a thick old wisteria root crawling up the wall. He hopped from branch to branch. These vines were beautiful, even in the late summer without their purple flower. Joan was beautiful too. She had very dark, shiny hair. It couldn't have been hard to attract the attention of several different men.

"Elisa!" I jumped. Eddie came tearing around the wall, his knees somehow already dirtied with mud. "Elisa! Mother said that I am to be with you until Samuel comes home." Eddie's tutor walked home from Church with the servants and the rest of the household. It was not a short walk. I sighed, summoning the energy for my little brother.

"Mother said we are having mutton for dinner." He pulled a disgusted face, clambering onto my lap. I looked down at the black hand mark on my white dress and bit my lip. I could already hear my Mother's admonitions.

Thankfully it did not take Samuel very long to return. I had been helping Eddie climb an old oak, and he was only halfway up when a rather windswept and very sweaty Samuel appeared.

"Lady Elisa, I ran!"

"I can see that!" I liked Samuel. He was lithe, with a crooked smile, though he gave it out sparingly. He was casual about everything, but always listened intently. Nothing was fussed over, but he consistently respected everyone's feelings, even Eddie's.

"I thought ..." He bent over, trying to catch his breath. His white shirt stuck to him. I could see his skin. I averted my gaze. "I thought, what with the happenings today that ... that ..." he took a few more breaths and swept his dirty blond hair out of his eyes "... that Eddie perchance would give too much trouble. Talking about ... Mistress Wright's ... travails."

"It was you who divulged the matter to him!" I said disapprovingly. The whole affair didn't seem so disgusting talking about it with Samuel. He spoke about it so easily, as though the drama at Church today had been a stray cat interrupting Communion, not a respected woman of society begging forgiveness in nothing but a sheet.

"I didn't mean to tell him. He heard me telling the ladies' maids." He pulled a face.

"Why were you telling the ladies' maids?"

"They asked me." He shrugged.

"Get me down, Sam!" Eddie yelled, now just a few feet off the ground.

"I'm here."

Eddie pushed himself off of the tree and Samuel caught him. "Don't talk to Elisa about Mistress Joan Wright and the three pricks!" he said hurriedly.

"Edmund!" I snapped.

"What? You're not allowed to hear about it! You're a nun!"

"Listen." Samuel got down to Eddie's level. "Your sister Elisabeth is far older and worldlier than you. She is more than able to hear these stories and still be bound to God as His loyal servant." Eddie opened his mouth to protest, but Samuel didn't allow him to speak. "You are going inside now; it is time to practise your music."

Eddie groaned but he did as instructed, stomping back to

the house, kicking the odd stone to remind everyone of his bad mood.

Samuel shook his head. "Much good do it ye." He smiled and inclined his head. It was a commoner's farewell, betraying his status.

"Much good do it ye, Samuel," I replied, despite myself.

CHAPTER TWO

"Elisabeth." My mother's pale face appeared like a suspended full moon in between my bed curtains. I had been so close to drifting off to sleep …

"Mother," I said softly, turning over, making sure she knew this was highly inconvenient to me.

"We have been praying. Your father and I."

"Praying for me?" I sat up.

"We want you to fast the coming days."

"Why?"

"You are vulnerable. More than most, after what has happened at Church. I wish we had never taken you. Had I known I would have demanded a private Mass at home."

"You think I need to fast, for penitence? I have not thought on it —"

"Of course you've thought on it," she snapped. How did she know? How could she know that I was so susceptible to these disgusting things? "You need to stay clean and pure for your calling."

"Yes, Mother."

"Fasting will bring you closer to God and further away from sin, wil't not?"

"Yes, Mother."

I spent most of the next morning reading the Bible. The first day of fasting was nearly always the worst. My stomach grumbled, but I took pleasure in it: each crunch of emptiness was what I deserved. It felt Godly, purifying, as if I were bathing in sweet-smelling water.

"Mother said you are to have a turn around the gardens to keep your mind entertained." It was Livia. "Agnes is coming and so is Lady Jane — she's visiting and you ought to show your face."

I was hugely reluctant to leave my Bible, but it was stuffy inside. I compromised by pocketing the Scriptures, so my hand could touch the binding even as we walked and discussed dull things.

It was a beautiful day for a walk, the sun golden but not so hot that my pale, sadly freckled skin would burn. The three women and their entourage walked peacefully around and around the manicured gardens. The air was scented with a glorious hotchpotch of flora and grass, but it couldn't quite distract me from the drivel from their lips.

"It's a cursed shame you're promised to Thomas, Livia."

I knew where this conversation was going: absurd dreams of becoming the next Queen of England and King Henry's fourth wife.

"They say he is still in mourning for Jane Seymour," whispered Livia conspiratorially.

"I think a bust like yours could snap any man out of grief," Lady Jane declared. "Even sad Harry." They laughed. I rolled my eyes. "Of course if I hadn't been married so young," continued Jane, "I would have been a viable choice, Father said so. Apparently Henry expressed some disappointment when I wed." She traced her finger along the red jewels that sat above her own décolletage.

"Don't your family maintain their allegiance to Rome, Jane? Are you not … Catholics?" I could not help myself. The rumours were rife.

"Elisa!" Livia snapped.

"God forgive you!" Jane cried. "My family are loyal to the King of England, Supreme Head of the Church!"

"My mistake," I muttered.

"And what a thing to say, from one about to attend a Nunnery! A catholic cess pool if ever there was one!"

"The nunneries, just like our churches, are reforming!" I snapped back. I had heard this accusation more than once. It unnerved me. I looked towards the house to see my mother watching us from an upper window. I raised a hand and smiled. I hoped she would be pleased with me, fasting, spending time with my sisters, but she didn't return my gesture. Perhaps she could not see me clearly.

My sisters had distracted flighty Jane with a new conversation. "No. Like this." Livia stopped, trying to demonstrate something. "Stand with this leg slightly in front of the other, so there is a smooth flow from the toe to the brow." She looked like she was standing normally to me. "Can you see the way my dress falls?"

"No," I said quietly beneath the other girls' declarations that yes, yes indeed they could see the way the dress fell.

"That's how all the women at court stand," Livia explained.

"All the time?" I asked.

"Yes," Livia shrugged, "of course."

"Sounds exhausting."

"Then it is your good fortune, Elisabeth, that you shall spend your life on your knees." There was an eruption of laughter from the three of them. "In prayer, I profess! In prayer!" Livia said, dabbing tears of mirth away from her eyes.

I didn't understand. "What do you mean?"

Jane was actually bent over in her mirth.

My whole body had become hot, tears threatened. This wasn't fair. It would have something to do with *tupping*. "Stop laughing!"

"You don't need to know, Elisa! It doesn't matter!"

I clenched my jaw together.

"So Agnes." Jane turned to my oldest sister. I had never liked Jane. For one thing she had grey hair, and she would've only been in her twentieth year. Plus she always wore weasels over her shoulders, and they were always bejewelled, with ruby eyes or sapphire tongues — hideous. "How much ... praying on your knees have you and John done?"

I groaned in protest, but I didn't stop listening.

"More than most. It is his favoured sport."

"Will you share your methods?" Jane elbowed her in the ribs.

"Just put it in your mouth —" Agnes started.

"And suck!" finished Jane delightedly.

I was quickly catching onto the topic at hand. I stopped walking. They would hardly notice me go. I remained where I was and let them walk on. I fingered the pages of my Bible. I should be thankful I was never going to turn out like them.

I walked down to the herb garden. There had been complaints from a few of the servants of a persistent ache in the head. I would make a mixture and give it to Samuel to distribute. I would need lavender, sage, marjoram, roses and rue. I opened the small wooden door to the kitchen garden. I hoped we had the rue.

"And when you're done blowing your nose you should not open up your handkerchief like that and look inside as if pearls or rubies might have descended from your brain."

"It's bright green. Like moss!"

"I don't care, Edmund."

"There's no law against looking into my handkerchief, Samuel, I'll do as I want."

"True, but these behaviours make people dislike us."

"This is stupid — looking at my nose goo isn't a sin."

"Sin harms us greatly, but lighter faults are a nuisance and this one in particular bothers me personally. It is not nice to watch you staring at your goo."

"How is it that this conversation is more pleasant to me than the one I've just had to endure with my sisters and Lady Jane?" They both turned to look at me.

"Which weasel did she bring today?" Eddie asked.

"Ruby eyed, with the spectral blue claws."

Samuel shivered. "An apparition I would be spared."

He had laid out Eddie's books on a large rug. The tutor was kind enough, or perhaps not brave enough, to keep my brother inside on a day like today.

"It is time for a break," Edmund declared.

"It is not," Sam disagreed.

My brother rose, looking Sam directly in the eye. But then Sam stood too, looking down at him sternly. Not willing to give up so quickly, Eddie got up onto one of the elevated garden beds, which I was about to protest, in defence of the trodden herbs, but he lost his footing and before I could say anything he fell awkwardly onto his side. Both Samuel and I made attempts to catch him, but neither of us were quick enough.

"My arm!" he wailed. "It hurts, Elisa! It hurts!"

Samuel propped him up. "Tell me where it hurts."

"Ma'arm!" he cried.

It was always hard to tell with my brother. He was born exaggerating everything, but it had looked like an awkward fall.

"We shall call for the healer."

"*No*! I'm fine! I'm fine! No healer." Edmund's breathing returned to normal. "I'm fine."

"Let me see?" I asked him. He nodded slowly. I pulled up his torn sleeve. "He's bleeding."

"Bl…b…bleeding?"

"The cut looks shallow but it's got a lot of dirt in it."

"I'll take him down the road to get it cleaned up." Samuel picked up Eddie, who was now repeating the word 'bleeding' over and over again.

"Don't be silly Samuel." I put a hand out, staying him. "I can clean him up. I just need water and oil."

"I have oil at the cottage."

I bit my lip. It would not be appropriate for me to go to his home on my own. "I could bring it back here?" he added, seeing my discomfort.

I imagined what my sisters might think if I went to Samuel's home alone. I saw their faces. Their shock. I saw Lady Jane petting her weasel frantically as she always did whenever there was a scandal. I shivered, annoyed.

"Don't be foolish: it will be fine. No one will object if they know that Eddie was hurt."

There was a second's pause and then he nodded.

I knew where his house was. I had been curious about it for some time, not least because I had heard he kept an extensive herb garden, but also because he seemed to have always only existed in the capacity of teacher. The thought of seeing where he slept, where he ate, where he did … whatever he did when he wasn't teaching Eddie, was arresting. We reached his cottage; there was a little hesitation at the door, but Samuel put down the child and held it open, and Eddie and I walked in.

It was small and simple.

"I didn't know you were a peasant, Sam," Edmund said loudly, forgetting to counterfeit his marvellous pain.

Sam laughed. I laughed too.

"I am a very lucky man to have a home all to myself on your grounds," he said, going to a cupboard and rattling its contents around.

Eddie sat down on Samuel's bed. It was a basic bed — the curtains were not ornate like mine — but it was big. Too big just for Sam surely.

"You shouldn't be here alone," Edmund whispered to me as I took off his shirt.

"I'm not alone. I'm with you."

Sam passed me the oil, water and cloth.

"Thank you …" I hesitated, about to dip the cloth. "I … I don't want to wet your bed."

Edmund couldn't contain himself. "Elisa wet your bed Sam!" he squealed, delighted.

I blushed.

"I have it on good authority that you yourself wet the bed not one week past," Samuel said over his laughter.

"I didn't!"

"Here, take him outside. Then we need not worry about blood and oil getting everywhere when we amputate."

We waited for a reaction but, unfortunately, Eddie knew not what amputate meant.

The garden was everything I had wanted it to be.

"Oh Samuel," I breathed.

"My pride and joy."

"How many different herbs are here?"

"Is anyone going to mend me?" Eddie asked loudly.

I ignored him.

"You have to taste my mint."

I had it nearly all the way to my lips when I remembered. "Oh!" I exclaimed.

"Is there a Godforsaken bug upon it? Something has been devouring my sage."

"I had forgot — I'm am fasting. Your garden distracted me."

"You are fasting? Have I forgotten a Saint's Day?"

"No. Mother and Father thought that I ... actually, *I* thought that I should after ..."

"Because of Joan," Eddie finished.

Samuel nodded slowly. "I see."

"I decided it would be best," I said, trying to reaffirm the decision in my own mind. It was best for me. "What with it being so soon before I go to the Nunnery, to focus ..." I drifted off. I just wanted to focus on God.

"I will make you a little satchel of all my favourite herbs so you can try them tomorrow." He smiled.

My stomach fluttered. Edmund coughed. We both turned to look at him.

"I have a question," he announced.

"All good students do," declared Sam.

"Do you think Joan and all the men were tupping at once?" Eddie's voice was innocent enough.

I crossed myself. I didn't even have the breath to yell at him, but was overcome by some sort of faintness. God forgive him. God forgive me.

I stared up helplessly at Sam, begging him to chide him. To yell. To do — something.

But all he did was shake his head, just slightly, as though Eddie had picked his nose again. He caught my gaze, and his expression changed. "Lady Elisa, are you well?"

"Don't let him say such things," I breathed as he gently eased me down onto the bench. Eddie was wearing a devilish grin.

"You are upsetting your sister," Samuel said seriously, taking over my task and cleaning the wound.

That was not the type of reprimand I was expecting. "No. I will not tolerate ..." I didn't know what to say.

"Ow! Sam! Stop!" Eddie cried.

"Stay still!"

"I won't." He got up and darted back inside. "Don't touch me!" His voice fogged up the cottage window as he glared at us from inside.

"You should not let him say such things in front of me," I snapped. "I am about be enclosed."

He lowered his head, the picture of servitude. "My lady, forgive me."

"If Mother knew what you let him say …"

He gave me a pained look. "Please my lady. Forgive me. God forgive me."

"Why are you not more affected, Samuel?" I demanded. "I … How could Eddie even think up something like that? You do not seem affected at all by these happenings."

Samuel indicated that he would like to sit next to me. Not seemly, but I nodded curtly. Since the tutor, only a handful of years older than I, had first entered the household, a familiarity had evolved between us, and it was relieving and easy, compared to all my other interactions.

"Whether it pleases God or not, I fear I place harsher sanctions on my young master, on myself, on God's people, when they engage in sin that hurts others. Mistress Wright was not guilty of any such sin."

I was interested, in spite of myself.

He looked at me seriously. "Joan's sins upset nobody. It was an arranged affair that, well …" he brushed his hair back, and shrugged "… it pleased all involved and hurt no one else."

"They arranged it? She wanted it to happen? Even Master Wright?"

He hesitated. "Some married people, including Mistress and Master Wright, enjoy such arrangements."

"How is that enjoyable?"

"I suppose —"

"No, Samuel! Keep close your lips."

He put up his hands defensively. "The lady's shaming chagrins me. The way Father Nicholas tore away her garb, paraded her by the Church. She hurt no one. Surely Christ cannot want a woman, anyone, treated so." He twiddled his thumbs in his lap.

"God would be angry. He would be angry at Joan for what she did."

"But did he wish her pain and shame? Remember: 'Let he who is without sin cast the first stone.'"

I thought about this for a few beats of my heart, and lowered my voice to a whisper. "I think I forgave her as soon as ever I saw her in her sheet. Oh Samuel, to see her crying and naked."

He nodded in agreement. "That is very Godly of you."

I blushed. We looked at each other. He did not fear my gaze.

"I have felt no anger at Mistress Wright, only with myself for thinking on … her sport," I confessed. He nodded, understanding. "It won't leave my mind! I am corrupt!"

"You are not corrupt."

He sounded so convinced. But if he knew what I actually thought. What I actually did …

"Samuel," I said, swallowing hard and conjuring my mother's authority with all my might, "whilst I understand your homily on sin, you are not a man of God. You are a scholar, but not of divinity. You cannot rank the sins from bad to good, for they are all despicable in our Lord's eyes. Particularly ones of this nature. They are disgusting. I am disgusting to think of it, you are wrong to think of it and Joan Wright the doer of these devilish deeds is most certainly revolting. To me and to God."

"I still do not hold you disgusting," he repeated. I picked at the dirt Eddie had left on my skirts. "I will go retrieve my young master and mend his hurts, and you can hie him home."

"Yes." I nodded. I was no longer angry. I was … I was tense in every part of my body. I was sweating; my breath was shallow. I had an urge to laugh or squeal or release something from myself. And then — I smiled. I exhaled and shook my head. Samuel was fascinating. I brushed down my skirt one last time and tucked a loose hair into my hood. I felt a hunger pain in my stomach, shut my eyes and revelled in it. It hurt, as Jesus would inside of me, having watched the whole exchange. He was reminding me of His presence.

A weight fell in my lap. My eyes flashed open. It was a package wrapped in a square of linen.

"The herbs," Samuel said, a blubbery-eyed Eddie holding his hand.

"Do not throw stuff into the laps of ladies," I snapped.

Samuel rolled his eyes. My mouth fell open indignantly, but I said nothing.

Mary, my lady's maid, was helping me out of my dress. She was tugging down my smock.

"This needs a wash, my lady," she said. "Won't be washing much at the Nunnery, I suppose."

"I know," I said defensively.

"You should wear this dress to London tomorrow. You shall not wear it again. Or this dress, this red velvet dress. You won't be allowed to wear colours either."

"I know."

She was pushing me. She wanted me to admit I didn't want to go.

I took hold of one of my bedposts. Delicately carved ivy leaves climbed up the dark wood. Of course I didn't want to leave this place. I didn't want to leave my tapestries. Especially not the one opposite my bed, with the bright, green rolling fields, the white castle with its blue turrets, and the hunting party with all the dogs. I had named all the puppies and their owners. I was attached to them. I liked that they watched over me as I slept. I didn't want to leave my books either. I didn't want to leave my big trunk full of my special trinkets. I didn't want to leave my constantly lit fireplace. Or the bunches of lavender Mary left around my room to make it smell good. I didn't even want to leave my mirthsome chamber pot. It had a frightened face potted into the bottom of it, and that amused me. I had heard that the nuns had to share.

"I'm going to miss you," she said softly. I looked at her. Her eyes were bright with tears. Mary had been my attendant — my bosom friend — for a long time.

"I'll miss you too." I would miss her more than anything in this room.

"The house will be so quiet."

"It's me that's leaving, not Eddie." She tried to smile but didn't quite manage it. "Will you be with me at Livia's wedding?"

"Of course, as much as your mother will allow."

"Good."

"You would have made a beautiful bride." Mary had sung that song before.

"It is not God's will that I marry, Mary." I stood tall, looking down at her, and doing that pursed lipped thing my Mother did to all our servants. I didn't like to hold my status above her, but when she mentioned marriage, I made sure she remembered who was what. "Jesus will be my bridegroom." I went to my bed.

Mary followed. "I just had always pictured you wifed and whelped."

"I don't want it, Mary."

"Would you with Samuel?"

My whole body became cold and clammy. I wasn't sure whether my heart was racing, or stopped completely.

I tried to exclaim, but I made a sound rather than a word.

She smiled coyly. I felt a rush of anger. The cold changed to hot, my humours shifting so quickly I was dizzy. "He's beneath me!" I managed.

How could I have been so obvious? How did she know?

"He likes you I think."

My body changed again. Now I was buzzing, like a hive of bees were within my body ricocheting off my organs and bones.

"He likes me?"

"He looks at you."

"He looks at me?"

"You like him."

"I don't like him."

"It's fine if you like him."

"It is not fine!" I got out of bed and began pacing. "And I do not." She looked at me. She had old wise eyes despite her youth. "I don't."

"The way you walk around, Elisa, with your body all folded in. Fasting all the time. Shutting your ears when we talk about men."

"I'm protecting myself."

"It's like you're fighting yourself."

"There is a devil within me! I cannot give it my soul."

To my surprise, Mary's eyes began to water. "There is no devil within you. What you feel about Samuel. It's … I …"

"Stop talking. You know not what I feel or think." It gave me shivers hearing her talk down to me. Like she could understand what I endured. "There is something rotten within me. Like Joan. The only place for me is the Nunnery. It is God's will. It is Mother's and Father's will. I am not made for this family life …" I was shaking.

"I don't think you should read this any more." She snatched up my favourite book. St Margery's writings, dog eared from my repeated reading.

"Give it back."

Mary stared at me, completely forgetting herself. "No."

"What?" I snapped.

She tried to backtrack. "I think another tome will do as well tonight."

"Give me back my book."

"Why don't you read the treatise on healing? With all the herbs and the remedies. You love that." I did love that book. She gestured towards it where it sat upon my bedside. "Sam also loves that book."

"Leave, Mary. Go from me." She hesitated. "Go!"

She backed out of my room, dropping the saint's book on the floor.

I looked at it lying splayed open on the hard wood. The book's spine would have been damaged. Curse Mary. I scrunched myself up and laid my chin on my knees, staring at my poor damaged manuscript, lying alone on the floor. I had perused the book repeatedly since it was decided I was to go to the Lacock. It was God's will that St Margery of Kemp would be secluded and devoted to Christ alone, like me, but she had been married to a man, forced to lie with her husband, night after night. It had nearly destroyed her, just as it would destroy me. But I would scape her tribulations; I would be straight into God's arms. An eternal virgin, like Mother Mary. An honour to my parents. I would be someone they could talk about to their friends. Their daughter the bride of Christ … If the King keeps the convents open. I cursed the intrusive thought. Of course he would, he would. The nunneries were being reformed to his liking, to my liking. Thanks to His Majesty the nunneries were now more chaste than any place in Christendom.

I should pray, and sleep. I should. I repeated the intention several times. But I didn't move. My thoughts were straying back to what Mary had said about Sam. Why had she told me that? I was not strong enough to keep my mind from this new bit of information. I forced myself to get out of bed, blew out my candle and prayed my prayers.

I prayed for the King. I prayed he may be relieved of his despair. That he may choose a good new wife. That he may keep his promise and leave the nunneries open. I prayed for the health of Prince Edward, the baby boy. Then I prayed for my mother. I had heard her complain of being tired that morn. I asked God to bless her with deep slumber. Then I asked that she might think good of me, and want me when I'm gone. I prayed the same for my father, and for his back, which was given to ache. Then I asked for forgiveness. That part always took the longest.

I had put Margery's book on the far table. I didn't want to read it that night. Not because of Mary. No. Because I didn't want to. Because I was too tired to read. I pulled my bed curtains closed and then I sat. In private. Just me. It had been a long time since I had been properly alone. Mary would normally sleep in my room, most of the time right next to me. Or Eddie or Livia would declare they needed my company to sleep well and squeeze in next to me. There had been some nights when we'd slept all four of us in my bed. But there was not a single noise tonight, no one roaming the halls. No gallivanting Edmund. Just me. I lay down but I wasn't tired. The thrill of the fight was still pulsing around me.

Could he like me? Did he really look at me? What did that even mean? I look at Mary all the time, I look at my parents, my brother, my sisters. Looking meant naught. But I could feel the iron grip on my imagination slipping. It was stronger than me. It had been since I was a child. I was ruled by it, tormented by dreadful visions — the execution of my whole family, pestilence coming to Oxfordshire, demons in my bedroom,

Lucifer whispering in my ear. I could see impossible things, faeries in the undergrowth, my life as a physician, what it would be like to be a peasant and to have Samuel Finch in my bedroom. We'd be married of course. Nothing un-toward. And perhaps he would be a lord, hiding from his responsibilities, and he has come to my room to explain that he has been living a terrible lowly lie avoiding his duties as a well-to-do man, and now will reveal himself for the sake of love of me. We want for nothing, least of all a dowry. As he speaks he gets closer to me, and he looks at me. He tucks a hair behind my ear. And then he kisses me.

The sheets covered me, pressing heavily against my body. I could feel my skin sweating; I ran my hand over my night gown, feeling everything beneath it. Was Mary suggesting that Samuel might want to touch me? In this manner? As I was feathering fingers to flesh in that moment? My husband, Lord Samuel Finch, hitched up my dress around my waist.

God left me then. Fleeing my body, knowing it would soon be defiled. He heard the rustling of my sheets, my sharpened breath and he knew. But God has always known of what I am capable. He knows the demons I entertain.

After I had finished I rolled over onto my belly. I couldn't feel anything. My soul had gone.

CHAPTER THREE

"Elisa! Elisa! Elisa!" Livia and Eddie tore into my room. The curtains were flung open. Eddie's somehow already dirty hands wrapped around my neck.

"It's the day, Elisa! It's the London day!"

I sat up in my bed.

"Where is Mary?" Livia asked.

I looked around for Mary and couldn't find her. I looked around for my own soul, for Christ, for a glimmer of divinity, but I did not see anything. I stared at Livia in the face, surely she could feel it too. She was in a Godless place.

"What's wrong, Elisa?"

"I am ... not well."

"No no no!" protested Eddie. "You can't be sick today!" He was right. I had been looking forward to our journey. We were going to London to buy clothing for the wedding. I would be buying all my cloth for the Priory too. We were to stay with the Burbages. Father and Mother would make an appearance in court, and we would go to the markets and purchase everything needed for the wedding. Livia's dress was going to have jewels and pearls and be garnished in gilt lace. We had discussed it at length.

"I cannot go," I choked. I could not see the room, or the people in it. In a haze, I could only envision myself lying in bed alone. Thinking about him, alone.

Livia was putting a hand to my forehead. "Shall I fetch the healer?"

"No, I need to be alone." I had done it before, of course, it was my nature.

"I'll get Mary."

"Don't."

"Maybe Sam will have some special plants," suggested Eddie, who had taken one of my blankets and fashioned himself a habit.

"No, Eddie."

"But Elisa … what about my dress? You said you would choose it with me."

I looked at my sister. Her thick eyebrows were furrowed.

Agnes's head appeared in between the bed curtains.

"Eddie. You need to go find Nanny Francis. She is waiting to change you," she said sternly. "Elisa. What's wrong?"

"She's not well."

"Livia, take Eddie back to his maid."

Livia grabbed Eddie around the waist and put him on her hip. "Come today. It is an important occasion."

"Pleeeeease!" I could hear Eddie's begging even after the door had closed.

Agnes pulled the bed curtains open. She was looking sternly at me. Like she knew. "You're not sick," she announced. "What is wrong?"

Of course she knew, because this had all happened before. And I had confessed in Church, and my private, stained words had been pried out of me in the confessional booth and given to my parents. For my own good, of course. According to Father Nicholas.

"Is it your dark fancies?" she pressed. "Your weaknesses?" Agnes had taken a step back, as if I were actually sick, possibly with the plague.

"Or have you done something worse?" I shook my head. "Has anyone been in your room?"

"No!"

"You have thought lustfully." She spoke in hushed tones. "You have given in to the desires of the flesh." The scales tipped and suddenly my anger at Agnes overtook the anger at myself.

"Why do you whisper now when yesterday you told the whole of Oxfordshire about getting down on your knees?"

"Oh Elisa," Agnes scoffed. "How young you are!"

"I'm only three years younger than you, Agnes!"

"You must confess. Zounds, Elisa! You are about to take your vows. How can you be so vile?"

"I don't know! I don't know why I do it!" I did not know. I did not know why I was so vile.

"I'm going to Mother."

"No!" But she had already walked out the room.

I flung the covers over myself. I will stay under here forever. This will be my hermitage. My priory. I would stay in my quilts until I slowly die of hunger and sin. Hot tears ran down my cheeks. My crying shook my frail blanketed nunnery.

I knew my mother's footsteps. The way her shoes and her small frame fell upon the boards of the house sounded the same no matter the circumstance. Her skirts always swooshed threateningly.

I stayed under the covers as my door opened yet again.

"Your mind should be grounded in the love of our Lord! You will stay at home. You will fast and repent. I will organise for Father Nicholas to come and you will detail to him what you have thought upon and … done." She was revolted. She could hardly stand the sight of me. I pulled back my blankets and reached for her, desperate for comfort, but she took several steps back. Her lip curled. I wanted her to embrace me, to tell me she could cure me. To rock me as she was wont to do when I was young and untouched by this lust. I wondered if she would tell Father. "Mary will remain to attend you. Fast, keep vigils and confess. All the while know that you've broken Livia's heart."

My nose was running; I could feel it on my lip.

She looked at me, made a sort of retching noise. Shook her head. And left.

Some time later I heard the carriages depart.

"My lady?" Mary was standing in my door way. Staring at her feet.

"I need nothing, Mary. I am sick in bed. I am fasting. I don't need food. I have my water. You can leave."

"I have a message from Father Nicholas."

"Leave it on my table."

"Are you sure you don't need anything, Lady Elisa?"

"I need nothing. Have the day for yourself. Go to town."

Her face lit up a little at this suggestion. My anger at her waned. "Go to town. I don't need anything from you."

"Are you sure, my lady?" I nodded. "Thank you, my lady." She smiled and backed out of the room.

Reluctantly I opened the letter. I read it slowly.

He would see me tomorrow for my confession. There were several Bible verses. Then at the end, another message.

In severe cases such as these, Thomas More, God redeem his soul, proved an exemplary figure of true repentance.

I knew immediately of what he spoke. Everyone knew about More's hair shirts, the scratches on his skin. And I had heard of even worse things that he had done.

I sat in bed a moment longer. Thinking of how alone I had

been in the night, but how everyone might as well have been in my bed. Agnes, Mother, Father, Father Nicholas.

I rose, my legs wobbly from a night and half a day of bedrest. Thomas More had been loved by God, respected by the King ... for a while. Of course now he was a headless corpse. But there was a time when he had been an emblem of Godliness in England. If I did as he did, then maybe I could be forgiven, cleansed and respected again. But I had done worse than Thomas More. I couldn't know for certain, but I assumed I had done worse than More. I certainly couldn't or didn't want to picture the great man abusing himself. Oh God. I thought of Livia, picking out her fabrics. Her jewels. Of my Father, going to court and having to know about me, picturing me ...

I stumbled out of my room, clutching the Priest's letter, heading towards the kitchens. The halls were quiet. I grabbed Mrs Smithe's very badly hidden liquor. It was another sin, but I planned to eradicate everything I'd ever done wrong and maybe even get some leeway with future mishaps. I went outside to the stables. The hot liquid burned my tummy, muddled my balance and started sloshing around with my thoughts.

I rummaged around in a trunk behind Mary's very large and threatening bottom. The horse called Mary, not my lady's maid. I found what I was looking for. I grasped it tightly, carefully side stepping around the little jennet, careful not to look her in the eye, lest the horse stop me doing what I was about to do.

I didn't go far, just around the back of the stable, where Mary couldn't see me. I held the riding crop in my hand and took a breath. I leant my head against a large oak. I could feel my knees getting soggy in the dirt. I felt my chest. Checking. It still felt cold, empty. God hadn't returned to me. I wanted to run from my earthly flesh. It were as if I had on soiled clothes, forced to wear them day in day out. My skin encasing me in

Hell. I uncrumpled the letter and smoothed it out in front of me. The whip was leather and well used.

I ran it through my fingers; the fresh air was waking me. I started wanting to go back inside. I was still in my nightclothes. The smell of the flowers and the warm sun on my skin reminded me of good things, of gardens, and herbs and blossoming trees. I was reminded of things outside of myself. But then my thoughts went to the morrow, when Father Nicholas would visit me and ask me to divulge my actions. And why. And what I felt.

I took a tight hold of the whip. If I could prove to Father Nicholas that I was serious about my repentance. If I could show my Mother and my Father that I was just as holy as Thomas More. I imagined showing them what I'd done. They would gasp in awe and pity as they looked at me, bent in repentance, blood dripping down my back. Holier than any Knolly has ever been.

I made a false blow. Like I was trying to get a horse to walk. It felt warm. I would take off my nightgown but I couldn't bear the thought of myself naked. My hand shook. I forced my thoughts back to last night, to this morning; I looked at the passages the Father had sent me. The first were the words of St Jerome.

> *Virginity can be lost by a thought.*

Well that was it then: I had lost my one treasure, my pass to the Priory.

I let the whip slap against my back, harder this time.

> *Ephesians. There must not be a hint of sexual immorality, or any kind of impurity, because these are improper for God's holy people.*

I tried again, harder.

Corinthians. Flee from sexual immorality. Whoever sins sexually,
sins against their own body.

The news of last night would travel through the house: I
wouldn't be surprised if the whole town would know. Samuel
would surely find out. What would he think of me? Young, vile
Elisabeth defiling herself in the night, because she would never
be with anyone, she would never be loved by anyone, and now
not even God would be her bridegroom. She was a child, alone
and rotten. My whole body seized. I let out a whimper and
dealt a mighty blow.

I could feel my back split. I did it again and again,
whipping the open wound.

I fell onto my front. My eyes rolled back. I could feel the
tickling sensation of dripping blood but it was nothing
compared to the bolt of burning fire running up and down my
spine. I had gone too far. This was too much. I breathed in the
grass, trying to stifle my moans. This was what I deserved, I
reminded myself.

"Forgive me, Jesus," I whimpered. "Please, I'll never ever do
it again. Please."

"Elisa?" I stayed prone in the grass. "Jesus Christ! Elisa!
What have you done?"

Surely this was some kind of a terrible joke. A test. From
God. Or from Father Nicholas. I grasped my letter and tried to
sit up. I yelped in pain.

Sam knelt by my side. "What have you done? Oh my God,
what have you done?"

I managed to turn my head to one side. I saw him. I did
not answer.

I could feel him prying the blood-soaked nightdress away
from the wound.

He was muttering my name over and over again. His touch was gentle but confident. I tried to focus on the pain.

I watched him pick up the cook's unidentifiable bottle of drink.

"Drink this. Two good chugs. I need to take you to a bed." I tried to shake my head. "Elisa." He spoke like he was senior, my superior. "You cannot move yourself; do not mind the propriety." He put the bottle to my lips and gently pushed my head back. I felt his fingers in my hair. I took three big drafts.

"I don't know how to move you. I'm worried the wound will get worse."

I pushed myself up into my kneeling position, whimpering as my skin tightened. He knelt in front of me. He moved to touch my face but stopped himself.

"Oh God, Elisa."

"Don't be blasphemous." I was dizzy.

"I'm going to put you over my shoulder. So I don't touch your back."

The pain, exhaustion and drink were too much. I let him move me. He heaved me over his shoulder. He carried me carefully but quickly to his home.

"I'm going to put you down. Can you stand?"

I slipped off his shoulder. He held me steady and looked at me, waiting to see whether I would collapse. He led me over to his bed and helped me onto it, propping the pillow under my head.

"Are you comfortable?"

I mumbled a yes. "Your pillow smells nice." I was drunk.

"Oh?" He said with his sideways grin. I watched him as he looked through his cupboards across the room.

"It smells like you."

"And what do I smell like?"

"You smell like the garden."

I was so drunk. After all this effort and pain purifying

myself, now I was going to do something stupid and need to do it all over again.

"I'm going to treat the … wound with lavender oil, Elisa."

"Do you have any leeches?" I asked.

He turned to me, looking worried. "I don't. I should fetch a healer."

"No. Lavender oil will do."

"Elisa, you're right. The leeches will numb the pain."

"No, Samuel! No leeches!" I said, grinning for some reason and speaking far too loudly.

He shook his head then put his hands over his eyes. "Why did you do this?"

I put my head face down in the Samuel-smelling pillow. It was silent for a long while. Then I felt the weight of the bed shift. I could feel his presence over me. "I'm going to clean the wound, then pour the oil." I made a noise of consent.

He peeled my hair out of my flesh, then poured something over the wound.

I cried out and grasped the sheets on the bed.

"I'm calling for a healer."

"No! Samuel! Please don't."

"Elisa —" He stopped without completing his rebuttal, distracted. "What is that?"

Gently, he pried my clenched hands open, taking the letter from the Father out of my grip.

My head spun, from panic, pain and the liquor. I made a noise to stop him, but I didn't have the will any more. This was who I was now. Everyone would know.

After minutes of silence I thought perhaps he had left, not wanting to look at me.

"That accursed man!" he barked suddenly. I turned my head. His hands were on his knees, and he was bent over as though in pain.

"It's not his fault, it's my fault."

"It is not!"

"You don't know what I've done!" I was angry now.

"Oh please, Elisa." He was pacing. "If your 'sins' mean you have to pry open your own back then I should be whipped into two pieces."

I had been about to fiercely defend my own vileness and sinfulness but his words stopped me.

"What do you mean?"

He had sat back down and was pouring the oil onto the wound now. I grabbed hold of my blankets.

"I mean that a prominent leader in this community, who knows his power and sway, has just forced you to hurt yourself."

"So that I can be saved and cleansed."

"Nicholas did this for himself. He gets pleasure from seeing women in shame and agony." Samuel pushed my sweaty hair out of my face. "Do you need more drink? How is the pain?"

I took another sideways sip, and then another. There was silence for some time; I was half enjoying, half wincing away from the feeling of his hands on my naked back. He had rough hands, from too much gardening.

"Do you know that the Greeks think sex is good for your health?"

I swallowed. "No …"

"They believe it is good for digestion."

"That is not relevant to me. I am to go to a Nunnery."

"Of course it is relevant to you." I felt tears threaten. "You are a woman, no?"

"I am."

"I know everyone in your life tries to exclude you from conversations about anything of this nature." He scrunched up his nose, annoyed. "But you are still a woman, and women, like men, are naturally lustful, and defying your natural way of being is like scoffing at God. Because he created you."

I had nothing to say. He had just … was it even legal to say that? Would the Church come in and take him away from me?

"You are always too bold about this."

"I heard you had a fight with Mary last night."

"You and Mary talk too much. You shouldn't gossip."

"What was it about?"

I took only the smallest pause, hiccoughed and then went on. "We argued about you."

"Me?"

"She said you look at me."

He smiled at that. "I'm looking at you right now."

"But are you *looking* looking?" I wondered how I looked, with my cheeks smooched against his pillow, blood drained from my face, night shirt torn open at the back. I wondered if my bottom was showing. "Is my — are my buttocks showing?" The filter between mind and mouth had fled.

Samuel looked unabashed at my fundament. "Not quite. Why would you fight about my looking at you?"

"She suggested that I like you, that I've … taken a fancy to you," I added.

"I see."

He had got out bandages now and was looking at them, trying to figure out a way to wrap my back, seemingly quite unperturbed by the conversation. Did he care that I might like him? Perhaps it meant nothing to him, seeing as I was a nun, a child practically.

"Why would this cause a fight? You and Mary are friends."

"Because it is shameful!" I spoke with too much vigour, my body seized in pain.

"Why? It is not shameful for other women to take a liking for a gentleman — your sisters have enjoyed the company of men."

"But Agnes likes her husband, and Livia is about to marry."

"What about the time Livia was obsessed with Mr

Boatman's son? Or when Agnes spent all that time 'going on walks' with the fair-haired man visiting from London. What do you think was going on there?"

"I can't be like that though!"

"Why not?"

I could feel myself getting worked up; there was a sadness, a tightness in my chest. My brow furrowed against the pillow. "Because all those things happened with the thought of marriage, with the prospect of a good Godly union. I am destined to be Christ's bride, so if I were to go gallivanting off with men, it would be like … it would be like I was betraying Christ!"

He pressed his hand lightly on the back of my head, stilling me as I squirmed in agitation and anger at the conversation.

"That blond man Agnes was with already had a wife and just about everyone knew it and Livia wasn't actually going to marry a commoner and we all know about King Henry and his favoured ladies," he took a deep breath, "and I personally have about a dozen stories that have nothing to do with the prospects of marriage." He did? "If everyone else can go around looking and liking and maybe even doing a little bit more than that, then you should be able to do so too, and without tearing your back open. You're no different from your sisters in body and mind, Elisa."

I felt tears in my eyes. I was seesawing between anger and shame. I wanted him to be right. He was right: why was I treated so differently just because I was the youngest and my parents hadn't the money to marry me off? Just because I was destined for God. That was circumstantial. It didn't change my anatomy, my desires. How could Mother look me in the eye and tell me to fast, to miss Livia's trip to London, when maybe Livia and Agnes were just the same as me, with similar desires, with similar thoughts. Maybe even she … but no. No. My sisters might have lusted after some boys, or even shared a kiss here or there, but they wouldn't have done what I did.

He could only see the side of my face, but he was reading me, seeing me.

"Whatever happened last night. I swear to you, everyone else has done it too." I looked up at him doubtfully. "I certainly have." He shrugged casually.

"Self ... self-abuse?"

For some reason he was laughing. I felt the colour run hot in my face. Maybe he hadn't realised what I had done. I buried my face in the pillow and wanted to become one with the feathers and die. He kept on laughing.

"No ... no, Elisa," he said in between his bouts of amusement. "Look at me." I turned to him. "I have a story for you." He recovered himself slowly. I continued to eye him suspiciously.

"I must've been perhaps fifteen years of age, or maybe sixteen. I was in my family home, where my parents and my mother's parents lived. I had been lusting after the baker's daughter. Alice. Alice Chapman." He looked wistfully into space. "She was the most beautiful thing I'd ever laid eyes on. She had hair like yours. Like autumn leaves, and wavy. With your freckles and green eyes. I couldn't keep my mind off her, and my imagination ... it was like Eddie's, maybe even worse."

"Goodness."

"Yes. Goodness. I don't remember the circumstances, but I had decided to ... to enjoy myself with Alice in mind." How did he make his own experience seem so lighthearted, so shameless? Perhaps it was because he was a man. "I go to my room and it all goes to plan, as it always did with Alice in mind. The only issue was that my bedroom, whilst my own bedroom, was also my grandmother's."

"No!" I shut my eyes, hardly able to listen. Sam's body was shaking with mirth. How could this be funny to him? But his joy at retelling the story was infectious. I was half cringing, half smiling.

"She was so tiny and so frail by that time, I hadn't noticed her little body lying under her covers. But, unfortunately, I wasn't so frail, or small. In fact, I was tall and standing in the middle of the room, with my breeches open, so it would've been rather hard for Nana not to notice me ..."

"No, Sam!" I moaned.

"Oh yes, Elisa."

"Maybe she was sleeping."

"Oh no, Elisa. She was not sleeping ... her eyes were wide open. Wide open. I turned around and she was just there. Glaring at me." His eyes were watering.

Whatever blood was left rushed to my face. "Did she say anything? Did she do anything?"

"She looked me right in the eye and she said," he put on an elderly accent, "'Samuel, you need to save your seed.' Then she turned over and went back to sleep."

I allowed myself a giggle. "What did you do then?"

"I tidied myself up and I went on a very very long walk around town and didn't return until well after dark, and of course, I never truly looked my grandmother in the eye ever again. She died a few months after that and I was, in part, relieved."

"Perhaps that's why she died," I suggested. Sam laughed so hard he snorted.

"Zounds, probably. No one caught you mid act did they?"

I recoiled. "We shouldn't be speaking so easily, laughing so wildly about something so ... so ..."

"So naughty." He was mocking me.

"Yes," I said firmly. "I thought my soul had fled me when I did it what I did. I felt like God had left me."

"Do you know how King Alfred the Great believed a woman kept chaste?"

"Shutting herself up in a Nunnery?"

"I think the exact quote is that you must use your fingers or another instrument."

Again, I recoiled. I replaced my face into the pillows.

"I don't think God will ever leave you, Elisa. You are too important to be abandoned by the Divine."

I felt myself want to cry as he said it. I swallowed several times, before changing the subject. "Will I ever be able to do anything other than lie on my stomach?"

"The wound is vertical, about a foot long down your back. It's shallow, but it's going to hurt when you move for a few days. I've laid bandages over it, but they won't stay when you stand."

"Have I stopped bleeding?" I should leave. If anyone heard about this, that I had spent the day lying on Samuel's bed …

"I think we should leave the bandages on for longer."

"Please, Sam." I reached my hand out to grab his. He froze and then his fingers closed around mine. We looked at our hands, entwined.

I pushed myself up into a sitting position. I winced and held my chest.

"We should get you some more clothes, perhaps."

I had thought the worst of the alcohol spins had gone, but as I sat up I felt a fresh wave of sickness.

"So do you like me?" I spoke quickly, before any sober part of me could stop my mouth.

He cocked his head as though he hadn't heard. I wasn't drunk enough to say it again.

"I think you are intelligent, humorous, capable," he said finally. I exhaled my disappointment. "And I also find you to be very beautiful." I sucked the air back in again. He sat next to me on the bed. I glanced at his lips. I could feel his breath on my face as he spoke. It was warm, and smelt like peppermint. "I also find you to be very drunk."

"And half naked on your bed," I added.

"That too." His gaze flashed to my lips. Our noses were surely about to brush.

"Are you going to kiss me?" I heard myself say it. Why? Why would I say that?

He shook his head and pulled away. He put his hands up defensively. As if he were reassuring me, as if I were scared of him. Scared of what he could do to me. But I wasn't scared. "You would do it if it wasn't me." I accused him. "I think you see me, just like they see me." I wobbled.

"I really don't think I do, Elisa."

"Are you sure?"

He sighed and tucked a hair behind my ear. The whole tiny house got even tinier, or perhaps it disappeared altogether. He took my cheek in his hand and turned my face slowly towards him, making me look him in the eye. My hand moved to his chest. I could feel his bare skin. He took a quick breath. He put his hand around the back of my neck. He looked at me. Not at my eyes. But at my face. He examined me. I could feel his gaze brushing over my cheeks, my freckles, my hair, my lips. I don't know how it happened. It could have been the alcohol or the burning need within me to prove myself, or maybe it was because I had thought about this a hundred times before and now Sam was holding my neck, and my hand sat over his heart. Whatever it was, we kissed. He leant forwards to my lips, and I met him, halfway.

I pulled away to look at him. To make sure it really was Sam I was kissing. He shook his head minutely, in protest of me leaving him. He pulled my head forwards again, kissing the edges of my lips, then moving up the side of my cheek bone. I could barely take a breath; his hand was on my bare back. But he had forgotten himself, and he slipped and touched my wound. I let out a gasp of pain. He jumped up and took several steps back.

"I'm sorry. I'm so sorry. Oh by God, Elisa. Are you hurt?"

I shook my head, trying to calm him.

"It is well, Samuel.."

He was looking at me as though he had only just seen me. "I'll take you to your room, I'll re-bandage you there, then I'll leave you."

He had realised. My kiss had betrayed me. My desirous, whorish nature had been revealed. He had seen what my mother saw, what the Priest saw, what God saw.

CHAPTER FOUR

"Mary! You told Mother?" My lady's maid was standing in the furtherest corner of the room. She was squished in between the tapestry of people at court and the one with the sheep that looked at me askance. Mary had managed to keep the secret five whole days. But I couldn't blame her for dobbing me in. If my mother had found out on her own accord, Mary would have been banished.

Besides, I had been hoping it would be revealed. My wounds would please them. I had taken steps to purify myself. To please God. To please my parents.

Mother had summoned Father Nicholas, my actual father and the town physician. Now all of Oxfordshire would know of my devotion, my holiness. I would be the Holy Knolly. Elisabeth the repentant. Elisabeth the redeemed.

"Show us what you have done," my mother snapped.

"And make it quick." My father turned towards the book shelf, plucking out a manuscript at random and aggressively flicking through the delicate pages. I flinched, both for the book and for myself. Their tones were short, angry. I had dreamed about the discovery and I had not been expecting this. I had imagined coos, pity and just a hint of awe.

Mary was called forwards. I was bent over the unlit hearth. She started unlacing my dress. My cheeks burnt hot.

"I'm sorry," Mary whispered. I frowned into the cold coals.

"Quickly! Father Nicholas is a busy man!"

"Yes, my Lady."

I had made a mistake. My wounds were just a reminder. A reminder of my lust. Eternal scars on my back. I stood in just my smock. My garments pooled around me.

I heard my mother's skirts brush against the floor. She snatched up my thin underdress, hooking the hem of my smock around my head. My naked backside was revealed to the room. My bottom exposed, like a child waiting for a spanking. I wished I had a bed sheet to cover me.

There were noises around the room. I thought some of them sounded impressed. I held hope.

"You have taken drastic action, Elisabeth." That was Nicholas. "You seem intent on repenting your lustful nature."

"I am intent," I whispered. I tried to relax the muscles in my bottom, but there was little I could do to stop the feverish shaking.

"Good. Good," he cooed softly. I felt the physician's hands on my back. They were cold. A splattering of my tears hit the stone hearth of the fire. I prayed that my father was still thumbing through a book.

"Will this redeem her?" That was my mother, asking Nicholas.

"For now. Though it won't cure her."

The doctor jabbed a fat finger into my back. I made a sad, helpless noise; it sounded like a rabbit caught in a trap.

"Will you put her dress down, for God's sake!" I could hear the anger in my father's voice. And he had blasphemed — in front of the Priest. Mary pulled down my dress.

I turned around and stared at my feet. I was still shoed despite my nakedness.

"You should be pleased, Lord Knolly. She has been brave and acknowledged the vileness of her actions." I felt Nicholas move towards me.

"I am not pleased at being force fed the sight of my naked daughter."

I will never be naked again.

"A necessary evil. For these marks on her back have saved her from an eternity in Hell."

From the corner of my eye I saw my Mother cross herself. I think she might have been thankful.

"What she has done is akin to martyrdom, my Lord."

Even in my humiliation, I raised a sceptical eyebrow and looked at Nicholas: he was trying to win my Father over — convince him of my Godliness — perhaps in case I ever told my father that it was Nicholas himself who had suggested my "cure".

"Martyrdom?" My father's eyebrow was also raised but Nicholas's words seemed to have impressed him. His daughter, the martyr. He would like that. A Knolly martyr. I could see him considering it.

"Yes, my Lord. Christ our God and His Highness King Henry would be in awe of her commitment to forgiveness and redemption. She has destroyed her body in God's name."

He didn't say anything. But he nodded. It was a final, abrupt jerking of his head. He was content. His gaze moved to me. I should've lowered my head, but I did not move. We made eye contact. I begged the tears that were threatening to stay balanced on the lower lids of my eye. Stay, stay. He grimaced at me. A smile. Of sorts. He got up and left. The door closed and the tears fell.

"Lady Knolly, I am afraid I have a flock to attend to back in town."

Mother seemed distracted. She nodded vaguely. The Priest left.

"Will you be needing my services my lady?" The physician thumbed his bag of equipment.

"No. You may leave." He had not been called to heal, just as a witness to my renewed holiness, a messenger who could take word to the Henley and beyond that I was whole again.

There was silence. The door closed.

My mother moved to me. She placed a hand on the back of my head. "Put on your clothes, Elisabeth."

CHAPTER FIVE

I was sitting on Livia's bed with both my sisters, my wounds healed. The windows were open. It was early, but it was already warm. It was the day of Livia's wedding. Our dresses were splayed out around us. I was entertaining Livia by putting on every single one of our jewels, including two headdresses. Livia was laughing hard, trying to add yet another set of pearls around my neck. Even Agnes was enjoying herself, flinging Livia's garter at her face, over and over again.

"Stop it, Agnes!" She squealed, as I attempted to balance the third headdress on my head. "This is meant for my leg not my head!" She caught it mid fling, and started twirling it around her fingers seductively.

Mother walked in. She looked at me. I smiled.

"You look absurd, Elisa."

"Wouldn't want to outshine the bride."

"Oh you won't do that." Thank you, Mother. She came over to Livia and petted her cheek. "You need to start getting ready!"

. . .

We started the parade from the house to the church. It was a crowd of musicians, kin I hardly knew, grooms singing songs and the maids all holding flowers, their hair adorned with ribbons. I looked around for Samuel — he'd be there somewhere but I couldn't see him.

I was dressed in a light blue, like the Virgin, of course. It had a line of faux-pearls at the bust line. It was old, but that meant it was comfortable. It didn't dig into my ribs.

As we walked through Farmer Henry's tall, unharvested wheat fields, the reveller next to me began playing *Greensleeves* on the recorder. It slowly became obvious that it was the only song he *could* play because he was playing it over and over again in one furious breathless loop. But strangely, it didn't bother me. I was in an odd mood. The air was filled with lots of sounds. There were horns, the halfwit on the recorder, laughter, clapping and incredibly dirty songs sung by dirty boys. Birds and rabbits were being scared out of the crops, making their own frightened noises. I watched Livia, dancing and jigging in the midst of the crowd. Her dress was beautiful. It was gold and red and made of silk. It flowed around her as she twirled.

Just before we had left the house Livia had told me the price of the beautiful material and jewels. All in all, it had cost twenty pounds. The figure was rolling around my mind. It was an absurd amount of money. It could have been my dowry. Not to some great man, of course. But it would have been enough. Agnes had taken me to buy everything on Lacock's property and uniform list the week before last, we had spent seven pounds. That was all it cost to send me to the Priory. Seven pounds.

As we wandered through town, our large parade holding up carriages and carts, I was doing the maths. If Livia had got a dress half the price, we could have saved ten pounds. Then add the seven pounds they had spent on the Priory list. Seventeen pounds. Then you consider all the new clothes Mother and Father bought themselves for the wedding. That was surely another seven or eight pound saved. And did they really need these musicians? They really didn't need Master Green-Blooming-Sleeves. How much were they paying him to play? How much had been the flowers? The ribbons? A dowry of more than twenty pounds was parading all around me. Not that I was set upon marriage, but the thought of the Priory was filling me with black dread. Perhaps my parents thought no one would take me and they wanted to spare me the embarrassment.

Samuel might have taken me. My mind harked back to his lips on my own. I felt the memory shudder through my body.

We arrived at the Church. It was extra colourful inside St Peter's today. The sun streamed through the glass and decorated the church in festive light. I took my seat. Perhaps my parents wished to send me to a Nunnery as a point of pride. An enclosed daughter is a daughter who is moral and devoted. A daughter who is married to a tutor is a daughter of poor parents. I looked at my mother and father. I knew Papa had several magnificent furs he could've worn today, but I didn't recognise this one and it was almost certainly new. He might have borrowed the money. It would not surprise me if he were in debt to all his closest friends, protected by his title and his lands. I tried to focus on Livia's smile and Thomas's devoted eyes but my mood had soured. I looked at the gift table in the Church: mountains and mountains of treasure and coins in a copper pot. All this abundance for Livia, and all I was afforded was a mattress, some sheets, blankets, one wimple and three veils.

I sat in the front row, watching Father Nicholas smiling at everyone. I had been made to confess properly of course. I could whip the skin off my back, but that didn't excuse me from the penitential booth.

'And where were your hands at that point?' I remembered the silky, smooth way he asked that question, again and again. I shivered. I could retch at the memory of his face when I explained to him the whipping. As soon as I mentioned the word whip he begun to quiver, his moist mouth wetting itself with spit. It was delight, or pleasure, or something — considering he was a Priest — entirely unGodly. My only solace was that I had not told him about Sam. Those moments were mine.

Eddie squeezed in next to me. He looked very handsome in his new clothes and when I told him so, he assured me he was fully aware of how good he looked.

"Where is Samuel?" I asked him quietly.

"He's at the back with the rest of the servants." He wiped his dirty hands on his new coat.

I turned around and saw Sam chatting animatedly with Mary. He threw a glance towards the front and caught me looking. He inclined his head. I nodded.

Before Father Nicholas had even started the ceremony the bride and groom were already kissing. People were giggling and whooping, my father's booming laugh overpowering them all. My mother was also smiling. I imagined them smiling as I left for the Nunnery. Proud of their daughters, who had each found her calling. I held Eddie's dirty hand tightly.

"Let go, Elisa," he said, looking over the other side of the aisle and smiling at a young girl from Thomas's family.

The deed was tied up with only some few words. It amazed me that all we needed to engender such a Divine Sacrament was the spoken word. I decided to leave a little earlier than the procession; I would aid in preparations at the house, find some small peace before the chaos. I informed my mother that the maids needed help with some of the indoor decoration and she didn't seem to care, as long as Eddie was taken care of.

"Samuel."

He was putting a ribbon in Mary's hair. "Lady Elisa." He bowed. I had hardly seen him since our kiss.

"Could you see to Eddie in the parade? I'm going back now to help."

"Of course, my lady." A part of me wanted everyone to know what had happened between us. I wanted to see my mother's face when I told her. I wanted to see her shock.

Mary accompanied me home.

"I hope you don't mind, Elisa, but I'll need help adorning the bridal suite; someone still needs to make the posset, and put the lavender oil on the bed."

"Has the Father blessed the bed yet?" I didn't want to be anywhere near Nicholas.

"He blessed it before the ceremony. He'll be too drunk to do it after the feast."

"Good."

"You look beautiful, Elisa."

I smiled at her. "Thank you. I feel it."

"Did you see Eddie with the Grey girl?" Mary asked.

"Yes! He was winking at her!" We laughed together. I ran my hands through the Queen Anne's lace that lined the roadside, enjoying the peace. "Will you get a chance to have fun tonight, Mary? Or do you have to work the entire evening?"

"Oh Elisa." She grinned. "The maids and grooms know how to have fun. At Agnes's wedding ..." She looked into the distance dreamily. "As soon as the feast starts everyone's too drunk to care what we get up to."

We went to the kitchen to collect the ingredients for the posset. The kitchen was the busiest I'd ever seen it.

"Oh, Lady Elisabeth!" squealed the cook. "You can't see us all like this!" She was smiling but her eyes told me to leave. Leave. Immediately.

"I must obtain the ingredients for the posset!" I called to her across the noise, trying to smile reassuringly.

Her eyes widened with understanding, and she thrust a few bottles and small sacks into my hands.

"OUT," she mouthed at Mary.

We made our way quickly to where Livia and Thomas were to spend their first night as husband and wife.

"Perhaps the King will close the Monasteries and Priories before you leave?"

I poured lavender oil on my palms and began plumping the pillows. "I leave in a handful of days," I say mournfully, now running my hands over the linen. "Besides the King has said they will be reformed. And even if he does close them, I warrant they will not close by Wednesday."

"If the King can divorce and behead his wives, he can do anything he wants, Elisa. This Anne ... she's going to be his fourth wife. Can you imagine, four wives!" Mary was pouring sugar into the jug. "It's a shame you never went to court," Mary added, wistfully.

I sat on the end of the bed. "There would be a lot of pretending and standing with your legs out in a line, and sucking up and all that."

"True." Mary nodded, flinging the petals over the bed.

"I suppose there will also be a lot of pretending and kneeling and sucking up to God at the Nunnery as well." Mary laughed, nearly spilling her jar of spices. "Maybe you've got it best, Mary."

"You forget I spend my days pretending it is my calling to light your fires, kneeling in front of you, and sucking up to your parents."

"Then it must be that all women are doomed." I leant over the end of the bed and adjusted a ribbon in her hair. I felt my throat constrict. I doubted I'd see her after I was confined. Maybe I would tell her about Samuel today.

"What's this posset about, anyway?" I said, my voice forced.

"Well, Lady Elisa, not that your parents would want me telling you, but we got some fortified wine here," she cleared her throat, "to relax the woman and invigorate the man."

"Oh my!" I pulled a face of mock horror.

"I have added the spice to make him last and we add the sugar to make him kind."

"Add lots of sugar. I want him to be very kind to Livia."

"She is giving him her maidenhead — I should hope he repay that gift with an abundance of sugary kindness." Mary tasted it, scrunched up her nose and shivered.

"Thomas will be giving her his virginity and virtue too, will he not?"

"Of course."

"Do you doubt it?"

"Only as I doubt every man."

I frowned. "Do you know something about Thomas? Does he have carnal knowledge of another woman?"

"If he is like all other men, I presume so."

I got up off the bed and brushed off my dress. "Well I hope not. For the sake of his soul, and for Livia's."

"Oh I don't know. An experienced man might be a better gift than a fumbling fool." She held the door open for me.

"Some days I wonder what you get up to, Mary. You sound like Samuel and it makes me worry for your soul and for your prospects." She slapped my bottom. "Mary!"

I sat on the top table during the feast, albeit on the very end. I was placed next to Eddie, of course, his minder more than his sister. The Great Hall had been decorated elaborately. Shining brass candle sticks and bunches of flowers cluttered the tables and I could hardly see for the giant roasted swan in front of me. The big bird's eyes shimmered as though she were about to cry but her long, elegant neck still managed to stay upright. Eddie plucked at her feathers. I told him to stop and pluck at the feathers in his cap instead.

"Of course it isn't quite Hampton Court." I looked down the table to see my father talking to a guest. "Although these tapestries are adorned with real gold and silver thread!" I peered over the swan's beak to look around the room. I wondered whether Father was telling a fib or not. The walls were glittering but was it just a facade? "Of course we don't have King Henry's tiltyard for jousting, his alleys for bowling or his courts for tennis!" Father laughed, his fake laugh, used for important guests. The smell of venison and roasted vegetables reached my nose. I spied the servants putting down even more platters on the long wooden tables. I spotted a tower of pies I hoped might come my way. "Though I would consider getting Grey's Court a tiltyard," he added loudly. I pinched the bridge of my nose and took a deep breath.

As the feast got on its way, people swirled about the hall, dancing and practising the art of flattery. My least favourite art. I was introduced to several of the Groom's kin. He had an abundance of brothers. My father stood behind me and introduced me to each one, ensuring each of them knew what I was destined for.

"This is my youngest daughter, Lady Elisabeth Knolly. Elisabeth is about to take her vows. She has known since a very young age that she was destined for confinement and for God's work."

He said the exact same words each time as if he had practised them in the glass. I had most certainly not known about this since a young age, but it reflected better on our family if I was leaving to the Priory to fulfil a vocation. He couldn't risk anyone assuming anything else.

Despite his carefully curated explanation, no one took

much interest in my impending enclosure; most drifted onwards to talk about how beautiful the house was or how well adorned my sister was. It was not until I met the fifth and final brother that someone finally expressed intrigue.

"Lacock Abbey, Lady Elisabeth?" He was another John. John was such a tedious name.

"Yes my lord; I wish to spend my days bent in prayer and devotion."

"And that is very admirable, Little Elisabeth." He must be only an inch taller than me, and at most a few years my senior. "It's a little Catholic but still, very admirable."

I looked up at my father, alarmed at this accusation.

"I can assure you, King Henry has full control of the religious houses. They are reformed." He was looking sternly at the young man.

John's body seemed to stiffen. "I didn't mean to doubt his Majesty, my lord."

"Of course you didn't." My father steered me away.

"Papa!" I turned to him, grabbing his wrists as soon as the man was out of earshot.

"Do not worry about John. He has a penchant for drama. He is not accusing us of anything." He touched my cheek. The movement was so slow and gentle. I wanted to grab him and bury my chest in all his furs and never let him go. "You are meant for this work," he said, as though reading my mind. "God has called you for it and he will look after you." I swallowed and nodded. "You present yourself very well around company."

I could feel my whole face flush with pleasure at his words. "Thank you, Father."

"Elisa, Mother has asked me to inform you that you are ..." he took a deep breath and shuffled uncomfortably "... you are only to attend the undressing of Livia this evening. Then you will leave. You will not be there when Thomas enters the room. Do you understand?"

"But it is tradition for the women of the family to be there with her."

"Your mother and I think it best." He was averting his gaze, as if I were naked again.

"Father —"

His mood changed drastically. "Elisa. Recall your vulnerabilities!" He shook me off and turned to walk away, beckoning Eddie to be with him.

The warm glow of his approval was steaming from its quick and brutal extinguishing. I was so livid, I couldn't yet feel that familiar burn of shame. I searched the gardens for my mother, and found her laughing with a group of court peacocks. I stared at her until she felt my presence. How dared she exclude me? She glanced in my direction, cocked her head at me, and raised her eyebrows as though to ask, "Anything wrong, Elisabeth?" But she knew. I knew she knew.

I sat alone for the rest of the evening. I had simmered back down to a numb resignation by the time the bride and groom were to retreat to their rooms. The balmy spring air had calmed me, the copious amounts of wine soothed my rage, and I had been watching Samuel for at least an hour, exchanging fleeting glances and small smiles. Mother might keep me from being there tonight, but she couldn't undo the past.

I gathered with the women of the family as Livia and Thomas kissed one last time before bed. It was traditionally the most raunchy kiss of the night, and they didn't disappoint. It encouraged a raucous rendition of a song about the different shapes and sizes of breasts. No one seemed to mind the obscenities, least of all Livia and Thomas. Agnes took my hand and we gathered around the bride with our cousins and aunts and friends; she was giggling and waving at Thomas as he was kidnapped by his own male kin, including young Eddie.

"Agnes, remind me how this goes," Livia whispered as we moved to one of the back doors of the house.

"We undress you in the bridal suite, and he will be undressed in the adjacent room." Everyone was giggling. I smiled. "Then Thomas will enter, having been undressed by his company." Furious noises of embarrassment and amusement were now coming from everyone. Even Mother. "Once you're both in bed we take turns in flinging undergarments at you,"

"Oh how amusing!" Livia clapped her hands together.

"Then you both drink the posset." I helped her up the stairs to the room. Her hands were shaking.

"Then we will not leave until your bridegroom has begged, pleaded and convinced us he cannot wait a moment more to have you!"

"Agnes!" said a chorus of scandalised voices.

"Lady Knolly! Lady Knolly!" There was a male voice coming from the bottom of the stairs. Mother looked down, frowning. The speaker revealed himself. It was Father Nicholas. He was propping himself up against the wall.

"Padre? Are you quite all right?"

"Perfectly fine, my lady, perfectly fine. It was only that I have noticed that Lady Elisabeth is in the party."

I felt my lip curl.

"She will be exiting before Thomas enters the room, Father Nicholas."

Everyone looked at me.

"A wise idea, very wise, my lady. But I have felt called to come retrieve her, perhaps at a bidding of Christ — it is better to be safe than sorry. And nothing good can come of her witnessing the undressing."

Everyone was there. Every woman I had ever known was

standing in this hallway. Listening to this. My mother paused for a long while. Slowly I turned to her. I shook my head.

"No Mama," I whispered.

"Seeing as she has proven herself to be so susceptible and vulnerable," the abhorrent man continued, slurring his words.

"Quite right, Father Nicholas," my mother said quickly, trying to cut him off mid-sentence. "Elisabeth, you will follow him down stairs and back out to the party."

"No, Mama!" It was Livia; she had grabbed hold of me.

"You don't understand her temperament," Mother said, detaching our hands.

I had no words. I was so angry. So truly enraged that if I did try to speak I would scream.

I turned and moved down the stairs.

"Quite right, Elisa. I will take you back to the party."

I pushed past him, elbowing him in the shoulder. He fell to the side, and the women called out, but he was too drunk to know what had happened.

"Do not fear, ladies, I've missed a step! I will escort Lady Elisabeth out." But I was already gone. I walked very fast, picking up a jug of wine and someone's empty goblet. I made speedily to the quieter parts of the garden, where I would drink this entire thing and pass out in the dirt.

Someone grabbed me by the arm. I let out a scream. They released me quickly.

"It's just me! My lady! I'm sorry! I shouldn't have grabbed you!" It was the groom, his name was Jakes. Or that's what all the servants seemed to call him — a nickname or a joke perhaps, seeing as he was the one who cleaned the 'jakes'.

"Jakes." I put my hand to my heart. "You made me spill my wine."

"I'm so sorry, my lady." He was crestfallen, hanging his head in shame.

"What can I do for you?"

"The maids and grooms are having our own little ... celebration." I gave him a small smile: he was nervous. "There is much more wine there. I saw you leave with the ... Nicholas ... behind you."

I held up my hand. I didn't need to relive that. "Lead the way."

CHAPTER SIX

There were plenteous good reasons for me to join this second, far merrier party. It would certainly vex my mother were she to discover my defection and Father Nicholas would definitely not approve. Moreover I had spilled a lot of my wine and needed more. And thirdly, well, Samuel would be there.

"Do you want what's left of the wine?" I asked Jakes, who was walking dutifully beside me, head down.

"Oh no, my lady. I could not."

"I can't be jolly with you if you treat me like your mistress." Jakes looked up at me bashfully. "Come, let us divide it in two." I drunk two gulps of wine and handed the jug to Jakes. He finished it and very manner changed. He smiled, his shoulders relaxed and his walk became bouncier.

"Where are you taking me?"

"To Samuel's house."

My body erupted with energy. My fingers felt like a blacksmith's hammer: sparks were about to fly out of them. I looked down to make certain it wasn't actually happening. Nicholas would have me drowned as a witch.

We approached the cottage. I could hear the laughing and

clinking of goblets from outside. The doors and windows were open and people flowed out into the garden. Samuel was standing on the front step.

"Elisa!" He inclined his head. "What are you doing here?"

"Father Nicholas …" I began, but sadness robbed me of the rest of my thought. I shook my head and looked properly at Samuel, tears spilt over. He moved quickly to me. I leant my head against his chest, and the sadness swelled again. "He stopped me going to Livia's room, before a company of kin." I could hear him mumbling curses into my hair. "Am I going to ruin your party?" I felt, rather than heard him laugh.

"I will warn everyone that they must behave just as if you were a maid. Scandalous behaviour will prevail. I will make sure of it." I looked up at him, still in his embrace. "Only if that pleases you."

I nodded. "It pleases me. I am in need of scandal, and wine. A great deal of wine."

He kissed my head. "Wine I have a-plenty."

A battle erupted in my mind as to what type of kiss that had been. Fatherly? Older-brotherly? Was it something more? It certainly wasn't tutor-ly. His lips brushed against my forehead. Oh Lord, Did I care? I looked up at him. "Are you ready to go inside?" I felt his breath on my face. Yes. I cared. I very greatly cared.

"I don't want anyone to call me lady, or to curtsey." I ducked through the small cottage door.

"Revellers!" Samuel called out. The room was filled with a dozen people — too many for such a small space, but everyone seemed happy, sitting on stools, the bed and at the hearth.

I smiled at everyone. I knew them all. They were, of course, surprised to see me.

"Elisa is here to overthrow her reason and be merry, and perchance talk shit about our masters for a bit." I laughed and everyone else followed. "She wishes, just for tonight, to be treated like a friend."

Mary bounded towards me. "Hello, friend!"

"It cannot be pretended you've ever treated me other than a friend."

She passed me a full goblet, took my hand and dragged me, to my great alarm, to the privy. She shut the door. The tiny room was attached to the back of his stone cottage. Lucky Samuel. Most of the servants just had to shit into pans. It was, like most privies, empty apart from the wooden bench with the hole in it. It was dark apart from a single burning candle.

"Mary! Why are we here?"

It didn't smell as horrible as most privies did. Verily the man was some sort of saint exempt from normal bodily functions.

"What happened?" Mary demanded.

"Why are we here, Mary?" I asked again.

"For privacy my lady. So we can talk." She sat down next to the wooden hole.

I winced. "Mary, people shit here. How much wine have you drunk?"

She shrugged, unperturbed, looking down the into the abyss of unspeakable waste.

"I clean up your shit each day." Fair enough. "Do you reckon Jesus shat?"

"Mary!" I crossed myself.

"I don't think Sam shits. It's so clean down there!"

I sighed and took a long, long draft of wine. "Can you take off my headdress?" I asked. I was wearing my cream diamond-shaped hood, with blue and gold jewels. Fake jewels, yes, but it was still out of place. She detached it from my hair and ran her fingers through my hair, unbraiding my plaits so the red tresses hung loose around my shoulders.

"Your hair looks so beautiful with the blue dress," she said wistfully. "Sam will —"

There was a rapping at the door. I jumped.

"Mary? You're not throwing up all over the jakes, are you?" It was Sam.

I opened the door. I could feel my face blush. "No purging in here," I assured him.

"Good. Now join the party. I must needs replace you on this throne here. The wine's gone straight through me."

I opened the door. His face was playful as he bobbed up and down, raising an eyebrow at Mary. She was giggling, refusing to move.

"Come, Mary! I'm absolutely overfull."

I took hold of her hand and dragged her out. We moved near to the hearth.

Nanny Francis stood up to offer me a stool. I almost took it before remembering.

"Is this a chair for Lady Elisabeth? Or common lass Elisa, a little drowsy with drink?" I took a large sip.

She smiled. "You're quite right — if you're not Lady Elisabeth then I'm going to put my big bottom right back down."

"As you should." I sat by the fire, Mary sat next to me.

"Do you care to talk over what happened?" Mary asked.

"No." I took another big sip. "I just want to enjoy the rest of my night."

"And do something rebellious," Mary instructed.

Sam brought over cheese and bread, and a woman called Beatrice. She was my mother's lady's maid and she had always frightened me. She was tall and formidable, but now she seemed different. Her hair hung lovelily around her broad shoulders, adorned with festive ribbons. She was expressing herself passionately, gesticulating wildly with her hands, clearly in disagreement with Samuel about something.

"It's not just about the words, Bea," Samuel said, "it's about what it says, underneath it."

"What're you talking about?"

"Poetry, Lady Elisa."

"Elisa." I corrected.

She didn't even wince, and she was normally a stickler for the rules. "Elisa. Samuel wants to see meaning behind everything. He forgets what's right in front of him. He thinks because he has been to university he knows more than me, but I can read those words and I am allowed an interpretation."

I smiled at her; she was red with passion. "What poem?"

"I will read it to you later," Samuel said. I flushed.

I sat, getting more and more dreamy with the warmth of the fire and the heat of the wine. I listened to the conversation meander and wind around poetry, touch on some local town gossip and then move onto the King's rumoured next wife, the other Anne. She was foreign and of middling beauty, according to most. Unlike the dead Anne, she was not rumoured to have any extra digits, but the more the conversation went on, the more extras this second poor Anne amassed (six fingers, twelve toes and an extra ear on the back of her head). Everyone spoke openly — our family would never have risked the Crown's displeasure by so much as mentioning the wife he'd had beheaded — laughing, asking questions and proffering ideas, saying silly things. They did not fear sounding foolish or blaspheming, even in my presence.

"Now, this has all been very interesting conversation," said Peter Thatcher, my father's groom. His face was round and happy. "But I think it's time for a spot of loggits!"

I was swept outside. Everyone got louder in the late night air.

"Now perhaps we should play regular old loggits, without …" Peter looked around the crowd "… the additions." Everyone snickered. They were like a little family.

"What be the additions?" I asked, swaying a little, leaning on Alice the kitchen maid for support.

"Well, the stick goes into the ground," Samuel began.

"That's normal practice for a game of loggit," I noted.

"And everyone throws their own stick towards the grounded stick."

"Still the same game as I play with Eddie ..."

"But whoever loses has to either tell a truthful answer to a certainly scandalous query, or perform a dare, that is most probably just as scandalous. The group can choose, truth or dare."

"That is different ..." I made my face look like my mother's. Stern and disapproving. I felt the air around me change. "It is a boon therefore that my throwing skills are excellent!" Everyone cheered loudly. I started wandering around the garden, looking for an instrument to throw.

"Choose one with smooth edges," advised Peter, "so you might launch it as you would a spear."

"Ah but that never works well for you, does it, Peter?" said a tiny little woman who I only knew as the wench responsible for lighting the fires. "I go for a short stubby one."

An inappropriate joke about the male member was made. I laughed, but mostly just revelled in the fact no one had worried about my soul as it was said.

I found my own weapon of choice. We gathered around a big yew. Sam inserted a tall branch into the ground, at which we were to aim. We lined up in a row. It was marvellous hard to see. There were lanterns in the tree, and around the garden, but the stick was just as dark as the grass below it.

"On three, we all throw."

"Fie! Lady Elisa hath stepped over the line!" Nanny Frances was pointing at the hem of my dress.

I stepped back, apologising.

"Thou knave, Elisa!" yelled Samuel, far too loudly seeing as he was standing right next to me. "Let us begin. Three ..." I was going to go for the spear-throwing technique "... two ..." I was nervous. Did I really want my servants to be able to ask me any question they want? Or make me do whatever they pleased? What if they resented me? "... one!" I threw my spear twig. It fell embarrassingly short, but it wasn't as short as Mary's. She had ventured a sideways fling and it had betrayed her. Everyone was bouncing around and pointing at her, and she was on her knees, wailing but also laughing at her own miserable failure.

"Drink!" Samuel instructed. Mary finished off her goblet of wine. I drank too, in solidarity.

"Do you want to answer a question, Mary? Or do you want a challenge?"

Her head lolled backwards. "DARE!" she shouted loudly. Cheers erupted again.

"Everyone gather near." Everyone but Mary gathered into a circle. Samuel put one arm about me and his other arm around Alice. He was very warm.

"What shall we make her do?" asked Jakes, slurring.

"No nakedness!" Mary yelled out.

"What's that, Mary?" said Peter. "Is't a bare bodikins you choose?"

"Nay, Peter!"

"What thinkest you, Lady Elisa?" Beatrice asked. "Surely after all these years there's something you'd like to make her do?"

I thought about it. "You are right. I want to ask her something."

"She said Dare."

"But it is our choice what we make her do," said the fires wench.

People murmured agreements. We broke our circle. Mary held her chin high, awaiting her sentence.

"I've chosen truth, Mary."

"Ask me your question, peasant."

I cleared my throat. "Have you ever kissed, or otherwise sported with, a member of the household." There was a conglomerate moan of protest. "What? What's amiss? It is a good question!"

"I'd warrant Mary has kissed every gentleman in this circle. It's a boring question."

I looked at Mary; she was grinning.

"And she's definitely had her hands down Sam's trousers!" Beatrice declared. Everyone laughed. Was that a jape? I looked at Mary, who was giggling with her hands over her face. Embarrassed, but not upset. Were they laughing because it was funny or because it was not true?

"Mary?" I spoke quietly, but it cut through all the noise.

"You're the one who wanted to know, Elisa." She tucked a dark lock behind her ear, and I saw how beautiful she was. I looked at Sam. He was looking at me. Was he waiting to see how I would react?

I took a deep breath. The air was filled with the vibrations of tiny wings, moths were hovering around the lanterns. I took a long sip of wine, trying to relax into the new information.

"Forgive me, I was knocked into silence by Mary's brave shenanigans!" A fresh cheer from the little crowd. I flicked my hair back casually, my face was relaxed, beautiful and unfazed, fingers crossed.

"Next round!" cried someone and we lined up by the tree yet again.

I decided to try again my spear-throwing technique, but this time, it truly did fail me. It had no power. It went up and then down, with the tiniest little thud you could ever imagine.

Everyone looked at me.

But this time their expressions had changed.

"I am ready," I declared, smiling wildly and sitting down on a tree stump. I took a long draught of my drink and crossed my legs under my skirts. A little more reluctantly, they gathered in a circle. I tried to o'erhear what they were saying. Their hushed whispers assailed me. It took a long time for them to decide. I wondered if I should also declare I would not disrobe. What would they make me do? They turned to me, their faces stern.

"We have decided to dare you to drain your entire drink."

"It has to be full," added Peter.

"Drink my entire drink?" I asked incredulously. "That is a dare for a child!"

"No it's not! You have to drink it in one draught."

"Art thou cozening me for being Lady Elisabeth?"

"We cannot dare you to run naked around, or kiss someone …" Mary mumbled.

"Why not, prithee? Samuel and I have kissed!" There was a stunned silence.

Samuel looked down at me.

"You've what?" whispered Jakes.

"We've kissed."

"But —" Mary started.

"But what? I'm only a child?"

"No —"

"I'm about to be a Nun?"

"Well —"

"I'm above his station?"

"You —"

"Don't make me drink as a dare! I don't have much time left abroad in the world."

Samuel slipped his fingers into mine. My breath caught in my throat. It was not panic; it was excitement. I didn't know if anyone else could see, as our hands were tucked in the ruffles of my skirt.

"Elisa —" Mary began, as though she were a million years older than me and wiser.

"Give me a proper dare!" I was determined. I imagined what my parents would think if they could see me now. Drinking, playing this game, with my hands entangled in this man's. In Samuel's hand. I felt another pleasurable vibration run down my spine. I was not a child. And I was not a Nun, not yet.

"I dare you to do it again then," Mary said.

Beatrice coughed uncomfortably. "The mistress ..." she muttered under her breath.

I did not need my mother mentioned. I would do this. Rules are rules.

I turned to look at Samuel. He was neither smiling nor frowning. I could not tell what he was thinking. There was a moment's pause.

"Well, will not you kiss me?" I asked.

"The dare is that you kiss me," he corrected.

It took only a second to summon the nerve.

I stood on my tiptoes and kissed him. It started a little chastely but the cheering and whooping spurred me on. I tried to make it look like Livia and John's, but it was surely so much better than that. Sam tugged at my lip with his teeth and his hand went to the small of my back. He tasted like sweet wine. People started whistling. We broke apart and I smiled, triumphantly. I looked at Beatrice. She would have to brush my mother's hair tomorrow morning and know about this moment. The thought gave me great pleasure.

The night rumbled on in a haze of wine. I seemed to blink and end up somewhere else. One moment I was throwing my stick, next moment I was back in the cottage, lying on the floor by the fire, listening to Samuel play the lute and Mary sing.

"I wonder if anyone hath noticed that I am gone," I say to the room.

I rolled myself onto my side and looked around. It was much emptier than the last time I had rolled over. How long had I been lying there?

"Well Livia's not going to check on you, and I'm not going to attend you, and Agnes will have gone to bed with John." Mary was dancing slowly.

"What of Mother?"

Mary shrugged. "Mayhap, but she hasn't come out looking."

"She thinks I am sulking."

"Thou lookest sulky, indeed," Samuel said, as I supped on my wine while lying on my back.

"How long until the sun comes up?"

"Not long. It will soon be time for us to start cleaning up," said Alice, her eyes shut. "We ought to sleep."

I was exhausted, but this mention of the feast ending saddened me. I sat up. The room was spinning, but I tried to see Alice in the blur. "Do not leave, Alice."

"I have to clean the kitchens this morrow, Elisa."

"I shall come and help," I promise. Alice laughed, as did Jakes. "I will!"

"Very well, Elisa, we'll see you in a few hours in the kitchen."

"Yes you will!"

It was just Mary, Samuel and myself left. Sam handed me some bread with cheese. Where did he get that from? Did he get that cheese out of his pocket? Do lowly people keep cheese upon their persons? In their pockets? One of my eyes shut.

"Are you winking at me?" Samuel asked. I shrugged. "You're going to feel horrible when you wake. Eat."

I did. My head cleared a little. I imagined the bread soaking up the red wine that sloshed around in my belly.

Mary was still dancing, despite Samuel having stopped

playing. I watched her get slower and slower, she was leaning more and more to her left.

"Sam!" I yelled out. I tried to get up, but tripped over my skirts. Mary was falling backwards, almost as slow as she was dancing. Samuel caught her. He gently lowered her to the ground.

"Fetch my sal armonyak, Elisa. In my trunk."

I knew what that was: a solution to arouse the unconscious. I found it quickly in a glass jar, uncorked it and put it under Mary's nose. She spluttered and coughed and her eyes half opened. She smiled at Samuel and me.

"You two should kiss again!" she declared. Then she dropped flat on the floor and started snoring.

"Shall we arouse her again?" I asked, bottle at hand.

"No, no … she'll sleep it off. But she's going to be in trouble tomorrow. Empty her cup of wine and fill it with water." I did as he said whilst Sam put her on the bed. Her legs and arms were each going in a different direction. I covered her with a blanket, trying to maintain what was left of her dignity. Not that she seemed to care. I had learnt a lot about her that night.

"And you …" I said, finishing my thought out loud. "I learnt a lot about you this even too." He smiled, putting a kettle over the fire.

"You and Mary have …?"

"Mary and I have." He nodded.

"Do you still … tangle with her? Do you like each other? Do you want to be married?"

I was sitting on the end of the bed, legs swinging like a child's. He took a long moment before he answered. "No we do not still tangle. Yes I like her. No I do not want to be married."

"But do you have a fancy for her?" I pressed.

"Why do you ask?"

"You know why," I said aggressively. I had felt near to sober when I saw Mary fall, but the clouds descended now once more.

Sam looked at me seriously. His brow crinkled. "No, Elisa, I do not have a fancy for Mary any longer."

"Why not?" I was barely audible now.

"I'm not sure. Perhaps it is because, of late, I've had instead a fancy for you."

I exhaled.

I wanted to bundle up the feeling in my heart in a package and then keep it in my pocket.

He was looking at me sternly from his stool by the fire. "I will be very sad to farewell you come next Sunday." Why did he have to say that? My body stiffened with sadness. "Perhaps you should go back to your rooms now. I can take care of Mary."

"No." I felt evidence of a tear on my cheek, damn traitorous drop.

"If you are found here, I will be ..." he searched for the word, "fucked."

"So you would want me to go?"

"Nay. I want you to go nowhere at all: not to your bed and not to the Nunnery."

I moved to him, I don't remember the process of moving but I was with him, his face inches from my waist.

He did not push me away but he did not touch me. I had never seen the like. He was the most relaxed, unbothered man in England, but his whole body was taut. I stroked his cheek.

"Elisa," he said, his breath shallow, "you should go to bed. This isn't Godly."

I laughed. "Since when have you been worried about Godliness? " He shook his head.

"You tore open your back ..." His voice broke. He rubbed his eyes. He looked exhausted. "I hated seeing you like that, Elisa. I hate what your parents and the Priory and Father Nicholas and ... I hate what they have put upon you. I don't want to create more pain for you. I couldn't be the cause of more pain, or more shame ..." His eyes shifted again. "I don't want to do anything that means I wake up tomorrow and find you in the stables with a whip."

I hated his fear. I hated hearing the word whip. I hated knowing he was scared for me. I went to move away but he put his hand on my hip. The jolt of him pulling me towards him created a sudden tension. I began breathing in short gasps.

"Do you want me to leave?" I asked again.

His head made a minute movement from side to side. No.

Then he pulled my head to his and kissed me. It was not like our other kisses. It was hard and messy, driven by something desperate. He yanked on my waist till I straddled him like a man straddles a horse, not breaking contact with my lips.

I could feel him underneath my skirts. I had that effect on him. Elisa Knolly out on a summer's night, making pricks hard. I almost started laughing.

I pulled at his soft curls and he let out a groan. I was so close to his body. I was reminded of how much older he was. He was so experienced. I reshuffled on his lap, and he made another soft whimper and I smiled.

"Elisa. What do you want? Why are you doing this to me?"

"I'm doing this to you?" His hand was under my skirts, on my hose, around the outside of my thigh. He was frowning.

"What do you want?" he whispered, as though it were hard to speak.

I tried to imagine myself tomorrow. If I let him touch me. If I touched him. I reached out and put my hand on his chest. I imagined what Margery Kemp would say if she saw me, or Christ ... He was watching, I reminded myself. Samuel moved his other hand slightly up my back, pulling me forwards. I felt him brush over the scab that ran up my spine. I didn't want to hate myself. I did not want to be disgusted by myself. But right now I did not feel disgusting. I felt like a woman. Like I was filled with something Godly. Like I was a kind of saint. I moved myself against him. He groaned yet again, and his head tipped back.

"Elisa. Do you want this? Will you want to have done this tomorrow?"

I leant my bust towards him and kissed his ears.

"Elisa!" he called out. "Yes or no."

I took a deep rattling breath. "Samuel, I'm about to be locked away for the rest of my life. I will die in a Priory an old woman. God can have me a prisoner, and he will have my whole life to mend or forgive me. I don't want to step from childhood to enclosure without this. I want you."

I watched his Adam's apple move as he swallowed. "I want you too."

"Christ," I whimpered, shocking myself. Lord, the next confession was going to take years at this rate. I smirked at the idea of retelling this story in detail to Nicholas. I imagined his face as I told him about how I reached my hand in between Sam's leg to brush against him.

I wished Mary were not upon the bed.

"I wish Mary were not upon the bed," Sam said out loud.

We got up off the chair. Sam held me, in all my heavy dresses, with my legs wrapped around his middle. He set me down against the wall. Slowly, painfully slowly, he began to undress me. He knew what to do. He shifted off my petticoat and girdle and bodice, no problem at all. And then I was standing there pinned to the wall in just my shift. He stopped there. Still breathing heavily.

"Do not doubt me now," I said, seeing it in his eyes.

"I cannot fathom I am looking at you. Like this." The memory of people averting their eyes from Joan crossed my mind, then the memory of revealing my scars to my parents surfaced too. I shivered. No. This was not like those moments. This was different.

I gathered the bottom of my shift in my hands and pulled it over my head. I had never been this naked in front of anyone — even when Mary ran my baths I would cover myself. But my hands were stretched up above my head, my whole body there for him.

I dropped the shift on the floor.

Livia had once said that I have big hips. I wondered if Sam was noticing that now. I hoped big hips was a good thing. He didn't seem displeased.

"It is not fair that I am bared and you are not," I announced.

He pulled off his shirt and then he pressed his body against my own. I put an arm around him and touched his back. Tracing letters on his smooth skin. I used my other hand to play at the tie around his upper hose. Samuel never wore a codpiece, despite it being the height of fashion. My sisters always mentioned his obvious rejection of the trend. I remember noting when they mentioned it that they seemed mildly disappointed. But right now, it looked as though he were indeed following the fashion.

He bent forwards and put his mouth on my breast, and I felt my whole body convulse. He stood up to kiss my lips; he looked so serious, his thumb slowly rolling over my nipple. I heard myself making small involuntary noises. He moved slowly back and forwards from my lips to my breasts. My whole body was vibrating. My thoughts were not coherent. I had just enough sense to check that Mary slept on despite our noises. She hadn't moved.

Sam started kissing my belly. I grabbed a fistful of his hair and he moaned into my skin. His tongue was dancing across my midriff. My eyes were darting around the room, frantic. Then, in my frenzy, I caught a glimpse of my face. It was my reflection, in a dirty piece of glass Samuel had hung near the door.

That damn glass. My body stopped shivering. I couldn't feel Sam's tongue on my skin any more but I could suddenly see very clearly. My long hair was scrunched up, sticking out at odd angles, my freckles were embarrassingly bright sitting atop of my ghostly skin, my mouth was parted in some obscene moan of pleasure. I was sweating. Even from here, even in that dirty tarnished glass, I could see that that child was kidding herself. Sam pushed me a little up the wall and I caught sight of my breast, small and stupidly shaped. I was immobilised with revulsion. It was as if Christ himself was showing me what he saw.

"Elisa?" Why was I doing this? How could I think to do this? I tore my gaze from the foolish child in the glass and pulled away, grabbing at a blanket and wrapping it around myself. I was Joan. I had become Joan. My lank hair, my shamed face and my sheet.

"Elisa," Sam said warily.

I had moved quickly, in a panic.

"We will stop. We won't do anything more."

"You do not want this," I told him.

"Elisa, I do want this."

"I am a virgin. A child. I am not like Mary. I am not sensual. I am made for a habit."

"No, Elisa —" I was scrambling with my clothes. Trying to cover myself. I could see the way I looked, naked, trying to put my leg into a skirt. My private parts open and vulnerable.

"Elisa." Samuel had one hand out as if I were a wild horse about to bolt. "Please listen to me. Please."

"I want to go back to my house and go to bed."

"You can go. You can go." He was whispering. "You haven't done anything wrong, Elisa. You needn't ask for forgiveness or seek penitence. Pray for me, if anyone. If you want to see fault here, find it in me."

I was backing towards the door. I felt the latch behind me and I opened it and then I ran.

The night filled with the sound of my name. He called for me. I even heard the sound of his feet on the grass, but then that stopped, and there was silence. I felt the long grass whip against my legs, my bare feet sore injured as I stood on twigs and fallen acorns, but I did not care. Grey's Court loomed above me, its red brick a soft pink in the morning light, welcoming me home, back to my family, back to my innocence.

CHAPTER SEVEN

I did not wake to tidy the wedding mess. I did not wake at all until Mary was sent for me by my mother.

I felt her touch my shoulder. I woke, but did not open my eyes. They did not feel able. They were stitched shut. Eventually, I strained against the goop holding them together and saw Mary, pale as a ghost with dark rings under her eyes, kneeling by my bed.

"Elisa?"

I stared at her, trying to remember who I was, what I was doing, what day it was. Slowly, as though trickling through all of time, the memories resurfaced. I stared at my lady's maid.

"Are you okay?" she asked gently.

I tried to push myself up. "What time is it?"

"Past midday, you little slugabed."

She passed me a plate of food and a cup of water and then clambered into bed next to me. My heartbeat was speeding up, flashes of last night scorching my vision.

Mary began to detail the different places she'd thrown up around the garden and how she'd been yelled at because she couldn't lift any of the chairs back inside. But I wasn't really listening. "My lady, are you well? You look to be in pain." She forced me to eat and drink. I debated telling her what had happened.

"I think you are in pain as much as I."

She buried her head in the pillows. "What was I like? Was't dreadful?" she wailed.

I stroked her back gently. "Not dreadful, Mary. You danced and laughed."

"And then fell asleep on Sam's bed?"

"More or less."

"Did anything happen between us?"

I shook my head tightly.

"Maybe it happened after you left?" she speculated. I hoped not. "I guess if something had happened, it wouldn't be anything new."

"Speak no more, please."

There was a pause, then more of Mary's memories resurfaced. "Zounds, Elisa, I just remembered!" She lowered her voice. "You kissed Sam!"

I felt a drop of sweat run down my side.

"I knew you liked him."

I didn't say anything.

Mary reached for my brush, pushed me forwards and began tending my hair. I loved to have my hair brushed: it made me feel young and safe. I cried, hoping she couldn't tell. I felt deep regret, but I couldn't determine whether it was from wanting more of last night or wanting less, much less.

"I hope you are not angry for letting yourself kiss him."

I started to shake with the power of my tears. "I don't wish to speak on it," I manage.

She started making shushing noises, cooing to me as if I were a baby. The brushing was rhythmical and calming. "They say the young Princess Elizabeth has hair just like yours, Elisa.

You've got princess locks," she said kindly, starting to plait my hair.

There was an urgent knock on the door. I jumped. "Yes?" I choked, confused. Everyone in this house just entered my chambers.

Samuel opened it and quickly shut it behind him, looking to have been running from someone.

"Samuel!" I tried to wipe my face on my bedcovers, but he had already seen. He started pacing, running his hands through his hair.

"Oh my sweet Lord, you laid your leg over me," breathed Mary. "Sam, I will come down to your house to broach this. Why have you come to Lady Elisa's room?"

Sam rolled his eyes wildly and flung his hands in the air. "No, Mary! I didn't have my leg over."

"Shhh!" I demanded.

"I need to speak with Elisa."

Mary was standing, looking from Samuel to me, trying to pin together our story.

"Does my mother know you're here?" I whispered urgently.

He shook his head. "Of course not. No one saw me. They are all in the withdrawing chamber." His face knotted in a frown. "I need to talk to Lady Elisa, Mary."

"Why?"

"Mary."

"What happened?"

"Go, Mary," I demanded.

"Elisa, what happened?"

"Leave!"

She backed out of the room. "What did you do to her?" she hissed at Sam.

I threw a pillow after her, suddenly furious. "Nothing! No one did anything to me!"

The door closed. I heard the latch click with precision. The room was silent.

"You were crying," Sam accused.

I was standing on my bed, sheet in front of my body. I gazed down at him. "Mary pulled at my hair when she was brushing it."

"Liar." He moved to stand at the foot of my bed, looking up at me.

"I'm allowed to cry if I want to cry."

"You are. But I do not want you to."

"If you are caught in my rooms, Sam —"

"I know what would happen!" he snapped. I reached my hand out, placing it on his head, wanting to calm him. He took a slower breath. "I know what would happen but I wanted to ask you ..." he swallowed "... I wanted to ask you not to go to the Nunnery. I want to ask you to stay and be with me."

Of everything that had happened in the last day and night, this was the thing that surprised me the most. I tried to retrieve my fingers from his hair but they were stuck in a knot. So I stood, hand in his curls, staring at him.

The door banged open and Eddie tore into the room. I jumped so hard I nearly slipped on my sheet; I yanked at his hair and came free.

Sam muffled a curse and rounded on him. "Edmund!" He scooped up my little brother. Looked at me pleadingly and then left.

I had seven more days at home.

CHAPTER EIGHT

Outwardly, I maintained my composure, but inside I was praying, near constantly. My thoughts did not belong to me any more; nearly all of them were directed to the Lord. I watched the world for a sign from God and I saw them everywhere.

I spent the next three days in bed. I came down with an illness. I was shaking all over. I spent my mornings shivering from cold and then my evenings sweating from heat. My head was heavy, and my eyelids too. It was a punishment. It was a call from Christ to stay in bed, to not go outside and find Samuel. I was never going to accept his offer. Of course I wasn't going to. But I had never planned on taking off my clothes and showing him what is meant to stay hidden either. I could not trust myself. God could not trust me. So the Lord was helping me. Keeping me hidden.

The next divine sign was that, when I felt better, Samuel left to see his mother. I felt supported — guided through the last few days of my secular life — protected. I even felt safe in Father Nicholas's sermons. I just stared at the roof and looked at the gargoyles. I named them all. My favourites were Arthigal the demon with the ruffles. He had endearing boggled eyes. And Pantalinom the Monkey Ghoul. I named the half-woman half-snake Boleyn. A nod to The Great Whore. I would conjure stories about their life in the Church when no one was there. They ran around the pews and played tricks on the Father. Such merry nonsense drowned out the Priest's voice. I retreated into my own mind. I don't think I looked anyone in the eye for days.

I was beginning to think I wasn't going to see Samuel at all. He had not been serious about his proposal. For he asked me and then left, not even awaiting my answer. Not that I had one. I had no answer, because it should have never been a question. But still, it seemed cruel of him to ask and then vanish.

But I did see him one last time, on my last day at home.

I was wandering around the gardens. I was doing this a lot. For hours and hours at a time. Reciting prayers, praying for my family, praying for the King, for the baby prince Edward. I was starting my transition. The wisteria had lost all of its flowers, but I still took great comfort from its ancient vines. I visited them often. But on this day, when I grasped the coarse, steady branch, I froze. Edmund had succeeded in his daily bid to get his lessons moved outside. Samuel was home and evidently feeling generous after his short holiday.

"Elisa!" Eddie ran to me. He had been very upset at the prospect of me leaving. I stroked his head and held him to me.

"Is your mother well, Samuel?" I asked, bringing Eddie back to his blanket and books.

"I'm afraid not." He looked drawn, paler than normal.

I reached out to him. "Is there anything I may do?"

"Nothing now. She died three days past."

"God rest her," I whispered.

His eyes glistened. He bit his lip. Then he shrugged.

"Is there anything I can do for you, Sam, anything at all?"

"You are to go to the Priory tomorrow?"

I wanted to tell him no. "Yes."

"Then no, there is naught you can do."

I looked down at Eddie. He was crying. He clung to my skirts.

"Please don't go, Elisa." Snot ran down his face. His bottom lip was wobbling impossibly fast.

I let out a horrible loud sob, one that had been sitting beneath my very heart all week long. What a miserable knot of people we were. All three of us, standing in a circle, crying.

I could not cover the sound of my distress. Just like my baby brother, I continued to weep openly. But I could not stay with them forever. I turned away and walked back towards the house. I could hear Eddie calling after me, making blubbering noises. Samuel was not making any noise. He did not call for me.

I was to say goodbye to my family at the house. I would be driven to Lacock Abbey by Jakes.

Mary dressed me in my new white postulant's tunic. I did not wear the veil yet — for that I would need to complete my postulancy and embark on my novitiate years. My bags were packed into the cart. My family stood in a line outside Grey's Court. So did the grooms and maids. So did Samuel. As I stood there, looking at them all, I felt removed not only from my house, or from my position — I felt as though God had lifted me out of time itself. I stood there, staring at them, and no time passed at all. They were frozen and I could examine them for as long as I wanted, my heart not beating. My father was stern. I saw the lines on his brow. I wondered what they meant. Was he being reverent and serious because of his respect for my choices, for what I was doing? I would like that. My mother was tight-lipped, angry. I hoped that she was angry with the situation, with her youngest girl being whisked away by their poor financial choices. I hoped she was not angry with me.

I looked to Mary; she was holding Livia's hand, something that would not often happen in public. But today was an exception. Mary held Livia's hand and Livia was holding Agnes's hand. It was a string of women who I loved. My small court of ladies. Perhaps, had I more control, if I were more chaste, then none of this would have befallen me and I would clasp my sisters' hands and we would stand in a circle, all connected, forever. But, instead I needed enclosure. I had to be taken away. I looked at Eddie, standing in front of Samuel's legs. Samuel had his hands on Eddie's chest, because he was squirming and crying. I guess time was still moving. Eddie broke free and grasped me around my middle. He wailed and protested.

My mother called for order. I soothed Eddie with hollow words. I pushed him back. Samuel took him from me. Our fingers brushed.

Then I was in the cart. I had not hugged anyone. I had not touched my family. As soon as the horses began to move I felt a panic, as if I had forgot something important at home. Why hadn't I hugged them? Why hadn't I embraced each and every one of them? How could I have just got in the carriage like this? Before I had said anything? Before I had embraced them?

I leant my body out the window: the world was foggy, not real, black and white like a frightening dream.

"I love you!" I called out. To whom, I did not know.

PART II

CHAPTER NINE

I did not want to attend to my thoughts. I could feel them in my mind, whirling around in a panic. The faces of my sisters. The grubby touch of my brother. Samuel. The knowledge I would never see them ever again was sitting somewhere within me, and I didn't dare go near it. I couldn't trust myself not to jump out the carriage and run home. I looked out of the window, trying to distract myself from the painful feelings. I listened to the rhythm of the horse hooves on the road, the occasional splash as hoof hit puddle. The scar on my back brushed up against the leather carriage seat. I started entertaining thoughts about my depravity, my nakedness. Perhaps I will turn up at the Priory and they will look at me, and they will see me. The ghost of Samuel at my breasts for all the Nuns to see. I tried to imagine leaving my sins behind. This carriage was taking me away from the transgressions of my corporeal life. I was new. I was about to be reborn.

I didn't want to leave it all behind, however, and a part of me, albeit a small part, did not want to forget what had happened between Sam and me.

I think I must have slept. A gift from God. A moment

away from the rattling in my mind. I woke to hear Jakes speaking with someone. I looked out the window.

Lacock Abbey. My parents had chosen my enclosure well. The Abbey was magnificent. It was grand, but not ostentatious. The large, sprawling building glowed gold in the evening light, the late summer vines still clung to its walls. There were small towers and eves dotted across the roofs: they were white with the fashionable crisscrossing of wooden beams. It wasn't the familiar red brick of my home, but it was beautiful. I slid my bottom to the other side of the carriage, looking out the other window. The gardens were expansive and well cared for. I could see forests in the distance, beyond the patchwork of fields filled with sheep. I craned my neck out of the carriage to locate the road to the village. It would not be a long walk to civilisation. We were not too alone. I took a ragged breath of relief. A part of me had envisioned being sent to the tower.

There were people standing at the front of the Abbey. A mirror of what I had left. It was such a similar sight I almost looked for Samuel. I shook my head, sloughing off my sleepy mistake. That must be the Abbess Catherine Wellys. She stood next to the Chaplain. He stood out in bright robes, surrounded by the sisters in their dark colours. Jakes helped me out of the carriage, then I stood still as he gathered my things. I did not move forwards. I had not thought this far ahead. Was I still to be treated like a Knolly? Were we all the same rank as before enclosure? Who was to greet me?

The Abbess stepped forwards.

"Lady Elisabeth." So I was still to be called Lady. "Welcome to Lacock." You'd really think they'd choose a better name for a place of virtuous chastity. "This is our chaplain, Reverend Father Peter."

"Reverend Father." I inclined my head. The short, stumpy man waddled forwards.

"Lady Elisabeth. I am so glad you have arrived safely in our hands. I have been praying for you." His voice was slimy, his words strangely elongated.

A horrible thought struck me: had Father Nicholas sent a letter ahead of me, warning everyone of my behaviours? I scanned his eyes for the look I knew too well. The look of shame and disgust. But they were glazed and self-absorbed. He did not know.

"These are your Sisters." They were not my sisters. The Abbess was gesturing to the rest of the greeting party. There were a dozen other women, all of whom looked similar in their habits, except one very large and short lady who stood at the end.

"Sister Constance!" Catherine barked suddenly.

A woman moved easily forwards. "Lady Mother?"

"Prithee carry Lady Elisabeth's bags to her quarters."

I looked Constance in the eye. She was beautiful, with immaculate pale skin, bright blue eyes and light eyebrows. I wondered why she could not have been married off. Perhaps she had no money. She winked at me before picking up my bags. I did not know how to respond.

The Sisters dispersed, the Chaplain left, and I was led away from the carriage by the Abbess. I looked around for Jakes, but couldn't find him to say my farewells. Perhaps he was tending to the horses. Would I see him before he departed? Tears formed in my eyes at the idea of not saying goodbye to him. The only connection left to my home.

"Of course there will be a lot of learning and getting used to practices in the first weeks. But you will be quickly accustomed."

The Abbess led me straight into the cloister, which shimmered with evening light. There was well-tended green grass in the middle of the courtyard and the passages were swept and clean. I could hear the hem of my white tunic on the floor, swishing on the stone. It had been made a little long for me in case I had any more growing to do, and then I would hem it when I shrunk with old age.

"Here we have the chapter house. For meetings, and readings." I nodded, peering into a large room with stools. "Up there is the refectory hall; you must wash your hands before you eat."

"Naturally."

"Now you must understand that as a Sister at Lacock the labour hours are different from those at other Priories and Abbeys." I nodded again, though I did not understand. We entered a small hallway and went up a large stone staircase. "According to the Rule of St Benedict we participate in the five divine services; we also have reading time and time to sew and spin. However there is also mandatory manual labour. We need help in the fields — there are many sheep in our flocks and we produce a lot of wool. But most importantly Lacock is an infirmary for those in need, and a sanctuary for travellers on the road."

We were met with a very large door. She opened it using her shoulder, putting all her weight into forcing it ajar. I looked into a great hall like that at Greys, with its tall arched roof, the stone walls lined with portraits of impressive-looking men, with the large fireplace and protruding chimney. Here, however, in place of sumptuous sofas and furs, armour and hangings, beds lined the walls. One dozen or so patients were tucked up in these beds. And Nuns in smocks were bustling around the ward, armed with bottles of herbs and remedies. The room smelt of peppermint and lavender, covering the miasmas of the sick, I supposed. I could see sprigs of it on patients' beds and on the tables. I had seen nothing like it before.

"We also have private rooms on the other side of the Abbey, for scholars who are visiting and the clergy men." I nodded. "I was told you have experience with some medicinal herbs and gardening?" I nodded again. "Then we will need you in the Infirmary." She tried to heave the door shut, but gave up half way.

"Sister Isabella!" she barked.

The large woman walked over at great speed. "Mother?" Her round face was flushed.

"Shut the door, Sister."

Isabella nodded and put her weight on the large piece of oak.

"Be wary of Sister Isabella," Mother Catherine continued to me. "Though most of our Sisters would not have received a habit unless found to be useful, teachable, discreet and chaste, Isabella is not … of that calibre."

"She isn't chaste?" I whispered.

Catherine laughed. "Of course she's chaste! What man would bed her?" I was liking the Abbess less and less. "No. She is …" The Prioress led us back around to the other side of the cloister. "She was cursed at birth. Her mother had probably sinned greatly," she was speaking loudly, uncaringly. "She has no hand on her left side."

"I see."

"It is required that we admit such postulants from time to time. Almsgiving. Like Christ, you know." I nodded. "The King is grateful that houses such as ours care for the debase and ill." I raised an eyebrow. She pressed on. "Rumours about the closure of religious houses are, of course, just rumours." My eyebrow remained raised. My heart beat a little harder. Dangerous conversation, Mother Abbess. "As rightful head of the Church, King Henry needs us now, more than ever before."

Her tone was tense. I wondered how much of her own drivel she believed. I found myself praying she were wrong. I prayed King Henry would send his troops here and carry me back home.

The Abbess continued. "All the rooms on this side of the

courtyard are bedchambers." The sun was creating shadows against the long row of doors. "That is my room. In the middle. And these are your quarters." It was a very small room, with a narrow bed and a window looking out onto the gardens. I saw the Greys carriage returning home in the distance.

I had missed my chance to say goodbye to Jakes.

The beauty of the Abbey was not powerful enough to combat the sadness of this realisation. I was not certain I could withhold my sorrow for many moments longer. I wondered if I was to be left alone soon. "Your parents have, of course, required you to have a private room, and this is the mattress they sent ahead of you. You and the widow Jane are the only two sisters with private quarters and they can be taken away if your behaviour slips, if you become indiscreet, unholy or, God forbid, unchaste." It was a threat. I looked at my feet. Unable to stop tears.

"You may stay here for now. I will send a Sister to get you for Vespers."

She shut the door. Huge sad gasps left my body. I sat on my mattress shaking.

"Sister Elisa?"

It was Isabella. I started crying more. I tried to say something, I tried to apologise but the words weren't making sense. I could feel tears and snot run down my face. I felt like Eddie. Oh Eddie … Another loud and shameless bout of grief rounded on me.

Isabella came and sat on the bed. She rubbed my back with her hand and made shushing sounds. Slowly, very slowly, the sobs ebbed away.

"I did not embrace my parents in farewell," I manage audibly. "And I missed my groom."

"Oh sweet sister." I only now noticed that she had a northern accent. "This is not an easy time for you." She continued rubbing my back. "Just breathe in and out. Slowly does it. There is time before Vespers."

I glanced at the hand she had in her lap. It was a mound of flesh. No fingers or palm. She noticed me looking.

"I presume Mother Catherine told you about her?"

"Her?"

"My stump. I address her like she's a Lady."

I smiled through my tears. "Lady what?" I snuffled.

"She has not a name exactly. I just refer to her as a lady." I wiped my nose. "I could name her though," she added thoughtfully. There was a knock at the door. Or not a knock — more of a scratch. I looked at Isabella. "I was expecting this." She hopped up and unlatched the door. "This is Arnold."

The dog was large, dark and shaggy. A true hound. He nuzzled into my legs. I petted him and he took away some of my pain.

"I didn't realise you were allowed animals," I said into his soft fur.

"We are not, but there are a multitude of forbidden acts common at Lacock."

I took a deep breath. "I have a lot to learn."

"You do, but no rush, chicken. You care for Arnold for the first few days. He can sleep in your room and keep you warm."

"Oh no."

"I think I shall be unable to take him away from you." Arnold had leaped up onto my mattress and laid his head on my lap.

"Well if he'd have me, I'd like to have his company."

Another knock. This room might be private but it had no lock, for certs.

It was Sister Constance. "Have you detailed to our postulant our schedule of prayers and meals, Isabella?" she asked abruptly.

"Not yet, Conny." The tall woman rolled her eyes, but she

was being playful. "I'll do it then." She sat down on the floor, looking up at me. "Are you letting her sleep with Arnold for a night or two?" she asked. Isabella nodded. "Good. It helped me wonders."

A third person entered.

"We might as well just leave the door open," I suggested. This woman was young, and had light brown eyes that were so bright they almost looked red.

"The Lady Mother suggested I come in because verily she knew neither Sister Isabella nor Sister Constance would give you the information you might need." She had a very highly strung voice. "I'm Sister Franella. Peace be with you."

"And with you. I'm Elisa."

"Sister Elisa," Franella corrected.

"Not yet." Constance was now lying on her back.

"She may be called sister after this evening, when her postulancy begins." Franella got out a piece of paper. "You two must go now," she instructed.

I begged them with my eyes to stay.

"It's alright. Arnold will stay with ye." Isabella got up. The hound looked at her, and it seemed she spoke, mind to mind, with him. I swallowed. Arnold put his paws onto my lap. The door shut.

"Firstly, a warning about your company here. There are lots of different reasons why these women have taken their vows, Elisabeth. There are, thank the Lord God, a handful of holy devotees at Lacock. But most of them are superfluous women who could not be married off. I know that Constance is said to have bitten the ear of the man she was betrothed to." I laughed, but managed to pass it off as a cough. "And of course there are those who have fallen from grace. You'll meet Sister Charity later. She has a child." I nodded. "You are not shocked?" Franella was vexed. "She is not a virgin! Yet she is here! I am trying to warn you of the decaying states of the order!" I nodded again, more seriously. "Then there are the widows. We have two widows; you will know them by their advanced age. And then there is Isabella; the Priory was obliged to take her. Mind you don't touch her," she shivered, "for she is cursed."

"She is not cursed," I said quickly.

Franella's chin retracted into her neck. "Have not you seen her hand?"

"Her arm is not a curse," I pressed. Her chin retracted further. "The Lord told me ..." I finished, not entirely convincingly.

"The Lord told you Sister Isabella isn't cursed?"

"Verily. Is't time to go to Vespers?" I asked, desperate to exit the conversation. She nodded and turned to leave, beckoning me to come with her.

CHAPTER TEN

All our prayers were said in the chapel of St Mary. It was Vespers, which happened just before supper. It was a small chapel, but we were small in number and it was by no means an undecorated or unsightly church. I filed into the mahogany pew, crossing the large stone slabs on the floor, many of which had engravings. The dead under our feet. I wondered if Lacock's nuns were buried there. Would I be buried there? I shivered and averted my gaze to the roof. It was ornate. Gold-painted flowers sprouted from the supporting arched beams. There were no gargoyles for me to name there. I was given my books of prayers and songs by the Abbess as I walked in.

"You will sit —" the Abbess began.

"Sister Elisa has asked to sit with us." Constance and Isabella had appeared beside me.

The Abbess's eyes became slits of suspicion, but she let us pass, saying only that I must be at the very end of the bench. We sat on the left side of chapel. There was a soft thrum of chatter. I thumbed through my book of prayers; I knew most by heart but I still felt nervous flutterings on the palms of my hands. I did not want to make a fool of myself.

Everyone stood. I tried to find the appropriate hymn. Isabella helped me, then in a very low whisper she said, "Just mouth the words for now. No one will notice."

I smiled at her. She definitely, definitely wasn't cursed, e'en if God had not directly confirmed it with me.

As it turned out, it really mattered little that I did not know the songs and could not hold a note. The hymns were performed ill. Even I could tell my new communicants were omitting syllables and skipping words. In one moment, one half of the choir was singing an entirely different part of the song from the other half. Mother Catherine and the Chaplain weren't even in the chapel. I could see them talking outside the entrance with another member of the clergy, seemingly unperturbed by the ghastly sounds coming from within. The song ended, at different times — nay, I wouldn't have called it so much an end as a dwindling. But in one way or another it finished, the Chaplain entered and the service proceeded. It was normal enough. Constance was reading a presumably contraband book the whole time and several sisters down my aisle were sewing. I would've relaxed if I hadn't known my Reception was quick approaching.

"Lady Elisabeth Knolly." Mother Catherine indicated I should stand at the entrance of the chapel.

I swallowed.

Constance pushed me up, and I stumbled to the font at the door.

The Abbess asked, "Elisabeth, thou hast petitioned to be received as Postulant in this community."

"I have."

"Thine entry hast been marked by discernment and testing."

It had not, but that was reserved for lesser applicants than a Knolly.

"Bow thy head and pray for God's great blessing as thou beginnest thy journey as Postulant in this community."

My hands were shaking as I obeyed. This was ... for the best. I was safe there. I needn't fear myself.

The Chaplain began the blessing. "May Almighty God bless thee in His Mercy and make thee always aware of His saving Wisdom."

"Amen."

"May He strengthen thine Faith with proofs of His love, so thou perseverest in Good Works."

"Amen."

"May he direct thine steps to Himself, and show thee how to walk in Charity and Peace."

"Amen."

"May Almighty God bless thee, in the name of the Father, the Son and the Holy Ghost."

"Amen."

There was more. The Abbess bestowed upon me my veil, and there were further prayers and exhortations. Some of the Sisters responded, while others continued in their clandestine pursuits. I looked up at my new family. Most of them were staring into space or looking at the sewing in their laps, but a few of them were watching me. A girl sitting behind Constance moved forwards to whisper something in her ear and they laughed. I smoothed down my skirts.

The Abbess gave a hard smile. "I'll see you in Compline." I nodded and went to sit back down, but as soon as I had put my bottom on the hard pew, everyone rose.

Isabella led us out of Chapel; we waited near the refectory for the meal bell to ring.

I caught my own reflection in a window. I looked so different with my hair tucked up under the folds of material. A picture of holiness. A fair sight better than my naked body being kissed by a man but still it was … sad, I think. Or maybe beautiful. I couldn't know.

"What do you make of our Chaplain?" The refectory hall was so noisy I'd hardly heard what Isabella had said. It was filled with people. Guests, churchmen, and nuns. I even saw a man from the Infirmary, waddling around on a stick. "Pardon, Isabella?" I whispered.

She pointed at the head of the table. "Father Peter. Our Chaplain. Mind, you cannot let him get too close to you if you're alone; he's a lonely man."

I stared down the table at him and he caught my eye. He smiled. He had waxy, almost green skin. I lowered my head. "I thought perchance there would be no men at the Priory," I mumbled.

Isabella laughed. "If it were that easy to be rid of them."

The food was far better than I had feared. Bread, turnips and a mutton pie. There was no limit on how much I might drink either. I took long draughts of wine, as I looked around. The walls were adorned with nearly a dozen tapestries, rendering the large room hot and stuffy, and the three long dining tables were cluttered with brass candles, goblets and food. Everything was in excess. One of the tables even had a game board. This was not the abject poverty I would vow to observe in my profession.

Isabella and Constance entertained me during supper, but when all was done, I hastened back to my own room. I wanted to be alone.

"Sister!" Franella called for me down the cloister, just as I put my hand on the latch. No one in the Abbey appeared to adhere to the vow of silence either.

"I recommend drinking much water before sleep — it will

help when you must rise at the second hour. I know I myself found it quite hard when first I came here." She passed me a large goblet and I drained it.

"Sleep well, Sister."

"Thank you — Sister."

I put my trunk against the door in place of a lock. Arnie welcomed me into bed and kept my toes warm. I worried about waking so early. I worried I wouldn't sleep.

CHAPTER ELEVEN

The first office of the day was four hours before sunrise. Four hours. Before even a glimpse of light. My days were clouded in a sleep-like haze. I swore I would never get used to it. The Sisters assured me I would. But seven weeks in and I knew they were all dissemblers. Though I was exhausted, the sleepwalk state came with the benefit of being too tired to think. I followed my feet, that followed the other Sisters' feet, from one office to the next. The only changes of note were those in the Priory's guests. Otherwise it was the same rhythmical pattern every single time I woke. The Abbess had decided I was not yet ready for the Infirmary and thus I whiled away my work hours in the kitchen garden. This pleased me greatly. I hoped I never would be ready for the Infirmary. I was given lists by the apothecary and the cooks and I collected, picked and plucked what was needed for physics and meals throughout the day.

Today I was to pick the apples. I had gone to the orchard the week before and the fruit had already been falling. The work was onerous, but I had not asked for help. I wanted only to be alone. My habit rustled the autumn leaves as I walked past Sister Constance in the kitchen garden. She was singing to herself, sitting contentedly in the dirt, picking the asparagus pea. She winked at me as I passed her. I smiled in return.

I unlatched the kitchen garden gate and walked across Lacock's fields. I could feel the huge sandstone Nunnery at my back, watching me. I wondered what would happen if I just kept walking. Into the village and beyond. Hunger and destitution, I suppose. I wrapped my cloak close around me and watched with amusement as Sister Charity made a run for a loose sheep, it was sheering day. She did a spectacular jump and tackle, and I witnessed a blur of black and white, wool, veil and wimple. I applauded when she got a grip around its middle. I think she may have given me a rude gesture in return. God forgive her. Yes, I was very content to be a gardening Nun.

I found the ladder and began my Godly apple duties, but it wasn't long before I longed for company. Since I had arrived, I had only been alone at night, and I had been so tired from the Offices that I had hardly noticed my aloneness. But as I made progress along the gnarled branches of the apple trees, inhaling the smell of churned-up earth and ripe fruit, I became very aware that all orchards look exactly the same. I found myself searching for Eddie, who often accompanied me to Grey's Court's orchard. He would dart between the trees, throw rotten fruit, eat rotten fruit, cozen me into also eating rotten fruit. Then I would call for Samuel, and he would rescue me from food poisoning and my growing irritation.

The sun came out from behind a cloud, and dappled, warm light hit my face. I took a deep breath and shut my eyes. I could not believe I was destined to never see them again, to never e'en hear from them again. I was in gaol, locked away from those I loved.

The bells rang. Time for Tierce. The fourth office of the day. Four to go. I looked down at my buckets of apples. Doing this alone had been a horrible decision.

The buckets bounced off the sides of my legs as I hauled

them in small increments back to the kitchen garden. I would be as bruised as the old fallen fruit by the time I graced Chapel.

"Sister!" I was learning to respond to this address now.

It was Sister Constance. Her lovely face was covered in finger streaks of dirt.

"Sister," I returned, thankful to see someone who could help. But she did not reach for a bucket.

She held something. Parchment. "For you."

"What is it?" I put the buckets down and massaged my shoulder.

"Take it. 'Tis a letter."

My stomach turned over itself. "For me?" I breathed. "How? I thought it was forbidden?"

"And wherefore you should read it now."

"How?" I repeated.

"Messengers leave them in the cracks in the wall of the kitchen garden." She gestured behind her. "The crumbling bit near the turnips."

My fingers numb, I unfolded the parchment.

Elisabeth my perfect poppet and most Godly daughter of Christ. It is your ever loyal maidservant Mary. Samuel is transcribing this letter for me, illiterate, poor woman as I am.

I choked and spluttered. Constance gave me a solid thwack on the back.

I heard rumours about a special and secret way of writing to Lacock's sisters. I pray it works. It is quiet at Grey's Court. Your parents are with the King in London and your sisters are in the palms of their husbands' hands. Eddie is our Lord and Master at the moment and today, upon his instruction, I built a tower, castle and moat out

of his bed pillows. Lord Knolly has never asked me to do
this and I enjoyed it a lot more than caring for your
father's furs. Do you know my Lord is requesting that I
clean them by spitting wine from my mouth onto his coat,
sprinkling flour on it and then leaving it to dry? Only
after this madness must I wash it as I used to! This is how
people at court wash their furs I am told. It is abhorrent
and only makes for more work. I have wished to complain
about it to you for weeks. I feel very relieved and I hope
you will find it as absurd as I do.
I pray for you every day, and hope that you are well in
body and mind.
Please find a way of letting me know that I have reached
you.
All my love in the world,
Mary

I was shaking with laughter and relief.

"There's something on the back," Constance said through a large mouthful of apple.

I turned it over.

Written with the hand of him which desireth as much to
be yours as you do to have him.

"You have to destroy it," Constance said. I shook my head. Or at least I think I did. I could not feel my body. I read the last bit again. He desires me as I desire him. I swallowed. I was clutching evidence of my lustfulness, but I could not destroy it. I did not want to destroy it. I looked up to Constance, expecting her to be disapproving, but she was not.

"Then you must keep it next to your breast, or you'll ruin it for everyone whose receiving love letters."

I nodded. Or at least I think I did.

"Good." To my surprise, Constance patted her chest. There was a crumpling sound coming from her breasts. "Always at my heart," she said.

I stowed my letter in the folds of my skirt, to be moved to my bodice as soon as I had opportunity, and we walked together, very late, to Tierce.

I thought of nothing but Samuel through Tierce, Sext, None and all the spaces in between. I should be in the confessional booth, covered in remorse, but all I felt was relief. I was relieved he still thought of me. My lust, my secret wanting — it had found me, travelled all the way across the English countryside and found me in my Abbey. These walls were not invincible: desire had slipped through the cracks.

A panic arose over not being able to write back — to let Samuel know I had read his words — and Mary of course. Poor Mary. Shame on me. I asked several of the Sisters how they replied to their illicit letters, yet none of their answers had been satisfactory. It was hard. You had to find someone who was going where you wanted your letter to go. Or you had to hide out at the turnip wall and catch the messenger in the first place. Turnip Watch, Constance called it.

I entered the hall in a daze, absentmindedly taking my seat on the long, wooden table for supper. I stared at the brass candlestick in front of me. The flame flickered. I shivered. He was so bold. So presuming. *Written with the hand of him which desireth as much to be yours as you do to have him.* The candle flickered again, dangerously bent in my breath. If he wanted me as much as I wanted him ... desire flooded through my body.

Isabella walked into the hall. Her smock was splattered with blood today, and I almost regretted saving her a seat. That was until she opened her sweet mouth.

"Oh my wee Sister. Thank you, dear." She sat down and scooped her ale towards her with her stumped arm. I saw the Abbess look at it alarmedly. "What a day!" Indeed. What a day. She waved at the Abbess with her stump. She knew exactly how to wind her up. Mother Catherine crossed herself.

"Constance told me ye got yourself a turnip note." I nodded. "The first one's hard. Like you've been tugged into the real world for a second, only to be bundled right back here." I brimmed with tears. Isabella nodded understandingly. "Listen, I've been thinking about what yer said on the first day. About calling this lady a real name." She gestured to her arm with no hand.

"Have you thought of one?" I manage, thankful for the distraction.

"I wondered would the Mother Superior be flattered if I used her name, like a namesake, or mayhap if we just called it Cathy."

I snorted into my drink. "I like it. Cathy she is." I shook Cathy with my hand.

"Sisters of Lacock." Chaplain Peter had stood, though he was so short you could hardly tell. Constance The Eternally Late squeezed in on the other side of me. Peter wagged a stubby finger at her. "It has come to my attention that silence is not being kept in due places, and the rule of St Benedict is not being observed. Might I remind you all that silence is part of your vow and if any word must be spoken for a reasonable occasion then it should be spoken lowly and gently so that it be scarce heard by the other Nuns." Ironically, he seemed to await some verbal recognition that we understood. We remained obediently quiet. "For the dinner table!" he went on, "I have a table of signs drawn up for you." He revealed a large piece of parchment with drawings upon it. They were, in my opinion, illegible. "The Abbess will now explain to you all what I have devised." He sat back on his large, cushioned chair and beckoned a boy to him. I had not noticed the child before. He would have been ten or eleven years. He brought the Chaplain wine.

The Abbess stood, and cleared her throat. "If you are to desire fish, you will wag your hand in the manner of a fish tail." Reluctantly, she demonstrated.

"Oh Lord. I cannot laugh." Isabella was rigid next to me, trying to keep a straight face.

"She who wants milk will draw her left little finger in the manner of milking." She mimicked milking a cow. On the other side of me, Constance started rocking back and forwards.

"For mustard, one must hold her nose in the upper part with her right hand and rub it and if you are desirous of wine you must rub your left fingers up and down your thumb."

Sister Charity started coughing to hide her giggles.

"The Chaplain has spent a great deal of time on this language, for your benefit," said the Abbess loudly. "He has created well over a hundred signals!"

Constance had done her best, but that was that for her. She held her belly and rested her head on the table as she laughed loudly and unashamedly. It was leave for the rest of the Sisters to join her, and there were several long minutes of laughing and spluttering, it was a marvellous wassail of disrespect and disorder. I could not even hear the Abbess trying to speak. The guests were enjoying the evening's mirth too. A visiting academic was doing the fish signal to his companion, who was doing the milk signal back to him.

But I did not join in with the woeful, wonderful disobedience because I could not take my gaze from the boy. He sat on the Chaplain's knee — though he was too big to sit on a lap. He needed his own chair. Someone should bring the boy a chair. His head was bent, looking down. He was not even interested in the illicit giggles and delight. Where was his mother? Was Father Peter his natural father? Did the Chaplain have a bastard boy? Father Peter was watching the scene disdainfully, shaking his head, barking instructions at our Mother Abbess, all the while stroking the boy's blond hair. My own hair was standing on end, and the ale in my stomach washed around. I turned to see if anyone else was worried about the boy, but no one had seemed to notice. I touched my hand to my chest. My heart beat under my letter. I wondered how many of these Sisters were carrying contraband against their bare skins. There were a lot of unHoly secrets at Lacock. I had thought these walls would expel sinners, sniff them out and spit them out. It did not seem to be the case.

CHAPTER TWELVE

It was not long after the hand signals supper that the Abbess found me in the gardens and informed me I was to work in the Infirmary now.

"You will start tomorrow." The breeze whisked my tunic into the air and my whole body stilled. I needed the garden. It reminded me of home. I needed to be near Turnip Wall. I needed to spend at least a few hours a day on Turnip Watch. What if another letter arrived? What if I could send a letter home? I had been asking the visiting academics and travellers if any of them were travelling towards Henley. But as God would have it, as of my removal to this Nunnery, Henley was the least popular place for anyone to visit.

"Please, Mother. Let me stay in the gardens."

"Sister Elisabeth!" She stared down her nose. "Must I remind you about chapter thirty-six of Benedict's rule?" I looked at her blankly. She did need to remind me. She proceeded with gusto. "He proclaimed that 'before all things and above all things' — 'ante omnia et super omnia'," she wiggled her thick eyebrows at me, "special care must be taken of the sick or infirm so that they may be served as if they were Christ in person."

I nodded, wiping my nose with my sleeve. The Abbess's face retreated under her habit. She had handed down her sentence.

Isabella came to collect me at the start of our labour hours. It was a Sunday. I hoped that meant it might be quiet, but as it turns out, the ill don't adhere to days of the week.

"Here, poppet, you take this apron." I recalled how hers was often splattered with blood. "They cannot make you do anything too filthy today, do not fret."

We walked across the courtyard: it was a crisp November day, the air cold but the sun warm. I desperately wanted to be in the gardens.

"I really wouldn't be so worried, Elisa," she pressed, reading my face. "The really poor and decrepit find shelter in the poorhouse in the village — it's the wealthy who are received here."

Isabella pushed open the large oak door. There were screens erected in front of some of the beds, but otherwise the patients were exposed to the room, lined up next to each other, one bed in each wall space between two arched windows.

"Ah, Isabella. There you are. See to Mr Leamington, if't pleases you. He needs fresh sheets. And you must be Sister Elisabeth."

I nodded. I was looking at a Sister I had never seen before. She was my mother's age, with a kindly face.

"My name is Sister Jane. I am provost here." I nod again. "I hear you have some experience with healing and medicines."

"A little, Sister." We were moving past the beds at speed. "I know how to apply leaches, and I understand how to make a handful of different remedies from herbs and oils. I spent my youth caring for my younger brother's cuts, bruises and breaks."

"That will be very useful. There are constantly scoundrels from the village in here, all banged up from tree falls and other naughty things."

"Yes, Sister." I paused. "May I ask a question, Sister?"

"Question everything and everyone in here, Sister."

"I wondered why I haven't seen you in prayers yet."

"I'm here night and day. This is my divine office."

"You must be tired."

Sister Jane stopped suddenly. "I am tired," she said, almost surprised. "I will be glad of your help."

"I will do my best to be useful." We started walking again.

"I warrant most of the time we only need you to talk to the patients, ask them a few questions about how they feel, keep them fed and dispense their herbs. Aye?"

"Aye."

"You will watch over these three beds." The ones near the back of the room. "None of them have had their medicines, or morning food. I also want a report on their ailments. Aye?"

"Aye."

I moved to go to them.

"Elisa," she called. I turned on my heel, nervous I had already misstepped. "I should inform you of their conditions."

I blushed. Of course she should.

She pulled a parchment from her pocket. Jane lowered her voice, tutting as she looked at her list. "In the corner we have a goodwife who hath only a few days past miscarried." My mouth went dry. "Next we have a slight pain in the foot." She rolled her eyes. "He likes it here a little too well. And then finally we have a feverous boy. His mother's worried."

Someone called urgently for Jane's aid. She turned and left.

I decided to address the mother and boy first. For she was formidable looking and glaring in my direction.

"Sister!" she barked. "I feel he is getting hotter. Check him!"

I was momentarily affronted by her tone of voice. The Abbess spoke rough to me of course, but she reminded me of my mother. This woman thought I was below her, and a part of me wanted to let her know exactly who I was. She would know of me. She would know of my family at the very least. But my gaze fell on the boy, and my arrogance faded.

"What's your name, child?" I asked.

"Edmund."

My heart gave a sad, lonely twang. "That's my brother's name." I felt his head. It was warm but it didn't alarm me. My own Edmund had got far hotter.

"How old is your brother?" the boy asked, lucid enough to be curious.

"He's eight."

"I'm nine."

"I can tell you have the advantage."

His red face swelled with pride. I smiled at him. "I would not worry. Though he is warm, he is not shaking or hazy in the mind. I will get him his herbs, and I will add some mint to cool him." The mother was still frowning, but she was also nodding, agreeing with me, trusting my decisions.

"I can tend to you in a moment," I quipped to the man in the next bed as though I had been at this work all my life.

I went to the store room with its different vials of different medicines. I shut myself in there. I could not see anything. It was completely dark, but it was what I needed. I took a few steadying breaths, then I opened up the door a little so the light could come in. I spent some time perusing the bottles and jars.

I fussed over the man with the imaginary ailment and then moved over to the woman closest the wall.

"My name is Sister Elisa," I said. I was finding it hard to look at her. "How are you feeling?"

I forced my eyes to her face: she was incredibly pale and very young. She didn't answer me.

"Do you feel any different today?" She was still looking at me, but she did not speak. "Do you want food?" Naught. "I will bring you something warm to drink." I would see if I might conjure her another blanket also.

I found one in the store room. I tucked her in like I tucked in Eddie. She responded to my touch, moving deeper into the covers. One of her legs was hanging off the side of her mattress. I touched her calf, trying to encourage it back into the warmth, but as I lifted up the sheets I saw the blood. I prayed my face didn't convey my panic. I replaced her covers. I looked at her again. Perhaps she wasn't talking because she was faint, she had lost too much blood.

"Sister Jane!" I said clearly, trying to keep the quaver out of my voice. I moved quickly to her. "There is a lot of blood on the bed of that lady."

"Get the screen from bed three and I'll get Isabella."

I did as she said, putting the wooden screen around the bed. "This is quite natural," Sister Jane said to me, pulling me close to her so I could see what she was doing.

Isabella lifted the sheets and rolled to woman to the side.

"She will bleed for perhaps another two or three weeks, on and off."

I nodded.

Sister Jane rolled up the nightdress. I averted my gaze at this woman's naked half. Jane noticed and slapped me hard across the wrist. "Put aside your useless shame," she hissed. "And put your hand on her belly, Elisa. Tell me if it seems swollen." I did so. "Lower down." The woman was moaning and sweating now. My hand touched her private hair, but I could feel a cramping within her lower tummy.

"Cramping of the muscles?" Jane demanded.

"Yes. There is a movement."

"She is still expelling the child."

The woman whimpered, whether in emotional pain or physical pain I couldn't tell.

"Get some hot water from the fire, and dampen a cloth with it. Lie it across her belly — it should ease some of the pain."

Isabella went to get it.

The woman let out a loud sob and one of her legs chicken-winged to the left, revealing herself in the most graphic way I have ever seen a woman's body, any body, not even my own. I went to put her leg back.

"Leave her. Let her find a comfortable position." Jane was looking at me sternly.

Isabella put the wet cloth over the woman's stomach.

"Where is her husband?" I asked in a hushed voice.

"He is on a journey, I believe," Isabella replied. "He will not be pleased upon his return."

"Watch her," Jane said to me, cutting off our whispered conversation. She left.

"We could physic the pain?" I said to Isabella.

"Aye — with what sweet drug, my sweet?"

"This is my first day. I …"

"You have no preference, then?" She smiled at me, stroking the hair of the splayed-leg, naked, bleeding woman.

I wracked my brain. Did I have a preference? I recalled Mary giving me ginger for my monthly cramps. My hand went to my chest, to my letter. Samuel had once given Livia fennel seeds when she ate. That could help too.

"Ginger? Fennel seeds?"

She nodded. "Your love teach you that?" She had noticed my hand on my chest.

I quickly removed it. "He is not my love."

"He sits awfully near your heart to be not your love."

"But I am a Nun."

Isabella shrugged, as though this was a stupid thing to say. "What was his name?" she asked.

I swallowed an uprising of emotion. "Samuel."

"Is that not a lovely name?"

I nodded. It was a lovely name. "It would please him I am working here. He is good with ailments and healing." My words surprised me.

"I don't doubt it he'd be proud. I shall get the ginger? You prepare the seeds."

Every day something happened that amazed me, that had me running for the cupboard with the herbs. I was crying more at night, but I was learning, and my appetite for knowledge knew no bounds. I even missed offices. Sister Jane had been teaching me to blood let. I saw my first ever male member. It was an old man's and it was gross and diseased. I thought it might be a sign from God that I should not meddle with members, but then I saw a young man's one and it was not nearly as frightful. I dealt with urine samples, faecal samples, blood samples. I saw my third male member and surely my dozenth female purse. Sister Jane even asked me to do an internal examination of a woman with child. After so many soiled beds, after nightly visions of pustulant undercarriages, after the tenth child to vomit on you in a week, your own functioning body seems like joy. I stopped averting my gaze from my patients' nakedness — if I did not see, how could I help?

CHAPTER THIRTEEN

The winter had been hard. Christmas had been joyless. There had been a plague of homesickness and an actual plague of the ague. There was a constant underlying thrum of mournful reminiscence about the festivities that happened on the outside. I checked the Turnip Wall every day: every crack in that crumbling wall. I had not received another letter. Nothing. In a bad bout of missing home I had written letters to Mary, and to Livia, and to Edmund, wishing each of them a Blessed Christmas. I had even tried to write to Samuel. I started and stopped, scribbled out and burnt several attempts. It was a shameful waste of good parchment. None of it mattered, anyway, as no one had been able to take any to Greys.

It was still bitterly cold at the beginning of March but I wasn't sure that excused Sister Constance sipping whisky through Mass.

"Do you want some?" she asked politely. I declined. It was no little temptation, though. It mightn't just warm me up, it could spice up the sermon, which was extra dull that Sabbath. As far as I could tell, and admittedly I wasn't giving the Chaplain a lot of my attention, he was comparing the seven

divinities of the Virgin Mary to the seven different parts of a
Nun's habit.

"So to recap," he said loudly, "the kirtle represents our trust
in God. This sleeve," he had recruited Sister Augustine to
demonstrate and was tugging at her left arm, "is representative
of the Virgin's righteousness. This one," he slunk around to her
other side, and tugged the right sleeve, "is mercy."

Oh Jesus save me. I tried to envelop myself in my own
prayer. I prayed for each of my patients.

"And now whenever you look at yourselves, you will not see
your stained smocks and bothersome veils, you will see the
Blessed Virgin Herself."

I doubted that. I rubbed my eyes and stood. We sang. Too
fast, and out of tune. Then we prayed. Then we sang again, and
then I was ready to leave. But the Abbess had stood to speak.

"We have a few announcements," she said, ushering the
women back into their seats. "We have visitors from the
Monastery of Stadhampton." She indicated the front row of the
chapel, and a handful of monks stood and bowed. "We
welcome you, brothers, we hope that you find refreshment and
hospitality at Lacock, just as Benedict would have commanded.
In further news ..." She paused, and looked anxiously at the
Chaplain. He nodded gravely. "We have the Commissioner
Thomas Legh and his men coming to Lacock within the
coming weeks." Noise rippled through the chapel. "They are
here by order of the King, to inspect our practices at the Abbey
and to extend the King's blessings." Again the Abbess
swallowed. "Therefore, there is no room, none at all, for the
licentiousness, noise and Godlessness that has pervaded our
halls!" Her volume had escalated, her face red. This was a
scolding and I had not foreseen it. "Punishments of the highest
order will be issued to those who —" she unfurled a long piece
of parchment " — sing too fast or too slow. Miss any of the
Divine offices, or Mass, confession or Chapter meetings. Speak

without necessity. Neglect to use the hand signals at the dinner table. There will be no frolicking or partaking in light and trifling pleasures such as singing songs that neglect to mention the Lord, or any sort of movement that could be construed as dancing. There will be no more communicating with the outside world." The Chaplain handed the Abbess a pile of letters. "Turnip Wall is no more," declared Catherine.

She brandished a bundle of notes, there would be dozens of them. Our letters. Any number of them could be from Mary, written by Sam. She handed them back to Peter. It made me sick to think he could touch our personal, private correspondence. I had nary a doubt he would read them. "We have known of this arrangement for some time, and have been collecting your illicit correspondence. Those who attempt to send or receive notes from outside will get the ducking stool." There was another shockwave of gasps. I knew for a fact the Abbess used Turnip Wall herself. This Nunnery of hypocrites. "Finally, I need not remind you that you will be thrown out of Lacock if there is even the slightest hint of deviant immorality or foul lust about you. You are servants of God, not whores."

Constance choked on her whisky.

I choked on nothing at all.

"Dominus vobiscum."

"Et cum spirit tuo."

No one could stop talking about Commissioner Thomas Legh. Even the patients were discussing him.

"And how do you feel tonight, Sir Barker?" Sir Barker was a viscount, the highest in rank in the Infirmary for the past week, and he had a bad attitude. He had fallen off his horse.

"Not good, Sister Elisa." He pulled a pained face. He was fine. We had offered to attend him in his own home, but he loved the fuss and constant attention he received at the infirmary. "I'm afraid the pain won't let me have a wink of sleep." Again he pulled the face. "But I am afraid none of you Sisters will be sleeping soundly either, what with the Commissioner about the place. No more naughty Nuns for Lacock!"

I smiled, pleasantly enough. "Would it please you to show me your calf?" It was bruised. But that was all it was, a bruise. No strain, no break, nothing. "I shall fetch you a calming spiritous drink and then apply some oils to it, Sir Barker."

"I fear I'll never be going home." I was afraid of that too. "Still at least I'll be here for the Commissioner's visit. You will tell me how it all unfolds, Sister Elisabeth."

"By God's grace you will be back in your own bed by then, Sir Barker." I tucked in a strand of hair that had escaped my veil. It must've been past midnight but still a few hours before Matins. My feet hurt. The night-time labour was hard, but it meant that in the daytime I could rest, or go outside in the gardens.

The door banged. I span around. It never made that noise: it was too heavy.

The Mother Abbess, Constance and Franella were at the door, carrying someone in their arms.

"Help! Please help!"

The Abbess, with no veil on, threw herself to the front of the pack. "Silence! We need a bed, with a screen."

"Put her on that one." I pointed to the bed nearest the door. I could tell now: it was Isabella. I got the screen, and then another.

Sister Jane was speaking to the Abbess and I took my first proper glance at Isabella. She was unconscious, ghostly white and covered in blood. Cathy, not the Abbess, but Cathy her right arm, had what looked like cooled wax encasing it. Had she done this to herself? Some dark spell for regrowth? But that was not where the blood was coming from. It soaked her skirts.

"Every one leave," I commanded, shooing the Nuns out. "Go. We will take care of her."

"She's going to die!" wailed Sister Franella.

"Leave Franella!" I snapped. "Con. Give us space!"

Constance took a hold of the Mother with one hand and Franella with the other and dragged them out of the Infirmary.

"The Abbess is trying to convince me she did this to herself," Sister Jane fumed, undressing Isabella apace. "I think not. She has been attacked and, if I am not mistaken," she took a sharp breath, "yes. She has been violated." Big black bruises in the shape of hands were on the insides of my dear friend's thighs. "We need pain relief, salve for wounds, and wet cloth for the burn. It seems someone thought it funny to wrap her arm in hot wax."

Her purse had been torn. I had seen similar wounds once before, on a mother, but they had been tears from a birth. As I put salve in between her legs, I felt her unconscious body stir. I did what Sister Jane had told me to do but I shook with sadness. As soon as I was done with the salves, I redressed her bottom half. Her virginity was stolen from her, but I could return a little dignity.

"Was it one of the visiting monks?" I whispered to Jane, now helping gently peel off the cooled wax.

"Perhaps, or another visitor, or the Chaplain ..."

I shuddered. "What? Peter?"

"Hush hush."

"But ..."

"Sister Marguerite has a child off Father Peter and I am certain it is not one she sought to bear."

"Oh my God." I crossed myself. I wondered if that had been the child on his lap.

"Wipe your eyes, dear, Isabella is in good hands. Together we will make her well."

．．．

We had been told first by the Abbess, then by Chaplain Peter himself that this ordeal had been self-inflicted, that Isabella was to stay shielded from the public eye. No one was to treat her apart from myself and Sister Jane. We were not to speak abroad. The Chaplain had made me promise to God to stay my tongue. I could not swear it was Peter who hurt Isabella so but as soon as he spake to me my body went cold and bile rose in my throat, like my physical body knew the truth. He told me to ask no questions.

When Isabella gained consciousness, she did not say anything. She could not move her legs for pain. Sister Jane thought there were more wounds deep within her, but there was little we could do for those. Only time would heal internal gashes but I worried that its march could not heal Isabella herself.

I got permission for Arnie to stay with her. Every time I walked into the infirmary, I trembled at the sight of them: Isabella staring into space; Arnie, sitting by her side, protecting her from further harm. She still had not ventured a word. She had not even noted her dog's presence.

I started spending most of my time with her. Sitting next to her. Missing nearly every office, despite Catherine's warning. I told Isabella what had happened each day. I told her about my feelings. She would listen. I would feed her. I got her up and walked her to the privy. She had cried in pain the first few times. I gave her water and wine. The hardest part was when I had to check her wounds, now that she was awake. Her face went red with shame. But she still didn't say anything, nor did she weep.

The first sign of change happened a dozen days after the attack. She reached out and patted Arnie on the head. He nuzzled into her and relief crashed over me.

"He's missed your touch." I half laughed, half sobbed as

Arnie got over excited, licking Isabella's face. She made eye contact with me for the very first time.

"I cannot go back, Elisa," she whispered to me. "Not with him there."

I didn't want to push her. She didn't have to tell me what happened.

"You don't have to do anything, Isabella. You don't have to tell anyone what happened. You don't have to go back. I will look after you."

Her eyes glazed over again. She looked confused. Then she shut her eyes. I watched her inhale and exhale. I was paranoid about her dying despite there being little reason it might happen. I didn't know if she was asleep, or counterfeiting, or had fallen into some sort of hell whilst still breathing.

Sister Jane forced me to start attending the offices. The commissioner would be there any day now, and everything had to be as the King expected. I tried to argue that one nun missing the Divine offices was a small thing compared with the Chaplain violating a sister, but she wouldn't listen.

I wasn't going to listen to the Chaplain in Mass. That would be my one sign of protest. I would bring a book to his sermon and read it whilst he spake. I went to the library just before the service in a hunt for my book of rebellion. I wanted to find a book that discussed what had happened. I wanted to know if Isabella's soul was ruined. Could she still be a Nun? Marguerite was a Nun and she had birthed a child outside of marriage. I needed more information.

I started perusing the stacks. I liked it there — the shelves overflowing, the desks cluttered with papers. The windows were stained glass, like at St Peter's back at home, and many-coloured light danced across the spines of books. I liked the crumpling sound of turning pages, I liked the whispers of the reading monks.

"Just throw it behind those books. No soul comes to these corridors any more." Constance and Sister Alice were down in the lower stacks, where the books were old and outdated.

They jumped as I revealed myself.

"Elisa! You frightened us."

I apologised.

"How is Bella today?" Constance asked. She had visited as often as she could, despite the Mother Abbess forbidding it.

"She is speaking and she is petting Arnie."

Constance grabbed onto Alice's sleeve. "Thank Jesus. I thought she'd never talk again."

"Do you know what happened?" I asked, glancing behind me to ensure we were alone. Would this please God? I had sworn I would not ask.

Constance sat down on the floor and took off her veil, and momentarily I forgot what I had asked. I had never seen her without her veil. She had long, golden hair. She looked like a very angel.

"I found her in the Chapter hall." I sat down next to her, Alice joined. We sat in a circle, staring at Constance's nearly finished candle flickering in the centre. "She was screaming." She swallowed. "I didn't see who, but the Chaplain ..." she shivered "... he's laid hands on me before, and he's..."

"Marguerite's baby," I finished.

She nodded. There was a silence.

"Oh, the Lord Himself help me. I cannot stop my tears up since I saw it!" She went to wipe them away, when I noticed she was holding something.

"What is that?" It was shaped ... Well, it was shaped like the male member.

Alice made a small groan of frustration. Constance half

sobbed, half laughed, and passed me a polished wooden phallus.

I held it. By the tip.

"We're hiding it because by repute the Commissioner will search our chambers."

"What's it for? Is it … art?" I flung it back into Constance's lap.

Alice laughed. "No! It's for us. So we don't … need a man."

I felt light-headed. "For self-abuse?" I whispered.

"Oh it's not abuse." Constance shook her head. "It's anything but abuse."

"You do things … to yourself?"

"Don't you?"

I spluttered and looked around, then shrugged, took off my veil, shrugged again, made another funny noise, and then, I spoke. "Aye, sometimes." I felt a power run directly up my back, right up the line of my scar. At first I worried it might be the hand of God, reminding me of my sins. But I was not so sure. My whole body let go of something, some sort of weight or pain that had attached itself. It detached.

"Well you must attempt to take this saucy fellow to bed some time soon. After the Commissioner leaves, we shall retrieve it."

The bells rang for Mass. We slipped the wooden member behind an unpopular copy of St Thomas Aquinas's essays.

CHAPTER FOURTEEN

I walked into the infirmary the next morning. It was still dark. I moved around the room lighting candles. I could see the shape of Arnie look up at me as I entered, he sniffed the air, then surprisingly, he jumped off Isabella's bed to greet me.

"Good morrow, Master Arnie." I bent down to him and he whimpered. "Art thou well?" He kept whimpering, a little louder now. I wondered if he were ill. I encouraged him back over to Isabella's bed.

I stopped. She was not there. I looked around the room to see who had been staying the night. A quiet and pious Sister Charity was sitting in the corner of the room. I hurried to her, not caring about my noise.

"Hush, Sister!" she reprimanded me, also looking round at everyone else in the room.

"Where's Isabella?" She was still making hushing noises. "Where is she?"

"She's ..." She took my hand and led me into the store cupboard. "She's been taken into the village. One of the women in town is looking after her."

"What?" I snapped.

"The Chaplain wished it so."

"Fuck!"

"Sister Elisa!" She looked like she would faint.

"Let me guess, the Commissioner has arrived?"

"Late last night." She was still trying to recover from my obscenity, clutching onto one of the shelves. "He must not see a woman who's mutilated herself here. And what about her cursed arm? Even you must have heard the rumours that she was more witch than Nun."

"She didn't mutilate herself! The Chaplain took advantage of her!"

"He didn't," she said weakly.

"Why wasn't she allowed to take Arnie?"

"I think they said something about putting the dog out on the streets. We're not meant to have them, you know."

I snarled at her, being of a sudden a Knolly, for the first time in moons. "Those curs! I will not countenance it!" I had backed her into the corner of the cupboard.

"Aye, yes," she whispered helplessly.

Light flooded into the store room.

"What is this?" Sister Jane was silhouetted in the doorway.

"They took Isabella!"

"I can see that. Sister Charity, would you see to bed seven, please?"

She squeezed out between us, giving me a fearful look.

"I've just been told she's been taken to the bakers' home. They had a spare room since their daughter died. I know Goodwife Crow."

"But ... her wounds."

"It might be a better thing for her to be away from the place where she was attacked, Elisa. This may be God's blessing."

"But what about Arnie? Why couldn't he go with her? She will need him. He has needs of her!"

"The Crows would not have him. I'd keep him hidden, were I you."

"'Tis an outrage, Jane!"

"I wouldn't put it past them to kill him. He's contraband, and this Commissioner is putting everyone into a murderous mood. The Commissioner and the Chaplain will be here in only minutes, and they will want to set a good example."

"Very well. It is my burden! I shall find a solution."

Jane gave me time off from the ward, and Arnie followed me obediently out. I prayed for preemptive forgiveness and hoped God would understand. I stole food from the kitchens and a big bucket from the granges. I walked with purpose as though my labour duties were simply taking me a little further afield. There were sheds behind the orchard, and the furthest from the house was for tools, but no one was doing any work outside at the moment; it was too cold. Where was Spring? Why had she not arrived? Oh poor baby dog.

Arnie waited patiently as I cleared out the inside of the freezing shed. I laid down blankets and filled up the bucket with water. I would come down every day just after Matins to let him out to do his business. Would that be enough? Constance could help me and we could work in shifts. He was going to be so confused. I could tell he was already perplexed, probably wondering where Isabella was. I knelt down, my knees freezing on the stone floor, and I explained to him everything that had happened and why I must leave him there. The blessed dog looked at me and listened as though he understood everything. Please Jesus may he understand. Perhaps God was allowing this, perhaps God did not approve of the things that went on in this Nunnery — perhaps this time, just this time, God was on my side. I snuggled with the hound for a few minutes. He stopped shivering. I gave him his food for the day: a lot of good meat scraps and bread. He was content. I shut the door, and walked away as quickly as I could. I was crying … again. This convent of tears.

We had a Chapter meeting. Everyone was fussing over everything; it all had to be just right for the cursed Commissioner. My hair was coming out of my veil just as it did every day. About seven different sisters told me about it, but I ignored them. We filed into the large room and I caught my first glimpse of King Henry's convent killer, Thomas Legh.

He was adorned in jewels and pearls and wearing a bright blue tunic. Behind him stood more than a dozen men. They all wore the same long black boots — it was eery, each man was a copy of the other. I smothered a snigger. Legh was smiling and nodding to us all as we entered. I distrusted him immediately. I shoved my curls back into my veil.

"By order of the King, I, Lord Thomas Legh, and my livery will be inspecting the convent at Lacock. We will be speaking with each of you, inspecting your places of worship, and of living. Service God as you would if we were not here. It should also be known that King Henry, Head of the Church, has blessed me with authority that supersedes the Bishop's. I have the power and will exercise my power to dismiss any of you from Lacock; I have the power to attain any of Lacock's property; I have the power to shut down Lacock for eternity, if it please the King, and if it please God." He smiled and threw his arms wide. "I will be taking private meetings with every single one of you, to ask questions about your Godly businesses and to inspect your moral fibres."

I looked sideways at Constance, whose chin had retracted into her neck in a comical display of disbelief.

·   ·   ·

His men crawled the halls. Legh was everywhere at once. There were reports of him inspecting the sheep fields, when I could see him, clear as day, inspecting the Infirmary. His boots made a signature sound on the stone, a two-toned *ca-thunk* that echoed everywhere I went. It took only one week for him to send for me. On the first day of warmer weather he plucked me out of my readings to 'inspect my moral fibres'. We sat in a room no bigger than a cupboard. Our knees touched. Legh was eating a piece of pie and drinking wine. I kept getting glimpses of the pastry swirling around in the French red. I tried to move backwards, wondering whether the knee touching some sort of trap. A clever cozening way to warrant throwing me out.

"Sister …" He looking down his stained list, trying to find my name, though he had only one minute since used it when greeting me. "Elisabeth."

"My Lord."

"You're from good stock." He grinned, offering me a piece of pie. Once I got over the initial effrontery of being referred to like a Lacock sheep, I realised no one had mentioned my family since I had arrived. I didn't like the fellow, but the thought of being able to discuss my past was enticing.

"Thank you, my Lord." I accepted the piece of pie for courtesy and took a conspicuous bite.

"Wash it down with this — it'll stick to your cheeks otherwise."

It had. I wanted the wine. I debated it for a long second, but it had to be a trap. Reluctantly I declined.

"I wonder why Lord Knolly would send his youngest filly to Lacock?" he pressed. I revelled at the sound of my father's title. "Does your father not realise the King has condemned the papacy and become the rightful head of the church?"

I started to sweat. He wanted me to confess to treason. To heresy. He wanted my father in chains, in the tower, headless. I regathered myself.

"This Nunnery is King Henry's, not the Pope's. My father would rather die than send me to a nest of heretics." Pie fell in my lap.

Legh smiled. "Of course," he cooed. "But the Pope has left his mark here. Godlessness and sins still stick to the Nunnery's walls."

"My Lord?"

"The Church. The Holy Roman Way. The Papists. The drinking and the frolicking, the food and the … encounters. His Majesty wants to put a stop to it all. Return to true piety."

"I hope that Lacock is not an example of what you speak. I myself find this a devotional place. I find God here." I was lying through my teeth.

"Do you find Sister Isabella here also?"

My breath caught. "Pardon me, my Lord?" I manage.

"Where is Sister Isabella?"

"She left, my Lord. She … was quite ill."

"So I keep hearing. It is my opinion that she might've got quite with child."

"No, my Lord!" More pie splattered my skirts.

"What of you, Sister? There's been a deal of misconduct at Lacock, whether you want to admit to it or not. Have you had any relations with any of the guests? The scholars tempt you into their rooms, perchance? Has a handsome scholar winkled you out of your habit, Elisa?"

He knew. He must know about Samuel. My scholar Sam. The letter under my habit was burning hot. How could he know? My mind was scorched with a picture of my nakedness, of Samuel at my breast. I saw us looked down upon from above: it was God, Jesus, showing me what They saw that night. Perhaps They had shown Legh too.

"Settle down, sweet. Settle down."

I hadn't said anything, but I must have looked a state. He forced the wine on me. I took a shaking sip.

"Now we will not discourse upon your particular transgression, if I can just get a little more information about Sister Isabella. Because you see, I don't like to be cozened, to have people think they can hide things from me. I have been given Godly orders by the King of England to discover the true state of these treasonous, blasphemous Roman houses, and nothing can be hidden from me."

I was having trouble swallowing the wine; the more I thought about it, the more my throat constricted. It was stuck at the back of my throat. A panic rose in me. I could not breathe.

"Settle. Settle," he murmured, sitting back. A little bit of the wine went down, then I managed a little more. Finally I swallowed.

"She was attacked," I half cough, half confess.

"Attacked? By whom?'

"The Chaplain. He … raped her, hurt her… They moved her to the bakery in the village. She did nothing wrong. She was just doing her duties to God, and he … got her. If it please you, my Lord, hurt her no further."

He nodded sternly. "It is my policy to take accusations such as these with a large, sparkling, grain of salt. Women are always trying to cover their whorish antics by blaming man."

"No!"

"But!" He held out his hand. "I am known for my knowledge of character, and I very much want to dethrone that slimy bastard. I can imagine him taking advantage of God's ladies in this way. I can see it in my mind's eye."

"He did it. I swear he did. I inspected Isabella myself, in the Infirmary — my Lord she could never have done it to herself. It was force, a man's force."

He stood up, opened the door, and began barking at his henchmen. I was so upset I did not move.

"Please don't hurt Isabella," I croak. But he was gone. I was no use to him any more.

CHAPTER FIFTEEN

I attended the next two divine services, but they were a haze and I would not have gone if not for the constant glimmer of bright blue Legh-men at every corner. I still had not stolen a moment to speak to Constance about Arnie — the rule of silence was being followed for the first time in any one's time at Lacock. I would see to the hound myself again the next morning. I saved scraps from dinner.

I ran to him the next day. He had consumed my thoughts all night and he been present in all my dreams; I prayed for him constantly. He was the only part of Isabella I could tend. Carefully and quietly, I went into the grounds the next morning. Before light of course. No one was awake. I had heard the Legh-men all night: they had been raucous, running up and down the cloister, standing at the doors of the chambers and shouting obscene things. I wished them a hangover and a long sleep. Stay away from us. Methought I had created something bearable here: but perhaps it had been too bearable. Perhaps Jesus had remembered my transgressions and was hauling me back to my rightful place, to penitent misery where my mortal body belonged. Familiar thoughts built, spiralled.

But then they stopped spiralling and the thoughts fell to the earth with a desperate, heart-quaking crash.

The door to the shed was open: I could see it now. It was definitely ajar. Arnie must have conned how to open it — or else someone had realised what I had done. Or else a Legh-man inspected it and had put Arnie on the streets, or beat him because they are cruel and love sport. Or killed him, because dogs are not allowed at the Nunnery.

Nay. Arnie *must* have figured out how to open the door.

"Arnie," I whispered. "Arnie?" I looked around, I felt the soft touch of day's break on my face, but I couldn't see any movement of a dog on the grounds. I reached for the open door. If I stayed my hand and looked not inside mayhap this would not be happening. But I must needs look. I poked my head around the door.

He was there. Whimpering.

"Sweeting!" I ran to him, and he nuzzled his nose into me. "Arnie you stayed!" I spoke into his fur, I could hear his tail beating hard against the floor. "I cannot believe it! You are such a brave sir!" I pulled myself out of his matted fur and looked at his long face. He was still whimpering.

The hairs all over me stood to attention.

The cool breeze turned to a hot breath. Hot breath right on the back of my neck. I would never forget the feeling. And some days even now, many years later, in summer, a particularly horrid, clammy wind will blow at my back and I will be once more in that shed, dying a death that takest me nowhere. I wished then, if not now, I had died an actual death, I wished for blackness and the abyss.

"Elisa." He grabbed the dog by the scruff. Arnie yelped in pain.

"Stay! Prithee do not hurt him!" Peter kicked him outside. He slammed the door shut and the shed quivered, shedding spiderwebs and old, old dust.

"I've been packing my trunk this morning, Elisa." I was cowering away from him, still kneeling as though Arnie were in front of me. He ran his hands through my hair. "I've been told I'm not just to leave my position as Chaplain, but that I'm to go to the clerical courts, to answer for a crime."

I was frozen, still kneeling on the ground.

He thrust his groin into my face. I felt him as I had felt Samuel when I sat on his lap. He was putting it against my face. I started to shake, violently. Why was I not on my feet? I should attack him. I should kill him.

"You must answer for your sins." I was relieved, for just a second, because someone else must be there — someone else had spoken to the Chaplain in a calm and authoritative voice. But no one else was there. It was me. I was speaking.

"You little witch, Elisa." He smacked me in the head. I didn't make a noise. I looked up at him, in this position of prayer.

Protect me, Jesus. Protect me.

But as soon as I had started praying, I knew, almost as though the Lord had told me. Christ wasn't going to be able to do anything about this. I was alone. I saw it in the Chaplain's eyes. I was going to be treated as Isabella had been treated.

I shut my eyes, and promised myself I wouldn't open them until it was over. I promised myself again and again, when you open your eyes it will be done with, when you open your eyes it will be over. But I worried I would never be able to open my eyes again, I worried I would only see blackness for the rest of my days.

I heard the thumping on wood. Mens voices. I was shoved to the floor and hit my head badly on the stone.

The light shone in as the door opened. I opened my eyes. It was over. It was over.

"Jesu Christe, it is Sister Elisa, with her skirts all up around her middle. And her sheath all on display. Have we been whoring?" It was Legh. I couldn't see his face. My vision was blurred and splotchy. But it was his gay, singsong voice. "Be not afraid, Elisa." I felt him take a step over me, and Arnie's presence at my face, licking me, nuzzling into me. "I see you're with the Chaplain. And we all know about Peter's perchance for tupping the unwilling, and doing it with a lot of blood, bruises and screaming." The dog lay down next to me. I felt his warm side against my body; he gave me peace; I let go of listening; I let go of sight; it all went black, with Arnie at my side.

CHAPTER SIXTEEN

I was in the Infirmary. It took me over a minute to understand where I was. I was looking for Mary. For my sisters. My mother. When I finally understood that I was in a Nunnery, in the Infirmary, I had to remember why I was there. My body didn't want to move from the curled-up bind I woke in. I felt a burning, stinging between my legs and a dull ache in the bottom of my stomach. My head pounded.

"Elisa?"

It was Sister Jane. She pulled up a chair next to me and started stroking my hair. And with each stroke, a memory fell into place. I tried to move but my body refused, as if I didn't own it or control it any more. I lay there, curled up, and I would lie there forever. Until I died.

I had lost my virginity.

God. Jesus. I was speaking out loud. I could hear my own voice, but I wasn't sure what I was saying.

"Shh, shhhh." Jane kept stroking my hair. I did not think I would bear it when she stayed her hand. "No man will hurt you any more," she whispered. "Legh has had the Chaplain escorted out of the Abbey."

My heart rate jumped as though I had run up a flight of stairs.

"It was a punishment," I heard myself saying, like a truth coming straight from God.

"It was not, Sister."

"It was a punishment for Samuel." I looked into her kind face, a multitude of lines crinkled with concern. She shook her head, but she didn't know what I was saying. I felt a sudden desperation for her to understand. "I let Samuel touch me. My naked skin. And ..." The pain worsened. I was whispering but I could feel words tumbling out of me. "I wanted him to. That is why this has happened. I wanted a man to touch me. And I have touched myself too. When I am alone. This is why it happened. I have been pretending to be a Holy person, lying to everyone who sees me in my veil, but now, this has happened, and everyone will know I am a liar. That was God's plan."

"But you didn't give yourself to this Samuel." Jane was listening to me, her face crinkled as she tried to understand what I was saying.

"No. And it doesn't even matter any more, because the Chaplain took it from me. Not Samuel. The Chaplain."

I was not even permitted to choose to sin. Sin was forced upon me. My grace gone, my dignity gone, my maidenhead gone.

She stopped touching me.

I made a noise of protest. She was taking a vial from the side of my bed. It would be the ginger and fennel mixture I had given to Isabella.

Arnie.

"Where is Arnie?" I sat up in alarm, pain rippling through my body.

Sister hushed me, pulling me back down into my safe curled-up position, and lowering her voice. "Sister Constance has him. She is hiding him." She forced the liquid down my throat, and it burnt. I had dispensed this to a lot of patients and I had never understood that to swallow it stung.

I stayed in the Infirmary for a long time. I had not wanted to part with Sister Jane, but eventually Constance convinced not any lock, and I had heard from whispers in the ward that Peter was still in the village, frequenting the alehouses, sleeping on the streets. There was nothing to keep him from Lacock Abbey, Legh-men or none.

"Constance," I whispered as we were walked into Mass. Silence was still enforced.

"Elisa?" She had doted on me, visiting me every single day I had been in the Infirmary.

"I do not want to sleep in my room."

She nodded seriously. "You can sleep in my bed. It is big enough."

Relief. Constance would be next to me. If he did choose to come to Lacock, he would have to fight a room full of women, not to mention this particular angry Sister. He had brutally attacked two of her closest friends in a matter of weeks. There would be no getting past her. Still … "Can I sleep on the side of you that is least near the door?" I had said it before I could stop myself.

"Of course." She squeezed my hand and passed me my office book.

The mind-numbing consistency of Nunnery life was useful to me. If no one interrupted me and if the schedule stayed the same, I could find a place in my mind where nothing hurt. Silence helped. I had been asked if I wanted to move from the Infirmary to another, less taxing labour. I was momentarily tempted to return to the gardens, to the earth and the smells of the spring. But the thought of being outside hurt — it would not be wonderful any more; it had been hopelessly corrupted. Everything was corrupted, but the gardens had been my favourite place. Their ruin overtopped the rest. So I stayed in the Infirmary where it was busy and my mind was occupied.

I did not speak to God.

I was not sure whether I was angry or ashamed. I did not commune with Christ. I pressed the cup to my lips in Communion but did not drink, I put the bread in my mouth but I did not swallow. I knew not whether I deserved God not, or whether God deserve me not.

Sleeping in the Sisters' dormitory helped; they prated on late, and other people's words filled my head rather than my own. If I was not asleep by the time they stopped talking, I would roll over to face Constance, and she would tell me tales until I slept at last. I built each day so I was outside of myself; Con even stood outside the water closet, talking to me as I relieved myself. I did not care to what lengths I went to ignore the darkness that stood waiting in my mind.

We kept Arnie in our room. He stayed under the bed for most of the day. We got up before the first office to let him out, and then he went back to bed. Legh's men did not seem to be at their most vigorous any more. They had made their kill. It was only a matter of time before they made a decision about the Abbey's fate as well as Father Peter's.

Even still, it was well over a month before Lord Legh called us into the refectory to announce his departure. It was out of schedule, which upset me. We were to stay there after supper. I had been sitting in the darkest corner against the wall since my emergence from the Infirmary, and hoped my vantage point would be unobserved, whate'er the men said during this infernal address.

Constance held my hand as the blue-robed men stood to surround their master. My breathing was ragged. What if they mentioned what had happened? I had heard it in passing often enough, people discussing it in the corridors. Legh and his men had made it common knowledge. Everyone knew everything about the unHoly state of my Holiest of parts; everyone knew I had been cut up, that Peter the Chaplain had forced me against the door. I gasped a little bit, and started trying to loosen my veil.

"I'm here, Elisa." Constance pulled my hand away from my head. She steadied me.

"What if they describe what happened, as a conclusion before they leave?"

"They won't. They won't." She had a way of looking right at me, into me. It was relieving. I didn't ever have to explain my feelings or my panic: she saw them. But I knew she could not promise me this.

"What if they close the Abbey?" I pressed.

Constance's face changed. She had been thinking about this possibility. I leant myself against the cool sandstone as Constance looked far away. "I don't know, Elisa," she said after a long pause, helping me up off the wall, forcing me to sit straight. "But we shall face whatever happens together."

"Sisters, Mother Abbess." Legh stood by the High Table, leaning over a pulpit especially provided. His hands dangling casually off the stone. "It has been a bustling few weeks!" He clasped his hands together, anticipating. "I will be making my full report to the King, verily, but it becomes me well, methinks, to acquaint you with the meat of it." Bile rose. "You will notice there are several who are not present today."

What if he explained what he had seen? I had not revised the night in my own mind — I didn't intend to visit it ever again. I certainly was not ready to have it spat back at me by the only witness. I started to sweat. I could see the shed in my mind's eye. But I was seeing it as Legh must have seen it. Moving past the barking Arnie, smacking open the door, seeing my body, naked, my parts splayed open, bloodied, covered in the Chaplain's seed.

"Your Chaplain has been banished from the Abbey." I could feel his eyes on me. Look up, Elisa. Look up. I raised my head. I stared at him. The man who had seen me, seen me like that. "The multitude of misdeeds and foul things in Chaplain Peter's history did not befit his role. He is the perfect example of the corrupt papist heresy still pervading these halls. You will not be seeing him again." He broke eye contact. "This is only just the start, however!" He smiled as his brother handed him a sheet of parchment.

"I want it known I will be reporting the following to Lord Cromwell, and by extension the King." He cleared his throat, flourished his sleeves. "The presence of a dog in the Abbey." I looked at Constance; her lip twitched. "The inability to stay silent during prayers. The inability to stay silent during Mass. The inability to sing in tune. The gluttonous theft and consumption of communion bread and wine to satisfy hunger not Holiness. The persistent holding of hands, whether standing or walking or sitting together. We will be reporting Sister Constance." I felt her stiffen next to me. I grabbed her hand.

"What did I just say?" barked Legh, exasperated. I let her go. "We command Sister Constance that in Holy obedience you must restore the statue of Christ you violently and drunkenly removed from the Chapel; if you decline to restore it you are required to make another at your own expense."

"Fuck." Con crossed her arms like a scolded child. Legh moved himself even further over the pulpit, as though he was going to tell us a great secret. "Finally, three sisters have required immediate banishment from Lacock Abbey, accused of behaviours that are not compatible with their vocations." Everyone looked around — who was missing?

"Firstly, Imogen Thatcher has been removed with evidence

she was with child." A ripple of shock reverberated around the hall. I shivered: Sister Jane had put herself in danger and given me herbs to rid my body of any child that may have found itself there. I had since got my monthly course. But I would never know whether the herbs had served their purpose or were not necessary. Was Sister Imogen bearing the Chaplain's child? I prayed not. One of my first prayers in weeks. I prayed she had wanted to tup some village boy because he was alluring and sweaty from a day out on the farm. I prayed she had given in to her own sin, and would now bear a child because of her own choices, and her own desires for flesh.

"Sister Marguerite has also been removed from the Abbey. She was found to have been having relations with laymen guests."

Oh, Marguerite.

Constance's blonde eyebrows were raised: she looked impressed.

"Finally, you will notice Sister Agnes's absence. After several interviews, Sister Agnes was found to be loyal to the Roman Catholic Church. She did not recognise His Highness King Henry as Head of the One True Church. She was detained this morning."

"Nay!" Sister Alice yelled out.

"Silence!" More dramatic hand waving. "Or I shall suspect you, Sister Alice, of not being loyal to the True Church of England either!" Con made a small whoop of sadness. "As you can see the list of discrepancies is long, and terribly serious. I would not be surprised if we were to hear that Lacock Abbey was to be dissolved. You will be released of your bonds of poverty and obedience." One of his men tapped him on the shoulder and whispered something in his ear.

"Ah yes. My mistake. You will be released of your bonds of poverty and obedience, but His Majesty has been merciful and all Sisters will be bound to their oath of chastity until the year of fifteen forty-nine." He smiled widely. I grasped the seat beneath me and felt the hard wood sweat under my tight grip.

Sister Franella started to cry. He looked at her somewhat affectionately. "I would ready yourselves for a life back in the outside. Life of a sort, at any rate. God bless and keep you, ladies."

CHAPTER SEVENTEEN

We made our way to bed.

No one spoke. We walked across the courtyard and the moon shone upon the Lacock Sisters, each of us trying to comprehend the possibility that our life sentence was not a life sentence at all and that our enclosure would be quickly coming to an end.

We readied ourselves for bed silently, and even when we were all under the covers, everyone was still. But the stirring in my mind was becoming violent. I didn't want a silent night. I could not have this soundlessness before I slept.

Constance's bed was nearest the door. I did not like this, but it was the only bed with room. I sat up. The bed was pushed up against the wall, so I could rest my back against the cold stone. I looked out over the dark room of sleeping women.

"What will you do if we are closed?" I spoke into the tension, snapping it. The whole room, the beds, the flagstone floor, the walls, everything seemed to exhale. The question everyone was holding tightly to their chests had been aired. It was out.

People sat up, coughed, reshuffled. In my room, there were Sister Franella, Sister Maria the Spanish widow, Sister Alice, Sister Charity and an empty bed where Sister Imogen had been sleeping.

"I do not know," said Maria; she was brushing her long dark hair with her fingers. The stray strands of silver sparkled in the candlelight. "I am old — I suppose I could try to remarry. But men are hard work you know."

Constance laughed.

"I suspect I'll go home," Sister Charity mused. "I could work the farm, find a husband."

"With whom you cannot lie," scoffed Con.

"Perhaps we can find another convent?" Franella asked.

There were murmurs of agreement.

"I heard the Mother saying the Crown has been dispensing money to dissolved Nuns, but due to our immoral and unchaste indiscretions we will not receive any at all."

"That is not just!" Alice said, throwing a fist into her mattress. "I have not lain with anyone this whole time!"

There was a chorus of agreement.

"I judge I shall go home and be married. My parents will be horrified at my return. They thought they were rid of me, but you cannot make Constance disappear forever, Papa." The Sisters laughed; everyone always laughed at Constance. "The poor old gentleman needs must find a lad to take me."

"A special lad willing to wait a decade for a tupping," added Sister Maria.

Something had been building in my chest. I thought perhaps it was tears, an outburst of sorrow, or wailing, but it was a bubble of words, rising unstoppably to my lips. "I am destroyed!" I exclaimed. "No man will have me, because … everyone knows! Everyone knows I'm cursed and — and violated!"

I could almost hear the bodies around me tighten with

embarrassment. No one spoke for a long time; my shallow breaths were the only sound filling the room.

"I am soiled goods too, you know." Maria looked ominous, the candle at her bedside flickering funny shadows on her face.

"No you're not," I retorted quickly. "You were married, you are a widow without virginity. You are not soiled. I am unmarried without my virginity. I am l-lustful and defiled." The words could not to be stopped.

"No no no," she cooed. "You misunderstand: certainly I fucked my husband, God rest his soul, and that was all very pleasing and proper. But I have fucked many men, and I have been married only once."

I could feel Constance start laughing next to me — she wasn't making sound, but she was shaking with mirth.

"And a lot of people know this of me, child."

Alice was the first to actually let a noise out. A true, merry laugh. And as soon as her laugh had touched the air, everyone else's followed. Except for Franella and myself. I wrung my hands in my lap. Franella made a tutting sound, and started puffing up her pillows. So Maria was what? A whore? Like Joan from Henley Church? Had she been made to stand in a sheet? My view of her shifted. I looked at her, brushing her long hair, her kind eyes. Her devotion to God was unparalleled by any Nun in the Abbey. Her worship was pure and true: I often saw her crying in a hymn or prayer. I had craved for a purity and a connection to Christ like hers.

"I am not as pure as the Abbess might think either." Alice was speaking now. "I am not as," she cleared her throat, "worldly as Maria."

Maria made a small bow of her head as though accepting a compliment; my mind reeled.

"But …" Alice shuffled her bedclothes a little "… when I was a younger woman, there was a boy in my village and his name was Tom Baker." She looked straight at me. "He made me get on my knees." I understood this phrase now. "I had liked him so much, I did not want to refuse him. But I think about it each night. I ... it haunts me. It haunts God too I would think."

Maria said something in Spanish. A knot in my chest was untying itself. I glanced over to the empty bed; we all knew that Imogen had her story.

Everyone looked to Constance — surely she had a tale to tell. I thought of the letters she held to her chest.

"We all know the ache of my heart — and loins — since I have hidden my instrument so carefully in the library," she joked.

"Thy what?" Maria asked.

"My phallus."

"Thou hast a phallus?"

Giggles. Even from me.

"I do not have a phallus attached to me, no. But I am the owner of a very nice wooden example of the tool: it's hidden behind Thomas Aquinas's works in the stacks."

"Oh I see," Maria understood, "I heard about those. Useful for Nuns and the ugly."

"Indeed, it is perfect for me," Constance joked.

I shook my head, no one could pretend Constance was ugly, not even for japes.

"You just ... put it in?" asked Alice quietly, curiosity overcoming her.

"Yes. And out and in and out and in." Giggles again.

"Have you ever been with a real boy, Con?" It was Alice again, saying more words in moments than I had heard from her in a year.

I felt Constance move under the covers. "No, Alice. No boys." There was something about the way she spoke that made me look at her. She seemed uncomfortable; she was biting her lip. I thought she might be lying.

Franella tried to make a noise. She had been looking at her lap, probably praying for us. I could almost feel her thoughts. She was an emblem of purity and piety in a room full of broken women, feigning virginity in a Nunnery. She radiated anger, or something strong and fierce.

"They know about me back where I come from!" she said, too loudly. "I couldn't go back home, my parents won't take me." She crossed herself, looking around at us all, the whites of her eyes glowing brightly.

"We all done things, Franny," Maria said softly.

"I wish I had been raped like Elisa."

I was so shocked at the statement I hardly heard it. Constance made an angry hiss, but I put a hand on her lap.

Franella went on. "Because I chose to do what I did! I have the devil inside me. I am wrong. I dream about vile things. Elisa may be just like me, we may both be defiled, and our virginities might be by the wayside but you ent got the disease I got. The hot lust. The want to touch myself, to touch men, to have them enter me." She couldn't stop speaking. She was panicking, gasping.

I got out of my bed and went to her; I took her shaking hands, and started making shushing noises. "That isn't true, Franny. That isn't true. You're not alone. Listen to the stories of these Sisters. We want. We all want. I want." There was a murmuring of agreement from around the room but she was shaking her head violently, her eyes frantic, her whole body vibrating, tears flowing. She started making a retching noise. I knew this state: it had possessed me. Poor Franny. Poor Elisa.

I looked around at my Sisters.

"Should she should go to the Infirmary?" suggested Constance.

"Look, Franny!" I turned my back to her, and shrugged off my nightgown.

Franny hiccoughed and went still. Everyone was stunned silent.

"You see the scar up my back?" I asked.

"What is it?" She hiccoughed again.

"I did it to myself with a whip." There was a small intake of breath from Constance. "After I spent an evening, by myself, having lustful thoughts, taking lustful actions." I turned to her, holding my gown in front of my nakedness, but unable to hide everything. My whole body was fizzing like a vinegar solution left to stand too long. "I was so ashamed, but the whip didn't stop what I felt. In fact it led me right into the hands of the man I desired." She was listening to me avidly. "I kissed him. I kissed Samuel and he's seen me as you've seen me now, and touched me, and I wanted it, and I still want it. You are not alone, Franny. Not in your guilt, nor in your actions." I knew it was true because I erupted in shivers. More strangely still, I knew it was true because when I spoke it, *I felt God*.

Franny's breathing had slowed down. "It is a deep scar."

"I was very ashamed," I answered.

"Are you still ashamed?" Constance asked.

I shrugged my shoulders. "I know not."

Sister Maria told a story about herself and a stable boy, the final confession of the night. Then she reached for a bottle of whisky in her trunk and we all downed a sleep-inducing draught.

But I could not sleep, even after the whirl of alcohol had set in. I had not felt like this since before the shed. I felt like myself. Almost more than myself. Above myself. Sharing the pain with the Sisters was like removing a peach-stone from a gullet. I looked around into the dark, making out some of the shapes in the beds. I loved these women. I did not want Commissioner Sir Thomas Legh to sack our home and send us far from one another.

The feeling of the room shifted as souls left to be in their unconscious slumber. The sound of breath became rhythmical but I could still feel Constance's wakefulness behind me. I turned to her.

Her eyes were open. "I'm sorry about your back," she whispered finally.

"It was tended very well." I smiled, soft with memory.

"By Samuel?"

I nodded. A tiny frown appeared on her face and for a moment I worried that she disapproved of my story.

"I don't want Lacock to be closed," she whispered. I nodded in agreement. "I don't want to be away from you," she added.

"I don't want to be parted from you either."

Silence. We watched each other.

"If I had given myself a whipping every time I pleasured myself I would be all stripes and scars." She swallowed, looking pensive. "Perhaps I should have been punishing myself."

"No!" I grabbed her hand under the sheets. "You deserve only good things."

"In your eyes … maybe not God's."

"My eyes should count for something."

She squeezed my hand. "Of course, they do."

I blushed. "And Constance, you are the most virtuous of all. I think that wooden phallus might be keeping you chaste."

"Not really." Her hair had fallen in front of her face. She wore it out as she slept, which left it tangled in knots in the morning. But she liked, she said, to feel it loosely around her face after a day in her veil. I moved a strand out of her eyes and felt her breath catch. I noticed her cheeks were wet with tears I had not seen fall.

"What mean you: 'not really'?"

She took my hand under the covers. "I am so sorry about what happened to you," she said, ignoring me.

I was surprised. I had not been thinking about the shed,

the door, the Chaplain. For the first time in weeks and weeks, I was not spending all my strength to prevent the night from surfacing. This night was consuming everything. My foot was touching Constance's under the covers, my hands in hers. My heart was racing, just as fast as when I had taken off my nightgown.

She moved her pillow. Our foreheads touched. Her blue eyes were grey tonight. I felt her breath on my face; I wondered if she could feel mine. Was it as sweet as hers?

She moved her head an inch closer, and kissed me. Her lips were so soft, it was all I could think about.

CHAPTER EIGHTEEN

I was confused. But it was blessed relief to have this thing ... this absurd happening take up all my thoughts. It was so relieving. It was so distracting.

Constance was her regular self the next day: speaking to me as normal, laughing, making fun and being merry. Legh was gone, and she was finally at liberty to be loud. The Nuns were back in their normal uniforms, the silk veils returned, the robes with long trains, and Sister Maria's fingers were once again adorned with jewelled rings and Constance had re-donned her golden broach and silver belt.

I spent most of Matins thinking I had almost certainly dreamt it.

I was so distracted by it all that Sister Jane told me to leave the Infirmary. I had given a patient three times the amount of echinacea root that was necessary.

I decided to walk outside. I walked far. After about a mile of taking short cuts through the sheep fields, I took off my veil, and tunic, leaving them by a stile. I felt more normal now. I might not have even been recognised as a Nun.

I recollected the evening before. Going through it, moment

by moment. She had kissed me. She had followed her desires, I supposed, and they had led her to my lips.

I sat beneath a large oak tree. I had climbed a hill. I could see the village spread out beneath me. Stone speckled in between the green spring trees.

Everything was always decided for me.

I picked up a fallen acorn and fiddled with its hat.

I was not allowed to be married. I was not allowed to go to Livia's chambers. I was to go to the Nunnery.

Sam kissed me. Sam took my gowns off. The Chaplain raped me. Constance kissed me.

Even when I did things by myself I chose my actions and my words because they were what I thought others would want me to do.

Father Nicholas had wanted me to whip my back. God wanted me to fast for my sins. Christ needed me to pray dozens of times a day.

When had I done anything because I wanted it?

I rolled the acorn down the hill.

I had wanted to go on this walk. I decided. I had not wanted to be in my veil or my habit so I had taken them off. I had wanted to wander the country and be in nature and so I had. I took in a warm, scented breath of air, and it was my breath, my own breath. In my own body. That belonged to me, even if no one knew it. It was mine. I hugged my knees into my chest.

I wanted to talk to Constance. She would be working in the stacks. So I got up and walked to the library, haphazardly donning my veil as I hopped over the stile, feeling, for the first time in my whole life, the architect of my day.

"Sweet Elisa!" Con was dusting books with a cloth.

I bowed my head. The Mother shot us a stern glare from

her table under the stained glass. She was wearing her contraband lace shoes.

"I have a book I want to show you," I said. Constance cocked an eyebrow. I led her downstairs, towards the prick-hiding book.

"Do you want me to recover it now Legh is gone?" she asked excitedly, seeing where we were headed. "Do you want to try it?"

"No," I snap sternly. "Ah, aye, maybe I do, but it is not the matter."

She looked at me, sucking her teeth, with one hand reaching behind the book, feeling around for the cock. "Here you go."

I looked down at it. "You are making me think I dreamt it."

She blinked, then nodded. "I doubt you dreamt it, unless we dreamt the same dream."

"What do you want?" I asked, brandishing the wooden male member at her.

"You." She was looking me dead in the eye, chin up, proud.

"Fine," I retorted shortly.

"What do you want?" She snapped back. "You do not know," she accused.

I bristled. "I do know."

"Nay. You have no idea."

"Be quiet."

"You can't decide if you want me or Samuel or God or —"

"Tell me not what I feel. I am wearied to death of people telling me what to feel."

She hung her head.

I balanced the prick next to a collection of St Jerome's letters. Good God, what had my life become? I thought of my mother. I imagined her face if she knew. Fuck her. Fuck them. I hope they would faint if they knew. They would not recognise me. That thought was ecstasy.

Con was standing very still. Frowning a little.

"This is my choice, my action."

I placed a hand on her hip. It was shallower than my own. Then I took my hand to the back of her neck. My face inches away from hers. She made a movement towards me. "Be still," I hissed.

I felt her uneven breath. Then I kissed her, and it was I who led the charge. She tasted sweet. I suppose I should have expected it. Constance let out a small noise and I pulled away.

"Do not stop," she said, almost angrily. I picked up Jerome's prick and went to find a table to sit down at. I would not be able to support myself for much longer. Constance followed.

It was one of the desks reserved for academics, but today two Nuns used it. Two Nuns who kiss.

"Are you well, Elisa?" she asked tenderly.

"I am beginning to think," I rubbed my eyes, "that if Chaplain Peter destined me to Hell, I might as well enjoy myself, indulge myself, in ways I actually want to. Because I already need a thousand indulgences to get me out of damnation, and I can't afford that right now."

We looked at each other across the desk. I was not certain what this all meant. From the look in her eye, she was not either.

"Why aren't you in the Infirmary?" she asked finally.

"Because I overdosed an old farmer with echinacea root."

"On purpose?" I grinned at her and shrugged. "I wonder how long we've got until we hear from Legh again." Constance looked up at the stained glass next to us, the different coloured light dappled on her face.

"If I were Legh, I would close us down."

"Elisa!" someone snapped. I fell off my chair.

"Jesus Christ!" I blasphemed. It was Sister Jane. Somehow she'd found me. "God forgive me," I added instinctively.

"Good God Elisa!" said Constance, who was belly-laughing at my fall. "The Lord's name in vain in the Abbey!"

"Oh please, Constance." I took Jane's hand and stood up. "This isn't God's house."

Constance stopped laughing.

Jane rolled her eyes. "I need you back, you old dope. Even if you are spending the day double dosing poor village men. Since Legh expelled Marguerite they've got Franny starting, and she needs someone behind her every step of the way. She has just been standing staring at Mr Johnson's leg for about an hour." I nodded. "Also," her voice lowered, "we have a new patient. A lady of the night, I believe. She has presented with ..." she stopped trying to be subtle "... with itching and burning on her purse. It's really very severe." I nodded again. "Franny has been avoiding her, but it'd be a good thing if you pushed her a little."

"Aye, Sister Jane." I stood, my legs steady again.

It amazed me it was not I in Franny's position. That Jane had found me to deal with the woman with the itch, because I, Elisa Knolly, did not have a problem with that sort of scandalous happening.

"I shall see you anon, Sister." I said to Con.

She winked.

CHAPTER NINETEEN

I only just managed to convince Franny to examine the farmer's leg wound. She did as she was told, and even went on to correctly apply the balm and re-bandage the leg. But getting her near the 'Mackerel', as she kept calling our strumpet guest, was another story.

The Mackerel herself watched, amused, as I physically dragged Franny over to perform an inspection.

"Just stand next to me, Sister, and assist me when I ask for you," I hissed, embarrassed at the scene she was making.

"Madam, may I ask your name?" I moved the wooden screen around the patient's bed. It was heavy and awkward, but Franny didn't move to help me; she was fixed to one spot, her gaze boring into the floorboards.

The patient still had not spake. I turned to look at her. I knew not if I had expected scarred skin, no teeth and alarmingly rouged lips, but I was surprised at her appearance. She had very dark, long hair and bright blue eyes. She would have been within a year or three of mine own age, and she was quite, quite beautiful.

"My pie hurts."

I flinched at her crude language. Her accent was common. I felt Franny's body buckle next to mine. Praise God, she managed to stay upright.

"Itches and scratches," she added, a smile creeping up the side of her face. She was enjoying terrorising the Nuns. But I had been handpicked for this task. I continued the examination of my harlot. I nodded and moved forwards, putting a brave hand on her forehead to see if she was running hot. Her cheeks were rosy and her skin very soft. I could tell she was laughing at me — behind those bright eyes was mirth.

"My name is Sister Elisa; what shall I call you?" I ask again. Her temperature was normal.

"I suppose you can call me Alby. Though your sister was comfortable calling me Mackerel." She spoke loudly, and Franny made a whimpering noise.

"Well I believe there is some truth in that," I quoth under my breath.

"And you will still treat me? When you know what I do?"

"We are all God's children."

"You might be, Sister, but I am daughter of the night, a goose, a whore. You know me as a Mackerel, don't you, Sister Franella?"

"God forgive your sins," Franny whispered.

"A turd in thy teeth, shrew," replied Alby, smiling.

Franny's gaze snapped back down to the floor.

Perhaps this woman's sins had given her a cruel, biting tongue. Perhaps my sins would do the same to me.

"Madam Alby." My throat was dry. "May I ask some further questions about your condition?"

"I'll just show you." She reached down for her blankets and hoisted them up; she was uncovered under the sheets. Her legs spread. Franny let out a wail of disgust and ran from the Infirmary — I heard the heavy door shut behind her.

I looked closer at the woman's purse. It was certainly inflamed. "You really should not be so vulgar," I muttered.

"I've paid your Abbess a small fortune to be here, therefore I be how I please." She spoke from behind her quilt, having lifted it over her head.

"You paid to be here?" I was surprised.

She uncovered her face, still split legged and unashamed. "Aye. Your Abbess needed a bit of convincing and I had the coin to spare."

"From your work?" I was thumbing through the notes Sister Jane had provided me on these types of illnesses, but I couldn't conceal my interest in her unusual occupation. I could feel, rather than see, her smiling.

"Aye from work."

Sister Jane poked her head around the screen. "Conclusions, Sister?" she asked firmly. Alby finally closed her legs and sat up on the bed, wincing and shuffling herself on the mattress like a dog with an itchy bottom. How could a face so beautiful hide so disgusting a heart? I made a note to burn rather than wash the sheets.

"Could it be Goose Bumps?" Jane pressed.

"No ..." Alby whispered. Her voice was so changed I wondered who else had spake. "No. It's not Goose Bumps, is it?"

I shook my head, but she was still afraid. With good reason. The stories about the disease were horrifying and always ended in an unsightly death.

"When did the symptoms begin?"

"Since last full moon."

"And you have not had fever or any other sores on your body?"

She shook her head earnestly.

Sister Jane nodded, agreeing with me. "It is not like Goose Bumps."

"It looks to me more like ..." I swallowed. I had seen this before, with Isabella. "... a rough, or perhaps violent experience has occurred. You have small cuts upon you; they should heal naturally — and itch as they do — but I would think that they may be ... opened again or aggravated by further ... use."

Alby laughed. I chided myself and looked to Jane, but someone had called her away. "You must abstain from work until the pain stops and itching stops."

"Is that all?"

I nodded.

"Will you make me leave?"

"There's not much more we can do here."

"Will they let me pay board to stay longer?"

"'Tis possible." I felt uncomfortable. "They ask for quite a price ..."

"Money is no matter." I must have given her a furtive glance. "You think I'm carrying around stolen money? Or money of my imagination?"

I decided to be blunt about it. "I did not know that your profession payed much money. I understood it to be poorly rewarded."

She smirked. "Not if one is clever about it."

CHAPTER TWENTY

"Have you heard of the green sickness?" It was late. The night was warm.

I felt rather than saw Constance shake her head.

"Does someone have it in the Infirmary?" she whispered. I felt her warm breath on my face.

"Not in the Infirmary," I said, giggling quietly. Wondering if they had brewed the beer too strong today. "But I'm sure our Mother Abbess has it."

"What mean you? What is't?" Constance pinched my arm.

"It's where a woman, most often a Nun, or sometimes the unsightly or smelly, get sick because they never lie with anyone, never please their hungers. They get unwell. Their bodies decay because of it." I had heard my sisters discuss it when they thought I was not listening.

"Surely it's a devil's lie … to tempt us." Constance fingers were interconnected with my own.

"It happens within the womb, Con. It is real." I placed my hand on her lower tummy. It tautened under my touch. "It leads to a madness of the mind."

"Terrible," Constance muttered. I kissed her. Our third kiss. I felt her lips smile under mine.

"That's it! God forgive me I cannot!" Franny yelled.

I jumped, we'd been caught. We were to be excommunicated. Hanged. I was to die.

"It's too hot! I am sleeping without my nightdress." Franny was standing on her bed in a mess of sheets and sweat. She had not seen us. She had not seen us. She was just hot. Too hot for her sheets.

"Me too!" Constance said. "This weather is unseasonable and unGodly." She wriggled out of her shift underneath the sheets, and threw it into the middle of the room. There were several other ghostly apparitions, as nightgowns floated through the hot air and landed on the floor.

"Abbess Catherine is going to get a cursed nasty surprise tomorrow morning," Widow Maria muttered.

"I'll get up early and make everyone cover up," I said, shoving my shift under the mattress, easy to access in case of inspection.

The warm, silly energy of the room dissipated as people fell back to sleep. A new energy arrived, if only in our bed.

We kissed again. But it was different. Obviously. This was kissing without clothes. But I kept my body away from hers, so my bottom was only just covered by the sheets. Perhaps we could move back to my private rooms together tomorrow.

"You will fall off!" whispered Constance. She put her hand in the small of my back and pulled me towards her. We lay, our bodies pressed against one another.

"I've never done this sort of thing before," I manage. She was silent. "Have you?" I pressed.

I felt her move under the covers. I stayed still, confused.

"Show me what you did to yourself." She whispered. She took hold of my hand. I shook my head slightly. "Show me." She said, firmer this time. Hesitantly, I guided her hands downwards. She pushed my legs apart. All my desire to say no went away. "What next?" She whispered. I didn't move. "Let me take a guess." Her hands wandered, slowly and intentionally. I felt her slide inside of me. I groaned and reached out for her, brushing her breasts, and clutching at her other hand. "You're going to have to try and stay quiet." she whispered into my hair.

And I almost managed it, until the end. It wasn't a loud noise and I didn't think much of it at the time — I hadn't been able to think much at all at the time.

Bells rang for Matins. Everyone moved around in bedsheets, protecting their modesty. In a daze I dressed myself. I caught Constance's eye and she smiled. I could not find my veil. I was going to be late.

"Here it is." Alice was holding it. Everyone else had filed out the room. She was standing near her mattress.

"Thank you, Alice."

She maintained a tight grip on the veil. "I was warned before I came here, Elisa, they told me that at the Priories there are *more who mimic Sappho than pray*. That's what they said. I just didn't believe it." I didn't understand what she was saying, "You know, of all the foul stories we revealed to each other, of all the sins we confessed, your little midnight moan was the most revolting of all." She left.

I shook. I wanted to be violently sick. I wanted to expel my experiences by throwing them up out of my body. But it was done. I could not go backwards. Alice was right. I had needed someone to remind me. I was the most revolting of all.

I only just made it to Matins, then I mumbled something to Sister Jane about my illness. Bless that woman — she might have thought I had an illness of the stomach, a runny tummy or a snuffly nose. She had no idea I was sick to my core with the devil's work.

I went to the library. I needed literature. I needed God to confirm I was Lucifer himself. Then I would treat myself accordingly.

As soon as I opened the Bible and started reading, I uncoiled. The frenzy lessened. I tucked my feet up on the stool and leant my back against the cool stone of the Abbey. I would just read the whole Bible, and when I found the passage describing what should happen to people who do things that I did, I would do it. A very hot tear ran down my cheek. This would happen to me. Only I could attract this shame.

After an hour or so of reading the panic returned, then it would subside again. It was frantic, tummy turning page rifling and then calmer moments of asking myself why I was so angry and wild. I pondered why Alice had spoken to me and not Constance. I wondered if I had made Constance do what she did. But I kept the pages turning whatever way my mood turned. It was at war, my heart. One moment all I wanted was to be under the good graces of God's eye. Lacock's eye. Mother's eye and Father's eye. The next moment, my humours were hot, and I wanted everyone to see me for what I was. I wanted everyone to faint at my choices, and recognise me as the defiant, deviant, ungovernable woman that I am. A force to challenge God. A force to challenge men. But then I was back to flicking Bible pages, my tears wetting the delicate parchment, asking the Lord for forgiveness.

Sister Charity was the only one who came across me. I snapped at her after she asked me what I was doing. Hopefully she would spread the news I had been taken by the spirit to read God's word in religious ecstasy, not that Elisa was a shrew, or, worse, that Elisa was trying to determine, just how bad her sexual deviancy was.

I rested the palms of my hands on my eyes. Colour

exploded in the darkness. I watched the purple lines moving, turning to red, then orange. I looked closely, making sure no words from God formed. I saw a blue squiggle that looked like the letter 'L', which could've stood for Lucifer. But I saw nothing else. Nothing abundantly clear.

I could find nothing in the Bible about what Constance and I had done.

If we had been men there would have been quite a lot about it. But we were not men. We were women. My lungs rattled as I took a few quaking breaths. Did I even have the energy to hate myself for what I had done? Why couldn't the Lord and I ever want the same thing? It was exhausting being always at odds with the Divine. My thoughts fluttered back to the event. How could He think of making something so pleasurable be a sin? The cruelty of it.

"Elisa. I'm glad you're well enough to grace us with your presence." The Abbess had to speak loudly over the prating of everyone at table. There were so many guests staying they had had to bring in another trestle, and the concept of silent Nuns had gone out the window. There was not even an attempt at sign language. "Are you feeling better? I hear Sister Charity caught you in quite a sweat."

"I am feeling much better."

She looked at me out the side of her eye but she didn't press me. "Constance wants to speak with you. She was worried she was not going to see you."

"What?"

Constance was downing a large tankard of ale by the fire. I moved to her quickly. I took hold of her hand. "Constance? What's happening?"

She was so beautiful. Her face took away all my disgust and pain. Who cared what God thought? Surely God could see this woman and her worth. I saw God in her eyes. I saw God in her sweet touch. I felt God last night when she … perhaps Christendom had got it wrong. God wasn't in Matins, God was in Constance. She was not answering me. She was staring into the dregs of her ale. Had she told someone? Or had Alice told everyone? She hated me. She hated what we did. She blamed me for what I did. This was my fault. I had forced my sinfulness upon her and I had made her like me. I was a plague. Nay.

"I am leaving today. Home to my parents. I am to be unenclosed, de-Nunned, un-sanctified."

"Why?" I knew why though: for punishment. From God. I put my hand on the cold hearth. Some of the guests started singing a crude song.

"They don't want me here when King Henry closes them. They want to be on the right side of this split."

"Split?" She nodded. "When do you leave?"

"A carriage is being arranged right now."

"This is punishment."

"No no no," she cooed, pressing her tankard of drink into my hand, encouraging me to drink what remained.

"It is."

We looked at each other for a dangerously long time until she cracked a broad grin. "Well maybe. But it was worth it." She squeezed my hand.

"I want to," I looked around the room, asking this damned nunnery for the words, "return the favour?" I tried.

"From last night?" I nodded. I could see the longing in her eyes. "Verily, I hath known for some time I must leave, Elisa."

"Then why did not you tell me?"

"I had not the heart."

"Constance!" Alice wrapped her arms around Con. I took a step back, alarmed. "I have written you a letter. For the carriage ride." She threw me a disgusted look. Constance did not see it.

But maybe she was not as revolted as her curled lip seemed: maybe she was jealous. She looked at Con the way I looked at her. It didn't matter any more — neither of us could have her.

An inebriated guest sidled up to us.

"Sister Constance, this is Brother Thomas. He's visiting from Oxford." Alice did not introduce me, but I had seen him before, cozying up with Alby.

"God … bless you, Sisters," he said piously, but with a hiccough in between the God and bless which robbed his greeting of its affect somewhat. "I was just sitting at the table, giving thanks to the Lord, and I felt called to come over to you and recite a little rhyme."

Con and I exchanged a glance.

"We would be honoured to hear it, Brother Thomas." Con smiled. I could not look away from her. I would never see her again. The brother was clearing his throat, looking at me, waiting for my response.

"Of course. I love rhymes," I said quickly.

"Good, good." He clapped his hands together in preparation, and other people gathered around. The brother cleared his throat dramatically.

> *"First a mornings take your book,*
> *the glass wherein yourself must look,*
> *your young thoughts so proud and jolly*
> *must be turned to notions Holy,*
> *and for all your follies past,*
> *you must do penance pray and fast*
> *and when your blood shall kindle pleasure,*
> *scourge yourself in plenteous measure."*

Applause. A few people muttered 'Amen'.

I looked at the man. I looked deep into his boring brown eyes. I debated. He was either a messenger from God, there to remind me of my place, of my sins, or he was just another example of hypocrisy in this crappy place. Another Godless person parading around in God's house.

"I heard you made acquaintance with one of our guests, Brother Thomas," I said suddenly. Loudly. He raised a drunk eyebrow. "Alberta — or Alby, I believe she prefers to be called."

"Oh." He was blushing. "Yes, I met an Alby yesterday I believe. In passing," he added.

"Indeed. Might I take a line from your eloquent poem, Brother Tom, and suggest that you *Scourge yourself in plenteous measure?*"

I left the refectory.

"What on earth could you mean, Sister?" he called after me, voice forced.

"She's a bloody whore!" I called out over my shoulder.

I stood in the middle of the cloister, where all the paths met. I was breathing heavily.

I watched in a daze as two guests embraced passionately on the North wall. This Godforsaken place. An escaped Arnold began to defecate on the lawns. No one cared anymore.

I could hear Con approaching behind me. I recognised her footsteps, light and graceful. I turned to her and buried my head in her chest. My tears wet the neckline of her habit.

"I cannot be here without you. Prithee do not leave me here. Can I come with you?"

I heard Constance sniff. I had never seen her cry. I turned my head up with a macabre curiosity to see what she looked like. It was beautiful of course. Her blue eyes extra bright.

"My parents would not allow it sweet Elisa." I hung my head. "Will you promise me something?"

"Anything."

"You must vow to botch up the rounds in prayers. Be'st

thou loud in the soft parts and soft in the loud parts and you must keep my wooden penis from being confiscated and you must not let anyone make you think you are not worthy."

"They will be my new vows," I promised, watching as she took off her veil. I smoothed out her hair. She gave the veil to me. I clutched at it.

"Thank you," I managed. I wiped away some snot running from my nose, trying to surreptitiously rub it away on my skirts.

"Thank you," she replied. The silver light of the moon was sparkling on her skin. I tried to capture the memory, imprinting it into my mind. Arnold squeezed his snout in between our bodies. "What will happen to Arnold?" I wrapped my arms around him, burying my nose in his neck. My big slobbery saviour.

"My parents have said I may bring him — but wouldst thou rather keep him by you?"

I took an inhale of his sweet-smelling fur, my body wracked in a new spasm of sadness.

"No," I said finally. "He shall be much happier somewhere he is not a stowaway."

"He will be able to go outside and run around," Constance assured me.

"Just as he needs."

There was a guffawing of drunken revelry, as a crowd of men and women, one of whom was almost definitely a Nun, another of whom was undoubtedly Alby from the Infirmary, whisked past. They were singing and tripping over their own feet. I caught sight of a rogue breast.

"Alby shouldn't be doing what she's about to do ..." I muttered.

"Go. Go tell her. Goodbyes are terrible when they go on and on."

I frowned; a physical pain sat high up in my chest.

"I shall treasure last night," she added.

I did not know if I could treasure it. I hoped I would not corrupt it with guilt, wash it out with shame. But I nodded in agreement. I would try my best.

I took her hand, and kissed her fingers.

Alby's flirtatious laugh came wafting out of the Chapter house's door.

"Go."

I kissed her.

Lacock Abbey was seeing it all.

CHAPTER TWENTY-ONE

As it turned out, my kiss in the courtyard was only the start of the scandals. My work in the Infirmary was undisturbed, but prayers were becoming unHoly in myriad ways. Whether it was the hangovers being nursed by the Nuns, the sleeping on the pews, the time Sister Janet threw up on her own hymn book. Then there were the evenings, wherein these hangovers were engendered. I watched, sitting in a chair in the corner of the hall, as this Tuesday night's pandemonium unfolded. I was watching Abbess Catherine with particular interest. She was … dallying. It was unmistakeable. For one thing she had taken off her veil. The Abbess, unveiled. I took a drink of my wine. It was diverting, watching her flick her greying hair, giggling like a small girl. She had seemed such an uptight Godly woman. So had so many of the people enclosed. So had I. Maybe it was this place. This place where I had been attacked. This place where I was constantly reminded I was sullied. This place that had taken Isabella. This Constance-less place.

My days were passing with a strange, pulsing consistency, as though I were in a carriage, destined for something. Moving towards something.

My eyes moved to a woman in the corner. I had my suspicions she was another such as Alby. She wouldn't leave the side of a man who was very overweight, very drunk and just about the least appealing person in the whole of Lacock, if not Christendom. Lord, I hoped she was being paid.

"Sister Elisa." A tall man in fine dress was looking down at me.

I stood and bowed my head. "Can I be of assistance, sir?"

"You're a Knolly." I didn't know whether to admit to it or not. But he seemed not to require a reply. He smiled and took up a seat next to me. "My name is Lord Sherrington."

"I recognise your name, my Lord."

He was a friendly looking man with a silver speckled beard and calm eyes. "I've met your father and mother several times at court."

My heart fluttered — I wondered if my father was in trouble for sending his daughter to a dissolving abbey.

"What brings you to Lacock Abbey, my Lord?" I asked, trying to keep my voice even.

"Oh are we at an Abbey?" I gave a tentative laugh, unsure whether he was angry and amused.

"This looks more like the King's court than the King's court does."

"It has been very changed place since the inquisition have left."

"People are expecting it to close."

I sighed. "That is the word."

"'Tis probably for the best. I have heard horrible stories. UnGodly." I nodded. "What is your experience of this place?" He looked down at me.

I could not be bothered to defend my Abbey. "UnGodly," I repeated.

There was a silence.

"I also heard tell of your abuse by the Chaplain." No one

had ever been so bold to just mention it out loud like that. Not even Constance. I was so shocked my hand had frozen halfway up to rearranging my veil. "I had him taken away from Lacock Village."

My hand remained still, mid-air. I tried to breathe. Was I getting any air? Finally the muscles unstuck and my hand fell back into my lap. "I thank you, sir," I mumbled, wondering if he was looking for gratitude.

"A woman of God should never have to experience these torments."

"Thank you, my Lord."

"What will you do when this house closes?"

"I don't like to think about it, sir."

He crossed his legs. "You should think on it, Sister. You will need to find someone to take care of you."

I looked at this Sherrington man. He held my gaze. If he had known what the last year of my life in truth looked like, he would not think I need another's care. I needed no one. I wanted no one to rescue me, to pick me up and fix me. I was already broken, and I was attending to my broken self gallantly.

"You have a defiant glare," he mused. "There is a fire in you." I took another swig of wine. "Will you show me around the property, defiant nun?"

I frowned.

"You don't have to fear me. I am not prying you away from eyes to seduce you. I would like a tour because I am Lacock's new owner. And I intend to examine what I have bought." He had whispered it. It was knowledge only for me.

"How dost thou buy an Abbey?" I whispered back, confused.

"From the King. It is the King's property, of course." We left the refectory. "What room is this?" he said after a moment's silence.

"The Chapter room. Perhaps you can use it as a

withdrawing room." I said it in jest, but he nodded as though the idea was worth considering.

"And this corridor?"

"It takes you to the courtyard."

"And what be in the courtyard?"

"The brewery, bakehouse, more bedchambers."

"Take me there." We walked outside. The pink evening sun created long shadows across the courtyard.

"When must we all leave?" The gravel crunched under my feet.

"Soon, very soon. I have no need for Nuns in my private house."

"And what will everyone do?" He shrugged. "Are all the Abbeys closing?"

"Eventually they will all close. I see little point in transferring to another enclosure, if that is what you mean. But I wouldn't worry too much, Elisa, I wrote to your father to explain your predicament when I told him about your attack."

I turned to stone, unable to take another step. "You told my father about … the Chaplain?" I asked.

"Of course, as soon as I heard about it." He opened the door to the bakery and sauntered inside.

"And how long ago was that?"

"I was informed by the inquisition as soon as it happened. I was kept up to date with frequent reports. Will you explain to me how this works?" He moved towards the baking oven. There was a knob of dough rising within.

I did not move. "No," I whispered.

"Excuse me?"

"If you do not know how a cursed baking oven works then thou art an idiot and deserveth not to know! I will not tell you how anything works, and I will not shepherd you about the home you have stolen from us." I tore the veil from off my head. My red waves sprang loose, thankful to be free. "I will not do anything for anyone any more!" I ripped the veil in two; it split easily. I threw it into the fire.

One single thought ruled me now. One single piece of knowledge.

My parents knew what had happened. They had not come to fetch me. They had not even sent word.

"Did my parents say anything about what happened to me?"

Sherrington looked amused. "They expressed concern."

My lip curled. Concern?

"It will be hard to marry you off now."

"Marry me off?" I swallowed. "I am a Nun, Lord Sherrington! I cannot be married! I am Christ's bride! I belong to God!"

"How can you be a bride of Christ after having the living daylights fucked out of you?"

I moved quickly, shutting the bakery door in Sherrington's face. Then I wedged the beam across the latch that was used to stop the sheep from coming in.

On the other side of the door, I heard him laughing.

I looked down at my worn leather shoes. I kicked at the crumbling wall. I let out a loud, angry noise. I had never made a sound like that.

"I told you you had a fire within you, Lady Elisa," he called from his bakery prison.

"Put your head in the bread oven, you prick!"

I looked up.

I had a witness to my crime. Sister Jane was watching me from her bedroom window on the other side of the courtyard. She beckoned me to come to her. I hurried inside.

. . .

"How long are you going to leave him in there?" We both glanced out the window. Jane gave me a strong drink that burnt my throat and stopped my shaking.

"I think I'd rather leave before he escapes. He's bought Lacock, Jane."

Realisation dawned over Jane's face. "I see." She plucked at a stray hair on her chin.

"I'm going to go find Isabella in town," I decided. "What will you do?"

"I shall stay until they force us out," she said pensively, "then — I know not. I have no connections. There is no sanctuary for me."

I pinched the bridge of my nose. How could Sherrington do this to us? How could King Henry do this to us? Just throw all these women out on the streets, with nothing left, with nothing to do?

"I wish you luck on your journey ahead, Elisa. I pray you continue to practise your skills with medicines and herbs."

"And you, Jane."

She hugged me, tightly, with a lot of feeling.

"I shall let him out when you have gone," she promised.

"Do not consider it an imperative."

I could not carry much with me. I fit what I could into my leather pouch and I put on all the clothes I could countenance in the heat. Even with all my layers, even with the summer night still warm, I shook with fear. Fear of hunger and destitution. Fear of the look on my parents' faces if they knew. Fear of the admonishments of Mother Abbess, of Father Nicholas, of Godly people. But this was my choice. I wanted to leave. I wanted to walk away. This was my own decision, for my own good. I governed myself now.

I could feel the Abbey at my back, watching as I walked

away. I wondered if she was ashamed of me. I heard the bells ring for Vespers. I turned around to look at Lacock one last time. Her sandstone glistened in the evening sun just as when I arrived, when I had every intention of denying my sinful ways, but I do not think she was disappointed. I think she was ashamed of herself. For all the promises she made of chastity and Holiness, I had found her out.

PART III

CHAPTER TWENTY-TWO

It was a strange thing to have lived in this village for a whole long year but never entered it. The cobbled streets were cluttered with dwellings, all neatly thatched with whitewashed walls and wooden beams. I could hear people at the alehouse in a nearby street and the birds hadn't yet returned to their nests, but still it was late. Nearly nine. I was looking for the bakehouse. That was where Isabella would be, with the Crow family. I recalled Sister Jane saying the goodwife was sweet, generous. I took a deep breath. The air smelt pleasant tonight. Like tilled fields.

The bakehouse. There it was. I could see the oven through the front window, its embers burning a deep orange. I could see candlelight upstairs.

What if Isabella had gone? What if she had died?

I knocked on the door.

There was a moment of silence. Then the sound of someone's footsteps coming down the stairs.

"Hello? Who goest there?"

The voice was unfamiliar.

"Goodwife Crow? My name is Sister Elisa. I am from the Abbey. I am looking for Isabella."

Another moment of quiet. Then I heard the heavy jingle of keys and the click of a lock.

A heavily pregnant woman with a pinched face appeared in the crack of the door.

"God bless you, Goodwife Crow. I am sorry to trouble you so late, but there has been a disturbance at the Abbey. Mayhap I could speak to Isabella?"

She squinted at me suspiciously but opened the door wide.

She spaketh not. Just stared. Perhaps she was thinking about how to tell me some dreadful tidings. Was Isabella … dead? Had she died of those internal wounds we could not tend? Perchance she was gone and no one knew where. Carted off to the poorhouse. Cozened by a wicked man. Would this woman say something?

I jumped as another person appeared behind her.

"Isabella, this Sister wants conference with you."

I took an audible intake of breath.

"Elisa," Isabella whispered. She pushed past Goodwife Crow and embraced me.

I wrapped my hands around her; her frame was smaller than before, her eyes darker, her skin, so pale. She took me by the hand and led me inside.

Mrs Crow went about remaking the fire at the back of the house, unperturbed by the nearly full-grown babe she was carting around. We sat down near the hearth on wooden chairs. I explained what had happened. I explained it all. Even the part about the Chaplain. I did not look Isabella in the eye as I told her that part of my story. But I do not think she looked away from me. I heard her humming and nodding as I orated.

"You left him locked up in the Abbey's bakehouse?" Isabella asked as I finished.

"I did. Though Sister Jane said she'd let him out eventually."

She laughed. Even timid Goodwife Crow tittered. I tried to smile.

"You can stay here a few nights, pet," said the pregnant lady. "Sleep next to Isabella. I'll fetch a few more blankets and leave them in the room."

"God bless you, Goodwife Crow."

"I'm sorry for what's happened to you, Sister." Mrs Crow paused, as though considering whether to say more. "You know, I'm glad King Henry's sold the Godforsaken place. Better that the Sherrington man have it than the devil." I gave her a small smile. "Much good do it to ye."

She left. Isabella brewed me a pot of tea.

I played with the frayed ends of my habit's sleeves.

"Have you supped?" Isabella asked.

"I've had some food."

I noticed her stumped hand; some of it had scarred after the Chaplain had burnt it.

"How is Lady Cathy?" I asked. Isabella raised an eyebrow, confused. I gestured to her arm.

"Oh I have not called her by her proper name since leaving the Abbey!"

"You cannot do that to her." I took hold of Cathy. "She deserves respect!"

Isabella shrugged; she was smiling, but the sparkle had gone.

"Th'art much smaller, Isabella," I said, still holding onto her arm.

She nodded. "I have been eating much less."

"Why?"

"I don't want to impose upon Mrs Crow."

"You have been ill?"

"I have not felt like eating since I have left." Now even her smile had gone. "Is Arnie well?"

"Con took him back to her home. She promised to care for him."

This gave her some relief. "Oh good."

"Do you have any plans, Bella?"

She shook her head. "I have been helping out the Crows with the baking and selling, but Goodman Crow ..." she indicated that he was upstairs "... he wants me gone soon. They want the room for the baby."

"Could you go home?" I asked.

"I got no home." I had forgotten. "Do you want to go home?" she asked.

I slid myself onto the hearth and stared into the sparkling embers. "I miss my brother. I miss my sisters, even Agnes. I miss my room. I miss ..." Samuel. "But I cannot go home. I am soiled. They know I am ruined. They were told of what happened, and I did not hear from them. My father did not come for me. My Mother did not write me. They are done with me. I am done with them." Sadness rattled threateningly in my chest.

Isabella moved to sit on the floor with me. She touched my knee and I began to sob. I grabbed hold of her shoulders and we held each other, both in convulsions of bitter sadness, clinging on as though someone would rip us apart. We both cried until my body did not have the energy to cry any longer, and we fell asleep on the stone, by the dying fire. Two Nuns destroyed by one Devil.

The next day I worked with Isabella, letting Goodwife Crow and Goodman Crow have a day off by way of thanks. We rose early from our stone bed and did not discuss the night before. Instead we went about baking. I let Isabella stand at the shop front and I worked the oven. It turned out that having two hands made it easier to remove bread from hot fires.

"Bella, I shall put the fresh ones over here." I placed the steaming loaves into a basket. "Next I will make more dough for some clap bread."

"Thinkest you I should become a witch?" asked Isabella.

I stopped halfway out the door. "Pardon?" I looked around, making sure no one could hear us.

"A witch. Me."

"Does one *become* a witch? Is it like becoming a baker?" I whispered.

Isabella looked speculative. "I suppose because of Lady Catherine here I might always have been one …" I could not know if she was being serious. "You can make money being a witch, my sweet."

"Hello, Sister Isabella." A frail old woman with a stick entered the store. "Can you cook up my dough, please? Burn it not this time, child." I guessed she was blind, as she seemed not to see me.

"Never again, Goodwife. I shall bring it you when it is baked." They exchanged coin.

I waited until the old lady was out of earshot. "It's risky talking about these things, Isabella, even if it is in jest."

"'Tis no jest," she said seriously, giving the dough another knead. "I think people would respect my services because of my hand, or lack thereof. I would be credible. Most people already think it of me …"

I thought about it for a moment. "I have heard of women selling potions and cures, and you know a lot about that already."

We escorted the bread into the oven and returned to the counter. I started rearranging the penny loafs and halfpenny loafs into neat stacks, but my mind was not on bread.

"If I could make enough money to rent out a little cottage

— it should not be in the village, but out of it, so cheaper, and safer. Then I could set up shop there. Sell cures. Help people."

She had always been excellent in the Infirmary.

"They could drown you if you do something wrong, Bella. If someone in the village dies, or gets sick and you've seen them … you will be blamed." A scone rolled off the table. "And drowned."

"Someone lost a runaway scone?" Alby entered the shop.

"That'd be us." Bella smiled.

"Oh!" The Goose pointed at me.

"Good morrow, Alby." I grimaced.

"They are all in such a fuss at the Abbey! Did you really put Lord Whatyouwill's head in an oven?"

"Nay!"

"A shame."

"Please Alby, don't tell any one you have seen me."

"No worry, Sister: I'm about to leave for London Town. I need only some bread for the way."

"What do you fancy?" Bella asked.

"A farthing loaf, please."

I raised an eyebrow at her.

"'Tis a long journey!" she said defensively.

I handed her a very large, warm loaf and she wrapped it up and put it in her travel pack. Then she got out her coins.

The small bag was full to the brim with gold. It was heavy in her hand, spilling over the sides of her palm. I averted my gaze. She noticed my embarrassment as she handed Bella the farthing.

"Coin maketh you coy, Elisa?" I said nothing. "Why do you not share my carriage to London? They will be coming down hunting for you soon enough."

"Do you think?" I asked quickly.

"I do think," she replied. "I also think you could be earning just as much as me in London, if you wanted to."

I looked at her face, expecting to see a hint of jest. But she was being serious. It was an offer.

"As a ... whore?" I confirm.

"As a whore."

"You should go to London, Elisa," said Bella suddenly. "There are more opportunities in London. More ways to live as a single woman."

"The baker's right," said Alby, smiling.

I looked at Bella. "I do not want to leave you. I do not want to be on my own."

"You will not be on your own. You shall be with Alby."

"I think you miscomprehend who Alby really is."

"She is a prostitute," said Isabella, "and a woman, an independent one at that, and she's giving you passage to London ... for free." I bit my lip. "I will be well. I have my plans to be an independent lady too." Still I didn't say anything. "Elisabeth. We are not the same anymore. We got less choices."

The words echoed.

I went to stand outside the bakehouse. Despite what Isabella had said, I felt I had more choices than e'er before. I had naught to lose. My virginity was gone. The Church did not own me. My parents did not want me. I had freedom to do whatever I wanted. To take myself wherever I pleased.

I could see her, the Abbey, peeking over the houses, spying upon me, maybe expecting me to come back. At least London had never feigned Godliness. Alby did not pretend to be something she was not.

"I am going to London," I told the Nunnery. She didn't even flinch.

I said my farewell to Isabella. I would pray for her each morning and night, I promised. She had only laughed. I sat in the carriage Alby had hired to convey us to the capital. It was as big as the one my family used, with a curved wooden roof engraved with twisting vines that wound around and around in leaved loops. The seats were soft and plush: stuffed full with the wool of a Lacock sheep, I supposed. I had warm bread on my lap, and my small bag of belongings at my feet. Alby was being quiet, reading a bound book.

She was the most un-whorish whore I had ever met. Actually, I corrected myself, she was the only whore I had ever met. But still, she was unexpected.

She looked up. "Want to read?" She rummaged in her bag and brought out yet another fully bound book. This woman was made of money.

"Thank you, Alby." I paused, debating my next sentence. "How do you feel today? I believe I saw you with Reverend Thomas before I fled?"

Her book covered her mouth, but I could tell she was smiling.

"T'was the strangest thing: just before I committed any indecencies last night, a voice, your voice as it happens, sounded in my mind, and I refrained."

"For moral or medicinal reasons?"

"Medicinal, poppet, I be way too far gone to be worried about me morals."

I snorted. "I am glad. You will be all the better for it."

"I feel poorer for it."

There was a silence. I looked out the window: the countryside was as green as I had seen it in years. "Thank you for giving me passage to London."

Alby smiled.

A breeze swept through the carriage and it soothed me, so I nestled back into the cushioned seat and read. The book was called *Prince Galehaut* and it was certainly not a text that would've been held in the Nunnery. But then again, the nunnery should never have been home to a wooden phallus either and now that I come to think about it, it should never have been home to me.

It was dark. I was tired. Why did travel make one so tired? I had done so little for so long. We had stopped at two different inns for food, water and fresh horses. But we had not stayed long. Alby wanted to arrive in London that night.

I was glad of her company; if she had not been there, I would surely have spent the whole trip crying. Or probably I would have turned around, requested to go back to my family.

Instead, I had read the entire book she had provided me, and successfully avoided thinking about anything important at all.

"Are you ready to think about what you might do when you get to London?"

Curse Alby.

"Where are you going?" I asked.

She was focusing on stitching the letter *B* into a handkerchief. "Southwark."

I was not surprised at her answer.

"Where specifically?"

"Mistress Hibbens's house."

"And she is …?"

"My bawd." She smiled a very big, toothy smile.

I had acquaintance in London. For all I knew my family might be in London. But I did not want to see them, and they did not want to see me. I wished that Samuel did not live on my family's land. I felt a pang of loneliness, bitterness, then it melted into fear.

"You may stay with me at Mistress Hibbens's." I raised my eyebrow at her. "Mistress Hibbens is a good woman. She provides refuge to those who need it. You will not need to work."

I let out a shaky breath. "I would appreciate that, Alby."

"But to be sure, you are not interested in making twenty shilling a night?"

I scoffed.

She smiled again. "Hibbens takes a cut, but you come away with around fifteen or so. Some of the wenches have clients who pay them thirty shillings for a thirty-second fuck."

It was an obscene amount of money. I knew my servant Mary got paid under twenty shillings for an entire year's service.

"What doth they with the money?"

"Whatever we want. Go to market, buy pretty dresses, travel, stay in nice inns, eat rich food. Get carriages all over England. There's a lot to do with money."

I was suspicious. It sounded like a sham. "I've seen prostitutes in London. Women who are thrown onto the street. Hurt. Given a beating instead of payment."

She nodded. "'Tis not all money and baubles. 'Tis hard work. Clients can be brutal. You get withchild. There is … damage." She gestured in between her legs. I rolled my eyes. "But I am fortunate. Madam Hibbens's House is one of the best houses in London. The Bishop of Winchester visits personally. So do many of the men at court. And Hibbens looks after us."

A sudden waft of London air — dirt, coal fires, people — rushed through my window, and almost as quickly out the other, but it left memories in its wake. I was young again, in my parents' carriage. My mother was fussing over my dress, my sisters redoing my hair, Eddie lying on the floor of the carriage giggling as the movement jiggled him up and down. And my father, in his black velvet doublet, the picture of fashion, laughing. I had been cared for. I shook my head.

Now I care for myself and better than they ever did. I swallowed and began twirling my loose hairs.

"You can meet my little daughter," Alby said casually.

"You have a child?" I wondered why she did not bring it with her. "Who looks after her when you travel?"

"My sisters."

"The whores?"

I could not read her expression. "My sisters."

CHAPTER TWENTY-THREE

I know not what I had been expecting.

I think anything would have surprised me.

We were on the banks of the Thames. The river had swelled from recent rain, and I could still hear its rushing pace from within the home, shop, whorehouse, Bishop's investment property — whate'er it was. If I were a little slow, I could have mistaken my whereabouts for being at Court. There was a large stone fire place, luxurious chairs, tables cluttered with crystal cups and vials of different coloured wines. A bird's cage filled with doves was strung to a beam. I could hear their cooing, and the soft lapping of their clipped wings. Flasks of ale seemed permanently attached to everyone's hands and there were people playing card games and board games, laughing and talking. A woman was playing Greensleeves near a stained glass window in the corner. It could have been Court. 'Cept the recorder player had her breasts out and the tapestries on the wall were all detailed with the male member.

"Alby!" A woman approached; she was maybe fifty year old, dressed in purple. Purple like a priest. Or a Queen. Her skirts were pleated, and she sparkled with a large bronze broach and a deep red hood. She embraced Alby like a dear friend. Her jewelled rings sparkling as she clutched Alby's back in a true embrace. "Alice is sleeping in your room. But you must go and wake her! She has spoken about nothing but your return!"

"Oh the poppet and peach! I cannot wait to wake her." Alby turned to me in excitement. I hardly recognised her. A mother's face. Since I had met her all I had seen was her profession. But she was a younger woman than she affected, and a mother to a little girl.

"How were your travels? And how was your dear mother?" Hibbens indicated we were to walk with her.

"She is well, Mistress Hibbens. Continues to believe me married and a weaver, but she is still well despite the deception." Hibbens laughed. Alby took my hand. "I was wondering if you would be so kind as to accommodate my friend for the evening." We stopped walking.

"Of course. And what is your friend's name?"

"Sist—" I stopped myself. "Elisa, Mistress Hibbens." She had grey eyes, almost as pale as if she were blind, but she saw me: she saw everything. "'Do you have a family name, Elisa?"

I inhaled. "Knolly, Mistress."

"I see." She did see. My name was not … common.

"Of course you may stay, Mistress — Lady — Elisa. A friend of Alby is a friend of mine. I welcome you humbly to our home." We continued walking. Hibbens moved through the air as though she were in water, fluidly, without hurry, Queen of all of this bizarre, Godless wonder.

There were a lot of rooms in this home. It reminded me of Grey's Court, except that my family was not there and people tupped in every room.

"My room's here," said Alby.

Hibbens unlocked the door with a key.

"Mama!" Alice was tangled in bedsheets. In her haste to get out of bed, she tripped and fell into her mother's arms. She would have been some seven or eight years old. I looked down at Alby, who a mere week earlier had been splay-legged on a bed at my mercy, now covering her child with kisses.

I smiled at a human's wondrous capacity for being a million different people all at once.

I introduced myself to Alice. She took to me quickly.

"Your hair is red!" she remarked, pleased at the fact.

"It is very red!" I agree.

"May I braid it, Mistress Elisa?"

I sat on the ground, listening to Alby and Hibbens, feeling small hands do masterful work. The room had a large window with a bay seat looking out over the river. I made a plan to sit there and watch the world go by.

"Will you go out with the other geese tonight, Alby? The culls have missed you. The Duke is downstairs and if he knows you are here he will not take no for an answer."

"Decidedly I will come down. I did some embroidery for Brandon on the ride home and shall give it him this evening." She flourished the handkerchief. "Alice, you are to give Elisa your mattress."

"I am more than happy to sleep on the floor with a blanket."

"Nonsense," said both the bawd and Alby at once. I had the feeling it was hard to shake the essence of being born well. People did not treat me like a runaway Nun finding shelter at a brothel.

"Fear not, Mistress Elisa." The little girl jumped up into her mother's bed. It was small, but the curtains were beautifully embroidered with gold fleur-de-lis. "I love sleeping next to Mama."

Mistress Hibbens and Alby left. Or went to work. I knew not.

I washed my face in the basin near the window. I ate a little of the bread and cheese that had been fetched for me and then

I got into the bed Alice had given me. It didn't have curtains, but it was comfortable. I smiled at her from across the room.

"Sleep well, Mistress Elisa."

The room smelt of roses. Alice fell asleep quickly. Then, underneath the soft hum of her breath, I heard the other noises. They were unmistakably not noises of Court. I could still hear the general merriment and chinking of glasses but I could also hear the bed crates shifting against wooden floors, the moans and grunts. I worried Alice would wake and her childhood would be ruined.

I slept through the grunting and the oomphing for seven days. I helped clean the bar in the day time; I washed tankards and helped make pies. I got to know Alby's "sisters". I was welcomed. People were kind. At night, I hid upstairs with Alice. We played games, dressed up in Alby's clothes, we painted pictures of the river. I even spent time drawing out the alphabet with her. She knew several letters already.

"You look like the little Princess Elisabeth!" Alice declared, dressing my hair with her mother's jewelled headpieces. Alby's headpieces would have cost a lot more than those I had worn as Lady Elisa. This one glittered with green jewels — real emeralds, not the paste I had been used to wear.

"Will you stay with us forever?" Alice twisted one of my curls around her finger. I stared at her. All my energy had been going towards not panicking about my next step, and here this little child was, chattering away, asking the one question that would ruin my peace. No. I could not stay there forever. I pursed my lips but didn't let her see my anger and panic. I tucked her into bed, and she was asleep before the symphony of tupping began.

I sat cross-legged on my mattress. I wondered whether I was going to cry. To have an attack of some sort. Should I find the next cart and go back to Lacock? Nay. But should I find passage home to my home — home? With Mary and Samuel and Eddie. If Mary or Samuel had known of my rape would they not have visited? Doubtless they would have written. Surely. I felt my memories of the Chaplain on the edges of my mind, but they were not coming for me. These moans of rapture and laughs of delight did not resemble what had happened to me. I sat washed in the sounds of sinful pleasure and I was … content. This fear in my mind was not fear of this place. It was a base fear: fear of hunger, fear of death, fear I had been cozening myself. That I could not actually take care of myself. That I needed the Nunnery, in all her hypocrisy, to feed me, to shelter me from cold and the rain. That I needed my parents to do the same. That I was not able to make my own choices nor go where I pleased. I had no coins to buy food. Alby had bought me some bread that morning out of the goodness of her heart, but she could not feed me forever. My tummy rumbled loudly, for all the world as if it were asking me the same question Alice asked me. Are you staying here forever, Elisa? Are we to starve Elisa? How will this fall out, Elisa? I put a hand on my belly, silencing it.

I shut the door quietly behind me, leaving Alice soundly asleep. I descended the steps into the riveting chaos. If Alby asked me why I was downstairs, I would tell her I could not sleep. A woman, very generously, gave me a glass of wine, her skirts billowing around me as she danced in between clients and courtesans. I found a seat in the far corner of the room and sipped my drink. I did not want to stand out. I was very aware I was still in my clothes of enclosement. I would like to be wearing dresses like these women wore: there were so many colours, so many jewels.

"Excuse me —" A boy, younger than myself, was looking down at me. He was struggling to find the right words with which to address me. I imagined his turmoil. Should he be polite and address me as a lady? Or should he not address me at all? For I, in his eyes, was just a plaything. A goose.

"My name is Elisa," I said, assisting him.

"Are you occupied for the evening, Elisa?" It was not an unexpected request. I was a woman in a whorehouse; what else could I be but a whore?

"Come. Sit." I gestured to the seat next to me. He hurried to the chair.

"How old are you?" I asked.

His bright blue eyes danced from my face, to my bust, to the people in the room. "I'm old enough," he said finally.

"And do you come here often?"

"It is my first visit. My brother has made me come."

"Which one is your brother?"

"He is occupied." He looked intently at a ruby ring on his finger.

"I see. And does he expect you to be occupied too?"

"He thinks I need to be experienced, before my wedding day."

"What is your name?"

"I am a Russell. The youngest son."

I knew who he was. My father had spoken about his family.

"You are betrothed to Arabella Knot?" He nodded, pleased that I knew. "You must be nearly wed?"

"We are, within the week."

"And you have not been with a woman before?"

"No." He sounded mournful.

"You wish for one of these women to fix this problem?"

"You could fix the problem …" he muttered.

"I could fix your virginity?" He gave a curt nod. "Virginity is seen by God as a virtue."

"I do not want to disappoint my wife on the wedding evening."

"No. You are right, that would be the greater sin." He could not tell if I was playing with him. Verily, I did not know if I was playing with him. "Do you think Lady Arabella will have sought experience too? So she can also be a good lover?"

His mouth fell open. I had gone too far.

"Elisa." It was Hibbens. "Not quite ready for bed, I see?"

"Not quite, Mistress."

"You have got a come-hither look about you, chit. And men are coming thither. I have had requests, but I see Lord Russell has found you first. You beat several men to her, my Lord; I am impressed."

The boy blushed with pride, forgetting his rage.

"Our crowd like new meat, especially auburn haired, well-proportioned meat."

"I am sorry for creating a confusion."

"Are you?" she asked pointedly, looking down her long nose.

"I beg your pardon?"

"Hast thou confused Lord Russell?" she pressed on. "I understand, my Lord, that you have booked out our royal suite?"

"Yes. Of course. I would not touch one of your other rooms." He had puffed out his small chest.

"Of course not, my Lord. I will send up some drinks and food to your room. If you stay there a while, I will make sure the evening is worth your wait."

He got up, and turned to me.

"You are very beautiful, Elisa."

I smiled despite of myself. He was trying so hard.

"And you are very handsome, Lord Russell." I replied, surprising myself.

He nodded and left.

"The Russell family pay thirty shillings for an evening here.

Per son. I can give you fifteen right now." She got out her purse.

"I'm not a whore, Mistress Hibbens."

"We are all whores in one way or another, Elisa. Whether we sell our bodies to God to be paid in salvation, or to our husbands in return for our safety and warmth, no woman is any different to another." She sat where the boy had been.

"But ... I'm a Nun."

"No, thou art not," Hibbens said plainly.

I opened my mouth to try again. "But, I have had ... I have been hurt. I'm not a — I have been ..."

The woman nodded understandingly as though I had just written her a detailed letter about my situation, not spluttered out a few odd words. "This is your choice, Elisa. But many of my girls have had their bodies used violently and they find that governing their own limbs and skin to earn coin is ... liberating."

"I would not be any good." A whisper.

"Elisa. He be a virgin."

"Fifteen shillings?"

"Yours, to do whatever you wish with."

It was a staggeringly large amount.

"I suppose I cannot ever get my virginity back."

She shrugged. "Not so: one of my ladies claims to have a good and marvellous recipe to regrow chasteness."

"Pardon me?"

"I believe, though I have not tried it myself, one distils sage and water, and then over several days, you shoot the liquid into your purse and eventually, voila! You are the Virgin Mary." I laughed. Hibbens did too. "Of course, no one can fool God."

"Perhaps a foolish bridegroom, but no, not Christ," I agreed.

"This is your choice. This is your body." My choice. My body. "Shall I take you upstairs?"

I bit my lip. What if I did it just once? Fifteen whole shillings. To start my life. With no help from anyone. Just Elisa, looking after Elisa. I could rent a room somewhere, and I could buy some new materials for clothes. Some butter for my bread. Perhaps London markets might have honey. I could try and get a job selling fruit after that. I had seen the fruit girls often enough on my trips to the town. I could sell fruit. This was my choice. Elisabeth the ungovernable, powerful goose. I liked this better than Elisa the broken, violated Nun.

I took a shaky breath. "To the royal suite."

The chambers were at the top of the house, up the winding dark wood staircase, past the collection of expensive tapestries and portraits that lined the walls.

"Are you certain about this, Lady Elisa?" Hibbens asked.

"I have made my decision." I wondered what Constance would think of this. I began compiling lists of everyone's opinions. What would Sam think? Livia? Agnes? What would Jakes think? I could veritably hear Eddie's inappropriate questions about what went where and who did what. He would definitely want to count the coins. I thought about my parents. The looks on their faces if they could see me now. I missed a step. Hibbens steadied me. I imagined Nicholas, watching me leave that bed, naked, carrying a purse of fifteen shillings. I smiled. I liked the thought that I could shock those innocents, that my own decisions could make my mother faint.

Hibbens stopped me outside the door. She undid my braids, placing my hair strategically over my shoulders. She gave me a piece of glass. I was pleased with my reflection. "Were you attacked from behind, Elisa?" I nearly dropped the glass. She steadied my hand. "If you have been attacked from behind, do not let him fuck you from behind. It will bring back ghosts." I think I nodded, I definitely made some sort of noise. "Flatter him, Elisa. Flatter him and he will be back for more, even after he's wed. Make him think he's God's gift to your hole."

"Holy God." I crossed myself unconsciously.

"Use your accent: you speak better than anyone on this side of the Thames, he will like it if he thinks he's screwing a noblewoman." She threw me a furtive glance. "And of course, don't reveal that last name of yours. Whilst you might like to imagine Lady Anne Knolly's face if she knew about all this, I doubt you want her hunting you down and taking away your well-earned coin and locking you in an attick somewhere."

My mother's full name made me shudder, but the Mistress shook her head. "Here." She gave me the satchel of money. "Think of the jewels."

Hibbens opened the door and pressed her hand lightly on my back. The room was very large, and more like a withdrawing room, with lounges and chairs, a thick rugs and a lit hearth.

The bed was also big, with dark red curtains and golden thread blankets.

The boy had undressed himself. He was sitting on the edge of the bed, swinging his feet. His twiddling thumbs hid his manhood.

"Lord Russell?" I said gently.

His pale skin flushed a light pink.

"The best I've ever had, my Lord," I said loudly.

"I guess you tell that to everyone." He was lying on his front. Chin cupped in his hands. Grinning from ear to ear.

"I haven't told that to anyone," I said honestly. He gave a short laugh and turned onto his back. Fully naked. Staring at the ceiling. I looked into my goblet. He hadn't been so confident about his prick ten minutes back.

"I knew I'd be good," he whispered to the roof.

"Well you are a Russell," I replied. He gave an outburst of triumphant laughter.

I rolled my eyes.

I was sitting on a long, soft lounge drinking wine. I was shaking a little. From adrenaline, not pleasure, that was certain. But I also was not shaking from fear. It had not been like with Constance but it was not like in the shed either. It hadn't been painful. His member had not revolted me. In fact, at the sight of wee thing, I had stifled a laugh. All throughout, the Lord had thought I was some kind of God, asking me to validate his every move. But of course, now that he was done, he was the God.

I wonder how long I was meant to stay there. I ate some grapes.

CHAPTER TWENTY-FOUR

The three of us were in a wherrie with red upholstered seats that was sitting far too low in the water for my liking. Despite the odd splash of the river on my skirts, despite the fact that last night I had sealed my fate as a woman worse than Eve, I felt a small bubble of joy, excitement.

Alice sat in my lap, Alby by my side, the sun shone and the sight was a spectacle. The Thames was full, river barges, passenger boats and maybe a hundred more wherries were on the water. We were being rowed, slowly but surely, across the river.

"We shall go to Cheapside markets, then to the London Bridge shops."

"I am looking forward to it." I had been to the London markets a few times in my life, with a multitude of servants and guardians. Today I could go where I wanted to go. "First I want to visit an apothecary."

"Do not you want to have a little Russell child, Elisa?"

"No, I thank you." I had most of the ingredients in my pouch, but I still needed oil of mint to ensure I was not got with child.

"We will go to Buckleberry Herbs — Alice! Take your hands out of the water. Verily, that's where your shit goes." Alice giggled. Her mother took hold of her hands. "Listen, it is long since you have crossed the river. Alice, you must promise me you will not stray. Not even when we get stuck in the people and the carts and you can see a way to widdle yourself through. Your mother and Elisa are too big to widdle. You stay with us. Aye?"

"Aye."

"Good. Now is there anywhere else you want to visit, Elisa?"

"I want to buy a wooden hoop!" Alice exclaimed, hand plunging back into the water.

"I want to talk to the women in the stores. Perhaps meet one of those ladies who has the fruit in the baskets? Or the flower girls. See if they would have me."

"You would make a beautiful flower girl," Alice said, patting her wet hands on her face.

London Bridge markets were my favourite. We could hardly move for the coaches and shoppers, but it no matter: there was always something to look at. The timber-framed stalls with the toppling brick chimneys were stacked on top of one another and the shops were filled with sweet-smelling things and colourful wares.

"A plague upon these parked carts!" exclaimed Alby as we manoeuvred our way in between packhorses.

I was eating fresh oysters from the Friday Street fish markets. My boots were crusted with London dirt, but I did not care. I'd just buy new boots. No one looked at me, got out of my way, or treated me with respect, but I cared not for that either.

"Mama! We need a cart — th'art making me carry too

many purchases." With every step, Alice crinkled and crumpled with the sound of her mother's parcels.

"Let me finish my last oyster and I'll take one from you." I threw the shell to the cobbles and relieved her of the packages with two new glittering broaches in it. Those were a purchase from Watling Street — I had even got a red piece of satin there: a noble's colour.

"Alby! The fruit girls!" I knew they would be somewhere. I remembered them from when I had come to town with my parents. Singing about their cherries and soft fruits. Carrying the wooden woven baskets piled to tipping point with food.

"Do you want some fruit, Alice?"

Alice wanted some plums. I squeezed my way through the crowds.

"Five plums, if't please you." I put the fruits in my pocket. The lady thanked me and started singing again. "A moment!" The woman stopped mid warble. She looked around the market, as though suspicious of someone watching her. "I have a question for you; I've recently lost my family." Fruit lady's eyebrows were raised: she was wary of me. "And I need a way to feed myself, to make money, find some board. I was wondering if I could become a market girl, like you." Again she threw a furtive look behind her. This time, I saw what she was looking at. About a hundred feet back, resting on the wall of a shop, was very tall, thin man. Watching us.

"He dun like me talking to customers too long, Ma'am. He's boss of all us girls on London Bridge." It was only now I was beginning to see the scratches up her arm, the dark bruising on her cheek. "Iffen you wanna job, talk to him." She walked briskly out of sight. I returned to Alby and Alice.

"Any luck?"

I shrugged.

"Let us find a place to sit and get some mutton and ale." Alby was red faced and sweaty.

"Where's best?" I took Alice's hand.

"Any tavern or alehouse. I need a cursed drink."

I had never been to an alehouse before.

"Let's go to the Adam and Even!" Alice had a knowledge of alehouses that did not suit her age.

But we took her suggestion and walked to Cheapside. The homes in Cheapside were all thatched, and they all dripped unpleasantly from the previous night's rain. I also noticed that the calibre of society slipped down a notch or two. I clutched my new broaches tightly to my chest.

"Just down here. On Milk Street." Alby said, leading the way. I saw the pub's sign swinging in the breeze. It depicted Eve with her apple, covering her nakedness in shame. It was crumbling with decay, I noted.

There was a crowd at the small door. We stood in the throng and waited. My eyes wandered, stopping on a short woman with a red-striped hood, sitting on the gutter by the side of the road. Her skirts were crusted in dirt, her face smeared with black. She looked at me and grinned toothlessly.

"Alby." I gestured discreetly.

"One of our sisters," Alby said, reaching in her purse and throwing the woman a coin.

We were pushed through the door. I wiped my feet on the rushes on the floor — the straw was already caked in shit from outside, but everyone else was doing it. I had half expected a dark cave, and angry men throwing bar stools, but the tavern was well lit with dozens of bracketed candles, and, though it was noisy, it was the thrum of a midday drink and pie. There was no threat of a fight. We nabbed a seat by the front window.

"What do you feel like?" Alice asked.

What did one order at an alehouse? Did they only serve ale? I was out of my depth. "An ale?" I asked, with a questioning inflection.

"And I," agreed Alice.

"And I," concluded Alby, petting her eight-year-old barmaid on the head.

I watched as Alice moved through the mass of people in the room, brazenly pushing legs out of her way. When she reached the long wooden bar she climbed up onto a stool, and started banging her little fists on the beer-drenched table until the maid paid her attention. She returned holding three big pewter mugs without a problem.

"Thank you very much, Goodwife Alice!" I accepted my drink and took a sip, peering out the mud-splattered window to see if I could still see the wench in the gutter. She was there, waving her pointed, striped hood at someone across the road. "Is she one of Mistress Hibbens's ladies?"

"Zounds no. Verily she works either for herself or in one of the Cheapside houses nearby. Hibbens's girls don't walk the streets — that is why we need not wear the hoods."

"But …"

"Mistress Hibbens runs one of the best houses in the area. We are Winchester Geese, cared for by the Archbishop. I count myself as blessed by God."

"You think God blessed you with your job?"

"So whatcher going to do?" interrupted Alice, sitting in my lap.

"I've been watching the women who sell the peaches and the cherries."

"Th'art to be a fruit lady!" Alice screeched gleefully.

"And where will fruit lady live?" asked Alby.

"Could I rent out a house?"

"On a fruit seller's wage?"

"How much would it be?"

"What did you pay for the plums?"

"A farthing."

She raised a dark eyebrow. "Most of those girls would live in a poorhouse."

"I see. 'Tis fine. I will not be a fruit lady. What else could I do?" Alby shrugged.

"Fine needlework?"

"Oh Lord, I have no skills there."

"Teaching?" Like Samuel. "Tricky to procure without a good reference." Alby added. "What about witchcraft?" I frowned. "You've got the wise woman's skills with the healing and herbs?"

Were these my only choices, a witch or a whore? "Of course, none of these will get your fifteen shillings a night," she added.

I frowned. Did not she approve of my quest for an honest, honourable living? "Alby, I only did what I did last night so that I could establish myself."

There were a few beats of silence.

"That may be. But you can stay with me for however long you need to stay."

I sipped my drink. Half angry, half thankful. "I thank you."

"Shall we peruse our purchases?" Alby put her packages on the table. I winced as the paper became soggy; there was not a beer-less surface in this place. Alice began unwrapping, and we admired our silk veils, lace shoes, our multicoloured collection of fabrics and, of course, Alice's wooden hoop.

The ride home was rocky and not as pleasant as the morning; the Southwark side had a cloud hanging over it, and I was suddenly eager for the peace of the Nunnery, or my old room. I had spent the whole day shoulder to shoulder with strangers, wading in dirt. I wanted Mary to bathe me, and then I wanted silence and solitude. But that was not what was waiting for me on the other side of the Thames. Though, truth have it, anywhere was better than the stupid, choppy water.

We were welcomed briskly through the door. It was about

four in the afternoon, so downstairs had no clients as yet. Just women. I felt myself relax — my shoulders retreated from their home around my ears.

"Elisa!" A goose who shared my name greeted me. Little-Elizabeth, is what everyone called her. She hugged me, and kissed my cheek. People kissed each other there. Cheeks were brushed by lips all over London — I even saw kisses exchanged between merchant and shopper. "How was your day in town?"

"It was good, I thank you! I have new clothes."

"Oh I cannot wait to see what you got!"

"Elisa." It was Hibbens. "Alby mentioned to me that you have experience with treating ailments."

"I do, Mistress Hibbens."

The Winchester Geese were awash with aches and pains, or more prevalently itches and burns. I set up my small Goose Infirmary in a cold stone room near the kitchen. It had no window, but we lit the stubs in the candelabra hanging from a wooden beam, and they provided enough light. Then we brought in a stool from the bar and laid down a spare pallet on the floor. I did not have my herbs and oils, but I could acquire them on the morrow. I met four geese that afternoon; I learnt their names and met them intimately — both physically, and emotionally. It seemed that everyone shared heartfelt stories when they had their legs spread. I might as well have worn a sign that said: *Bare your cunt and your soul.* But I came across nothing I could not treat, though there was little to do for a pregnancy in its fourth month; how she had not realised, I would never understand. Denial is a strong medicine, but it will not stop an eventual birth.

"You been kept busy!" Alby was braiding Alice's hair, getting her ready for bed.

"I have." I felt happy. My bones ached from tiredness, but it was a satisfying soreness. My time at the Goose Infirmary had even made me forget my day's purchases, and I felt my bubble of happiness swell even greater when I saw Alice had placed my packages neatly on my bed.

I jumped onto my mattress and started unwrapping my presents.

"Th'art bouncing with happiness, Elisa!"

"How can I be anything but joyful when I look like this?" I pinned my new gold broach onto my dirtied, unrecognisable habit. It had green jewels, and they glittered in the evening light. I couldn't take my eyes off it.

"You should wear it tonight."

"You mean it's not morning yet? I swear I have been up all day and all night."

"Do not you want to make another handful of shilling?"

"I want to go to bed."

"On your own?"

"On my own."

"Aye, love. I'll see you in the morning then."

CHAPTER TWENTY-FIVE

I went back over to London the next day, this time by myself.

I sat in the wherrie. It was just as beautiful as the day before, but I could not feel any joy about the sun on my skin. I hardly even noticed the shining rivets in the water. I kept my eyes on my lap, away from the horrible stare of the wherrie boatman. He had kept quiet yesterday, with the three of us. But

—

"So are new whores cheaper to buy?" He had no teeth.

"I am not a whore."

"Why'd you come from the whorehouse then?"

"I am visiting a friend."

He laughed. I heard his lungs wobbling around in his chest.

"There ent a single woman going into London from Southwark, dressed like you are, who ent a bloody pricey Winchester Goose."

I tucked my newly slippered toes under my skirts. Zounds, I looked like a woman from Court, but travelling from a quarter where such women never ventured. Why was I dressed like this? I had been so elated by my purchases, I had not realised how stupid they made me look. I could feel myself burning a hot red; I shoved the money at the boatman and got out as quickly as my big, stupid skirts allowed me.

But the walk to Cheapside was worse than the boat. By the time I reached the apothecary I had witnessed the second by second destruction of my new white shoes. I actually shook with anger at myself, for being so stupid, so infatuated with my new things, my ridiculous whorish purchases. I had been like a child. Elisa, the child who wore white shoes to Cheapside and cried when they were destroyed.

But the shoes were not nearly the worst part. I had been invisible yesterday, but now I was a woman, well dressed, young and on her own. There was no honest reason for me to walk alone on the London Streets, and I begged for the attention of every single disgusting man who inhabited London. The hobble of houses on London Bridge were no longer colourful or magic; they were refuges for poxy old men who wanted to yell at me, to follow me around, to jump out of crowds and ask how much I was. To pinch my arms, and pull my hair. If it hadn't been for a particularly nasty cut on one of the geese's back, I would've given up and gone home, but that infection would spread. I needed to purchase my remedies.

The keeper at the apothecary knew what I was — even though I was not really. Everyone seemed to know what I was, or was not. I wanted Constance, or Isabella, or Livia or Alby, or any of Alby's sisters. I wanted to be surrounded by my sisters, by my Nuns or my whores: I did not care. I wanted the presence of women. Where were the women in London? The vials of liquids and bunches of herbs were packed into the shelves without care. Nothing was labelled. But I knew what I needed — I was only pretending to browse. I needed only time to collect myself.

The Apothecary wrapped his knuckles on the desk, making me jump. "You know there's naught no one can do about Goose Bumps?"

"I suppose there be nothing here to fix a rude mouth either?"

He sneered at me. But I stood my ground. I did not want him to speak to me so. He would not speak to me like that if he knew I was a Knolly, nor even if I was in my Nun's habit. Bastard.

"I know what I need." I pressed my list into his hand. "I am in a rush."

"Then why'd you spend five minutes crying into my rosemary?"

"I know other apothecaries who are not afflicted with disgusting manners. I can take my well-earned coin to them if you wish." His lip curled. I pointed to the parchment. "You can start by getting my Goddamned mint leaves."

He did as I said and I was out the door a few moments later.

I steadied myself near the window of the store and gazed long at my destroyed lace shoes. Fix your eyes on your shoes and walk quickly, but do not run.

Everything had been fine until Milk Lane, or as fine as it might be when you stand in what is of a cert human shit. But the men on Milk were far worse than poo flung from a window.

I saw the first one in my peripherals. He was not actually a man; he was younger than me, in very dirty clothes. He had been begging, his hat on the muddy cobbles, asking for coin. When he saw me, he scanned the crowd, expecting to see a chaperone.

"Hey! You!" Not original. Not specific. I could have kept walking and pretended not to hear. He could have easily been calling to anyone else on this street. But I turned. I turned, curse me. And I looked the begging boy right in the eye. He licked his lips and made an obscene gesture with his hands. He called out again, but this time he was not yelling to me. I do not know how I noticed them in a crowd already swarming. But I saw them both immediately, two more paupers with hungry eyes.

I moved quickly to the busier part of the street, scanning each face I saw in the throng, looking for kindness, someone to protect me. I could pretend I was a Lord's daughter. I *was* a Lord's daughter. I could scream, and tell them I had been separated from my family. Surely someone there would want to stop Lord Knolly's youngest being raped. Again.

Someone pulled at my skirt. I lashed out, swinging my hand behind me, making contact with one of their faces. He was crouched, like an actual animal, leering up at me. He tugged at my skirt again. I pulled against his grip. But he had only been a distraction. The other boy had come up behind me; I felt his arms slither around my waist and lift me off the ground. Something sharp poked into my belly: a knife. The third boy stood directly in front of me. His arse pressing up against me, hiding the silver blade from view. "Don't make a sound, harlot. Or I'll stab you right here on the street, and you can die on Milk Lane like a hundred other whores." The feeling of the one behind me reminded me of the Chaplain. I could feel his breath on my neck. I thought I was going to be sick. Would he stab me if I vomited on him?

We walked in amongst the crowd. I tried to make eye contact, to plead with my eyes. But the three of them repelled people like they were oil and the crowd were water. They were disgusting, smelly and obvious thieves. I wondered if by any chance they just wanted to kill me, not rape me. Just a death. Please just be death. Memories from the shed, moments I hadn't remembered were resurfacing, as though warning me about what might be about to happen. How the Chaplain had shook and sweat with the effort of prying open of my legs. How he held his hand over my mouth and I had tasted his disgusting flesh. I was still grasping hold of my remedies in one hand. Mayhap if I dropped the heavy bag it would distract them? Or perhaps I should just give into what was going to happen to me. Perhaps this was revenge. This was my just desserts. Love from, God. For being a whore. For fucking a man for money. I could not fight this. This was Divine intervention. They pulled me down a quieter alley. Closer to my fate.

The knife against my tummy was released. I got a shove in the back.

Did I really, actually deserve this, God? I do not know anyone deserved this.

"What you got in the bag?" The one I had spotted first spake.

I did not deserve this.

"Aphrodisiacs. To sell. At the brothel."

They stopped and gaped.

"Knew you was a whore."

I nodded.

"Let's have one then," said the biggest one. Thank God they were not bright. The three of them had pressed me against a wall. I put my hand in the bag and reached for bottled liquid I had bought for Margaret's stagnant tummy … it was fiery, spicy on the tongue and should only be consumed in a very small amount.

"Right. Me first." The big one pressed his groin up against my skirts. He didn't need the supposed potion. Bile rolled around my mouth. I wanted to spit. He unstoppered the vial.

"I dunno how I'm going to be harder than this, boys!"

The other two guffawed.

"Dun drink it all! Save some for me!" one choked in between his laughter.

But he did drink it all. He downed it. The bottle smashed, he retched and grabbed his throat, and had I stayed longer I would have seen him shit his breeches, but I was gone. I could hear one set of feet behind me. That was better than three. But my slippers, soaked with mud, were slipping over the cobbles.

"God forgive me. God forgive me. Give me an escape."

I ducked down a smaller, short street, and was spat out at the foot of a Church. I allowed myself a quick glance behind me. He was feet from me. I ran into the cloister. Mass was being offered. I ducked into a side aisle and sat down. Surely he would not dare to venture into the house of God to grab and rape a whore.

I waited. He did not enter.

I tried to steady my breathing.

A Church. Right when I had needed it most. Right when I had asked for forgiveness. My breathing steadied. I inhaled the familiar smell of pages, incense and communion wine. God had forgiven me. He had given me his house, his home as refuge when I had needed it most.

"Dominus vobiscum."

"Et cum spirit tuo."

It was the end of the ceremony. Hesitantly I looked around. It was larger than my Church in Henley; the roof towered above me and the priest was so far away, I could hardly hear him. I looked to my right. The pew's occupants had shuffled several feet away from me. The woman nearest me was shaking with fear.

I had slept with one man. For one sum of money. And now I reeked of whoredom.

The congregation began to move. Talk. Go. The Mass had ended.

I started to pray.

"You defile this space."

I opened my eyes and turned my face to the speaker. He could have been Father Nicholas, he looked so much like him. "You defile the House of God with your sins!"

"Nay! I do not." My voice was so small. "God hath forgiven me."

"He hath done nothing of the sort!" he assured the crowd. "Take her out. Make of her an example."

I was thrown out of the Church. My head smacked down onto the cobbles. Someone put their foot onto my back. I tasted shit. My body was crushed into the pavement of London.

The congregation were watching. I heard them laugh, clap. A rotten tomato was thrown at me as if I were in the stocks. It exploded against my cheek, and the seeds slid slowly down my face. The Priest yanked me to my feet by the scruff of my new, destroyed dress. The mob cheered.

I shrugged myself free. I could feel the Priest's breath on my neck. I turned to the sallow-faced man, and grabbed him by his pristine white robes. No doubt these dirty fingers would leave a smudge. The congregation inhaled.

"I thought Christ washed the feet of a whore?" I hissed into his ear. I felt his body constrict in fear. He tried to say something, but he could not get the words out. I gestured down at my ruined shoes. He glanced at them. "My own feet could do with a fucking clean."

CHAPTER TWENTY-SIX

If I shut my eyes and ignored the pain I could imagine I was back at home with Mary. And she was bathing me, brushing my hair, readying me for bed.

But I was in a brothel.

Still, I felt nearly as safe as if I *had* been back at Grey's in Mary's care.

As soon as I stepped my dirty foot over the threshold of the whorehouse I had felt safe. I was immediately surrounded by the women. I surrendered to them. I would take no responsibility for caring for myself today. I trusted they would be my mothers, and they were.

Alby had not asked anything yet. She splashed some of the warm water up around my breasts, cleaning the dirt from my collarbones.

"I ruined my shoes," I whispered.

"Ah, hen. Plenty more where they came from. Prettier ones too." I swallowed and nodded. "I pray you climb into these warm clothes now, deary." Little Alice helped clothe me. Then the child tucked in my blankets and kissed my head before scurrying off downstairs, leaving me alone with her mother.

"What did they to you? Did they get into your skirts?"

I shook my head.

"Oh bless you. You fought em off."

"I made him drink Margaret's mixture. The peppery one, to get her shitting again. I told him it was to get him hard."

"What?" She was aghast, her big blue eyes bulging.

I managed a chuckle at her expression. "He was not bright."

"He did it?"

"He drank the whole vial."

"Jesu Christe, Elisa! You are the best babe ever born to England! Zounds, he'll still be shitting himself now — he'll be going till morning!"

"I ran into a Church to get away from the one who chased me."

"Ah, child. They like us not in there. It vexes them we wear bigger jewels and look more beautiful in our dresses."

"There I was thinking they do not like harlots because they tup for coin."

"That does not help, true." She sighed. "I am just glad you reached home safe."

"It was a cursed close thing."

There was a soft knock on the door. I sat up.

Mistress Hibbens put her head within the room. She was carrying food and drink. She floated in and placed it by my side.

"Thank you, Mistress Hibbens."

"Prithee let me know if I can do aught at all."

"Th'art too good to me." I took a deep swig of the red wine and it spread its calming wings across my chest.

Hibbens threw a look to Alby. Alby gave Hibbens a little nod.

"We have a spare room, with a proper bed, with curtains, a lounge, and a wash basin. It is yours if you would like it."

Hibbens had not been explicit, but I knew of what she spake. She was not offering me free board. I would work for it. "This is your choice. Take your time." Both women left, leaving me alone. My choice.

Hibbens's words reverberated, echoing again and again. I was tired. A deep sleepiness that went beyond my physical body. It was an exhaustion of the soul. I thought about crossing the river again, of trying to get a job in a city that hated me. I did not want to go there. I did not want to be alone. I did not want to leave this place. The Church did not deserve me. My family wanted me not and London had spat me out like I was a bad piece of chicken.

I had been sitting it seemed on my bed for hours, but when I got up and opened the door, Hibbens and Alby were still standing outside.

"Do you need anything, Elisa?"

"If you wouldn't mind, would you help me bring my clothes to my new chambers?"

I would have three tutors and several lessons before I began.

Hibbens herself would teach anatomy and technique.

Margaret was in charge of pruning, including doing one's hair, painting one's face and dressing one's self.

Maisy was to teach me self-defence and house rules.

I was lying awake in my new room. In my new bed. My new bedclothes were a blue damask, embroidered with intricate stars and moons. I had the same aspect as Alby, and I could see the wherries on the Thames from my large window. I had art in my room too — more than I had had at Grey's Court. One of them even depicted Eve, doing something I swore I would never try. Today, I was having two lessons: one from Margaret and one from Hibbens. Maisy would take me tomorrow. I took a deep breath. I waited for panic, I waited to see was I going to run away. Was I about to climb out my window, scale down the wall, bolt? But my breath came easy; it was deep and satisfying. I had made my decision, and I did not have to hold my head above water any more. I was not paddling for dear life, desperate in a sea of sin. I was completely submerged now, I had surrendered to my true nature, and it turned out I could breathe easy underwater, in this deep ocean full of whores. I was no longer stringing prayers together to survive.

After my morning with Margaret, I successfully dressed my own hair and my own face. I was not displeased at the result. It was fashionable to be pale at court, or so said Margaret. And I already had pale skin. I enjoyed the methodical painting of my face with creams that would soften the skin; we started with lightly massaging sesame oil into my cheeks, then after that had been absorbed, I plastered a mixture containing honey and beeswax into my pores. It felt good. My skin felt plumped and youthful. I hoped I would be able to do this every morning. But resigned to my fate or not, I would have rather been in Matins at the Nunnery than where I came next.

"This is Antonio." Hibbens, Antonio and myself were in one of the bedrooms at the brothel. It was a smaller one, with dark furnishings and black bedsheets. For the moodier, ravaging client. I stood by the window in my new red and cream gown. The Antonio in question was entirely nude.

"God bless you, Antonio," I mumbled.

Antonio nodded enthusiastically.

"He is Venetian, and speaks no English."

"Si," he said, smiling and nodding.

"I see."

"He will be helping us today in our first lesson. Stand near the light, Antonio." She dragged him over to the window.

I swallowed.

"It is merely anatomy, Elisa, this be nary a time for the Nun in you." She sat me down in a chair opposite the Venetian. Everything was most ... eye level.

"So!" Hibbens whipped out a long pointing stick from her skirts. "What do we have here?"

"Antonio's prick!" exclaimed the Italian proudly.

"This isn't a lesson for you, Antonio!" Hibbens slapped his thigh.

At the end of the class I had a test. I was to label, point to and demonstrate:

Item the first: sensitive areas.

Item the second: too sensitive areas.

Item the third: areas to avoid (unless requested).

Item the fourth: seven (*seven!*) different tupping positions.

Item the fifth: a pleasant and alluring post-tup massage. (Which Antonio seemed to enjoy.)

The next day, once again, I sat with Margaret and did my hair and facepaint. It was a meditative way to begin the day. Then I went to my first lesson with Maisy. Upon my arrival, she presented me a wooden bat.

A bat. To hit people with.

"You will keep it in your room. I hath used mine properly three times, and threatened to use it seventeen times as of the Wednesday just gone."

She showed me where to keep it: behind the bed post. Accessible, but out of sight.

"Now, we are whores," she declared. My heart missed several beats. I was not used to this declaration. "So when we use our bat to defend ourselves we needs must ensure we do not kill or visibly damage the client, because no matter what he is trying to do to us, we'll be the ones on the gibbet iffen he brings charges agin us."

I opened my mouth to protest. That would be impossible. I

was a Knolly. A Knolly would never be hanged, nor e'en put in gaol. The client would be in chains for laying hands on a Lord's daughter.

I shook myself. I shut my mouth. It was not true any more. My family was not the armour it had long been. I had said yes to this. I had lost my Knolly-ness. I was just like Maisy now.

She went on to point out parts of the body I might with impunity hit, and with what force. Then we went outside to meet a hay-bale dressed in men's clothing, and we spent a rather enjoyable morning of whacking said bale with my bat.

The next few lessons with Maisy were spent on a more sombre note, and my newly beloved bat was stowed away. Instead, we discussed the rules that the law enforced upon these ladies of the night. Me. Enforced upon me. I was to know the rules, despite the fact we disobeyed nearly all of them, just in case we were to be inspected. We were not meant to work on feast days, we were not meant to solicit outside the brothel, we were not to deviate from girl below, man on top, we had a booklet of sumptuary laws to follow and we were not even allowed to have board at the house. They taught me about the Bishop of Winchester, the protection he offered and what to do if he, or one of his people, arrived at our home.

We were in Alby's room, eating dinner. Alice was performing a show for us. She had her mother's jewels on and a large feathered scarf wrapped around her head. As far as I could tell, she was performing some sort of dramatic dance, where she seemed to be playing several roles at once.

"Bread, please." Alby pointed at the loaf nearest me on the table.

"Mama! I am doing a show! Do not speak!"

Alby mimed sowing her mouth shut. I passed her the bread. The play was long and Alice was lucky she was endearing. Hibbens entered before it had finished, and even she showed due deference and waited until Alice had curtseyed before she spoke.

"Bravo, Alice dear, how we love your plays," Hibbens said above our clapping.

"Perhaps I can perform in the parlour soon?" the child added hopefully, sitting down to eat.

"One day, dear," said Hibbens and Alby together.

I shivered.

"Elisa. I have two options for you."

I shivered anew.

"You can audit Alby's appointment with her Monday night gentleman."

"Audit?"

"Watch. Take notes."

I started shaking my head.

"Or you can see your friend downstairs."

"My friend?"

"He wants … just a bit more practice." She put the fifteen shillings into my hand.

"The Russell boy?"

"Lord Russell."

And so it began.

Of course, it wasn't all like Russell: five minutes of action and ten minutes of vanity and strut. Some of the men were bullish, some were cruel. I was always ready to fight, to protect my body, yet there were many who were lovely, gentle and polite. There were a few bizarre requests, including a returning customer who liked to pretend we were King and Queen. Then there were some experiences that were pleasurable. One had e'en been very pleasurable. A scholar, of course. With hair like Samuel's.

No one paid as well as Lord Russell either, but the boy returned frequently, even after his wedding night.

There were also those who wanted to do it with my face pressed against the wall, with their bodies pressed up against my back. This was the only thing I would not do. I could not do it. Nothing else upset me. But when I felt their breath on my neck …

The first time it had happened, I crumbled. I fell down the wall and wailed as I had in the shed. I had to give him a cursed refund, and Hibbens had been furious. I had been furious. I had squalled at the Mistress and she had yelled back.

But I was getting better at avoiding it.

"Do not deprive me of looking at your face …"

"Only poor people tup like that, Monsignor …"

I would do a dance, or get on my knees. Anything. Anything but their warm, clammy lips on my neck.

Despite this, I was well liked, as Hibbens had predicted. My incurable air of nobility appealed to many of the clientele and so I was kept busy. Not just by the men either, but by my sisters: I spent my days caring for the geese, distributing ointments and tonics, monitoring pregnancies, cleaning cuts. I was even given permission to grow my own garden, and a feeling of actual contentedness uncurled when my herbs grew.

CHAPTER TWENTY-SEVEN

I was in the small drawing room, a chamber through a pint-sized door in the main atrium. One had to bend down and stick one's arse out to get through. It was part of the appeal. It had space for a single chair and a table, but the walls had an abundance of candlelit brackets and several of our visitors liked the privacy. I could hear a cold autumn breeze whipping against the stone outside. Winter was on its way and my knight needed me to keep him warm. I sat on his lap and rubbed his back with my hand. "Any better, sir?" I asked. I was tired tonight.

"Yes. Much better." He was young, with a beard of no more than a few blond wisps. He was also, almost undoubtedly, a member of the clergy. He had not so divulged, but he had a guilty look in his eye and he smelt of Church. I was good at picking out the religious men.

"Could you—?" He gestured awkwardly towards my breasts.

I sighed, then tried to pass it off as a moan of yearning. Obediently, I pulled down the corset, letting my breasts sit out on top of the pearled hem. I smiled at him. Then, in slow motion, as though my breasts were a frightened animal, his hand made the treacherous journey to my chest. There was a few seconds' pause as he struggled to choose between the left or right, but he successfully landed on lefty and managed several uncomfortable squeezes.

"Does that feel good?" he asked, scared blue eyes glancing up to mine.

"Divine," I whispered into his ear.

Oftentimes, it was the shy men who were verily the most aggressive, and unsurprisingly this fuzzy-faced clergyman left a bad taste in my mouth and bruises around my abdomen. I washed myself thoroughly, and rummaged through my box of remedies in search of salves. Then I returned downstairs to the tavern, hoping I was finished for the night. No more men were at the bar. I smiled.

"No one left, Elisa!" said Alby, beckoning me over to join the women on the chairs around the fire. I got myself a stiff drink and joined them.

This was one of my favourite parts about living in Hibbens's brothel: when the tavern had cleared out and the hour was late, when the Mistress had gone to bed and the drinks flowed, when the conversation meandered easily, and when Maisy bought freshly baked bread from the bakery in the street behind us. These were the magic hours.

Maisy tore the loaf into six equal parts and handed it around to the women. I had the seat nearest the fire and I was warming my toes close to the embers. I had cocooned myself in my starred and mooned blankets, like an oversized cloak. I was listening to Little-Elizabeth discuss her family.

"I see them once every week. I take them money, buy them a few treats. Some fruit. A new piece of fabric. They never been more proud."

"But do they know what you do?" asked Joanna, a dark-skinned woman from Spain. I enjoyed listening to her speak:

her accent was smooth and rhythmical where Sister the Widow Maria's had been sharp and gravelly.

"I am hardly selling cherries in Cheapside, not when I turn up with a basket full of chicken eggs and bread and butter. They do not mind; they are proud of me."

I gave a low, bitter chuckle. Maybe if I bought my lovely mother and father a big basket full of custards and tarts, wrapped up with whorish ribbons and paid for by whore money, maybe then they would be proud of me.

The women were looking at me.

"Your parents don feel the same?" asked Joanna.

"Do yours?" I asked incredulously. What, did everyone's parents condone our lusty living?

"I send money back to Spain, they are happy." Joanna shrugged.

Most people there had climbed up a ladder to find a home in this house. I had fallen off the ladder, spectacularly.

"Mine know not what I do." I wrapped my blue and gold cloak tighter around me. "Fain, they are ashamed of me thinking only I was a wayward child raped in the Nunnery where they cloistered me."

The door opened.

There was a collective groan from the women as everyone turned around to see what late-night time waster had wandered in off the streets.

There were four men. They were jolly. Inebriated. The usual early-morning client. But there was a difference.

"HIBBENS!" The voice echoed sonorously off the beams.

Alby rose to greet the guest, only to promptly fall to her knees, skirts billowing around her.

Little-Elizabeth, bowing continuously, went to fetch the guests drinks.

Joanna pegged it up the stairs, presumably to notify Mistress Hibbens.

Anne and Mary stood with chins tucked in, looking at the floor.

I had ducked behind a chair.

"Reverend Father in God," Alby began, "how can we serve you and your good company? Mistress Joanna has gone to fetch Mistress Hibbens."

His white religious robes had wine stains on them. He swayed, but managed to maintain his threatening stance.

"We are here to inspect the conditions!" The group of men laughed. "I see that you women are in forbidden colours!" The Bishop of Winchester, the Reverend Stephen Gardiner, walked over to Alby. He stroked her purple headdress with a finger. "I suppose you are serving forbidden foods too? And when we go upstairs will we see women who have residence here? Will I see tupping in unorthodox manners? Will I see tupping on Feast Days?"

"Reverend Father ..." Alby whispered.

But the Bishop started laughing. "What a house I run! Full of miscreants. I am lucky they are beautiful miscreants of whom His Majesty most justly approves!" He ran a finger under Alby's chin.

"I'm here, Reverend Father." Hibbens. Hair undone. Pillow mark on her left cheek. "Does His Majesty need a goose tonight? I can get the rest of them now. Line them up. You may pick." She turned to go back up the stairs.

"Stay, Hibbens. We shall select the whore for Henry in the morning. For now, my companions need ... companions." His company had been chatting with Little-Elizabeth at the bar.

"And for you, Reverend Father?"

"Send your best to my quarters."

All the men went upstairs.

Alby, Joanne and Anne with them.

There was silence in the tavern.

Hibbens's gaze snapped to me. "What were you thinking?

Hiding like a child? It's the Bishop of Winchester! Our owner, our protector, our God!"

I stood up. My bed-cloth robe fell to the floor. "I understand, Mistress Hibbens."

"Then what was the matter?"

I tried to swallow. "Because our God, our Reverend Father, Patron Saint, Christ-like Stephen curse-him Gardiner, brought company."

"So?"

"So he bought Lord Knolly of Grey's Court." I whispered.

Hibbens's head snapped back towards the stairs. The stairs my father had just ascended. With a whore. To fuck.

The Mistress told me to go to my room. To stay there until she sent for me. I promised I would but I did not. I stayed by the fire in the bar room. I stayed there until day broke.

As the fire dwindled and died, something was lit anew in my heart. Like I was sucking the hearth's heat right into my soul.

What. The. Fuck.

That goatish, fly-bitten scut.

That wayward, half-faced bladder.

That. Fucking. Prick.

I was parading the hallway, putting an ear to each door, possessed by something, maybe righteous rage, maybe the Devil.

"Elisa? Are you well?" It was Joanna. She was going to the privy.

"Who took the man with the dark hair, and the eyes exactly like mine?"

She bit her lip. "With hair that comes to his shoulders? With the red doublet?"

"Yes," I hissed.

"I had him," she muttered, scared. "In the library room." She pointed down the hall. "He is asleep."

My gaze swivelled to the door behind her. I pushed past her.

I banged the door open.

He did not wake.

He rolled over in his bed.

I think he was naked.

I locked the door. Then I found a vase.

I picked it up and smashed it as hard as I could on the floor.

"God's toes!" He jumped upright.

Yes. He was naked.

"What … what?"

I dragged a chair towards the bed. It scratched the wooden floor.

I sat in it. My father held the sheets against his chest. Staring at me.

"Elisabeth?"

"Father."

I crossed my legs and glared at him.

"What dost thou here?"

"I work here. What dost thou here?"

"You do not … work here," he said, voice croaky from sleep and a hangover.

"No? Seems strange I hath tupped a dozen men in this very bed for a lot of money. Very strange, if I do not work here."

He looked down at the sheets he was entangled in. "You left the Nunnery to come here?" I watched as he pieced together the mystery of his daughter's life.

"Yes."

"Why?"

"So that I can wear headdresses with real pearls, and buy clothes my parents couldn't afford."

He bristled. "I knew your Devilish ways would get the better of you."

"And you yours." I gestured to his prick. "Where did you think I would go, when your bosom friend bought my home and sent my Sisters to the winds?"

"Why did not you return home?"

"Why did not you fetch me when I was raped?"

"You were a Nun!" His volume was getting louder. "You were not my responsibility!"

"I am your daughter, much though we both regret that fact."

His Adam's apple was wobbling.

"Th'art a hypocrite," I whispered. "You stripped me naked in front of a room full of people because I touched myself." He winced, still disgusted by my actions. "Why should you not now stand naked in the street for your sins? I would defrock you in front of Mother, in front of the town barber, in front of the King himself. Adulterer."

His faced darkened; he was incredulous. "Oh please, child! You do not know this world." Villainous beetle-headed maggot. I knew more of this world than he ever would. "If I am to be punished for my sins then the Bishop of Winchester should be hanged. God forbid, the King would be publicly naked for an eternity."

I got up onto the bed. My father backed himself against the furtherest bed post. I grabbed hold of his wrists, bringing him close to me. I could feel his pulse under my fingers. Continuous, fast beats of fear. My face was close to his.

"Why am I subject to rules upheld by no one? Why am I shamed and beaten and humiliated by those who do the same as me, worse than me?"

Something changed in his face. He had not been listening to me.

"Has the King ever requested to see you at court?"

"Oh!" I clapped my hands together in excited delight. "Do

you think I could help the Knolly name if I ride him really well?" Opportunistic Father. I was not even surprised.

"He would like you, Elisa, I know he would."

"Of course he would. But I would do nothing to please you Knolly. You are uncovered. I know you now. I see you."

I got up and took a deep, cleansing breath. I had my hand on the big brass key when I turned around for just one last goodbye. "Perhaps I will write to Mother." I bit my lip in contemplation. "But no doubt she is tupping someone else too. Lord Francis used to visit often enough when you were from home."

"Elisa —" His voice cracked.

"Papa." I curtsied and left.

CHAPTER TWENTY-EIGHT

"Elisa?"

I was in between clients, redoing my hair. We had been busy over this festive season. It was only the fourth day of Christmas and I was exhausted.

"Yes, Hibbens."

"I have a letter here." She came in and sat next to me. "It is a slightly different proposal."

"More than two?"

Hibbens shook her head. "No. Not like that. Sir Chiswick wants to take you to a Yuletide feast."

"And then we tup?"

"No."

I stopped brushing and turned to her. "Do I get paid?"

"Handsomely."

"Why does he want me?"

I put on my newest ring, a large garnet encased in gold. It had the letter E engraved on it.

"He wants you to pretend to be," she scanned the letter, "Lady Mary Chiswick. His wife. Her information is all here." She handed me the thick pile of paper.

"Why?"

"We ask no questions. But I presume he does not want a bachelor's desserts. He must be in want of a wife, and unable to wed one."

"I see."

I scanned the missive. Chiswick had gone to some length to create a faux wife: he had even writ down Mary's favourite foods. "Could I get in trouble?"

Hibbens shook her head. "He's invented her; you are not impersonating anyone. I would say the only one at risk here is Chiswick, and only of severe embarrassment."

"And you want me for it?"

"I assume you know how to behave at such occasions? The rules? The dances?"

"Unless something's changed over the last year and a half."

"That is always possible, but I am sure you will catch up. It is this Friday evening, at the invitation of Baron Edwards at Holdsworth Manor."

"Will people of Court be there? Will Father be there?"

"I've been informed that there is no risk of royalty, or your parents. It will be relatively modest. The Court is at Hampton for Yuletide tonight."

I nodded. My parents would be *there*, I did not doubt.

"It means th'art breaking nearly all the sumptuary laws." Alby was helping me get ready. She was the only woman I trusted could dress my hair in the most secure and fashionable of plaits. I was wearing a gold corset and kirtle, with silver-threaded detail, and my cloak gown was a deep green, with a dark fur around the hem. It was thick and warm against my skin. I wore a very large gold necklace, with a green jewel in the middle. It matched my dress perfectly.

I looked in my reflection and I saw a beautiful woman.

Like a lady of the Court. I looked a tiny bit like my mother, but I was softer. I had rounder cheeks and redder hair. My blue eyes looked darker, and deeper than they had been when I was young. I would please this Chiswick lad, I didn't doubt that.

"Now I know you are the important one tonight, but I got news too."

"Spill! I will be your secret keeper." We were both in very good spirits.

"I'm seeing a man tonight." She flung her dark hair over her shoulder.

I laughed. "Are you verily, poppet? And is he paying you good coin?"

"Most good coin, Lady Chiswick. He is one of our most prestigious visitors and he asked for me!"

"Prestigious Alby! Tell me! Tell me who? Are you going to Hampton Court? You are, are not you? Hath the King requested you?"

"Ah!" She twirled around. "I cannot tell!"

There was no amount of badgering that would make the pretty rogue tell. I wished her well, and prayed she might give up more information in the morning.

Chiswick said about three words to me the whole carriage ride to the house. He was a short man, with a big balding patch and a sulky affect. He smelt ripe. Like he'd smothered himself in rotten apples. I wondered if it was intentional, a perfume to hide another even more repugnant odour. It did not surprise me that he couldn't convince anyone to be his betrothed: his foul stench would do it alone.

Still I played my part, and my excitement bubbled as we arrived at Holdsworth House. The guards at the front, the torches outside — it was rich and I had developed a taste for rich. I was just about to allow the footman to hand me out of the carriage when my dear husband grabbed me firmly by the wrist.

"Don't embarrass me, whore."

I stroked his face, which was oily. "Never, my husband."

He winced, and I was helped down the carriage step, wiping my hands on my kerchief.

It was the twelfth day of Christmas, arguably the most important feasting day of the season. Lord and Lady Edwards had bedecked their manor accordingly. The roof of their great hall was now a sky of green holly, punctuated by an abundance of red berries. The tables had more than the usual amount of candles, and a much greater than usual amount of food.

I perused my fellow guests. At a feast in any lordly household, at any time of year, the hosts and their most important guests sit at the head table. Then the tables to their left and right create a horseshoe shape, and they are the second most important people, and so the rank descends down the tables until the very last, nearest the door. My family had never sat lower than the second table, and my parents were often honoured guests. Tonight, however, my husband and I were seated at the very, very end and it became abundantly clear, very quickly, that no one liked Sir Chiswick.

"We are so pleased that the Baron invited you, my Lady." Lady Sidney was sitting on my left. She was old and hard of hearing.

"Oh, I am forever indebted to the Baron, Lady Sidney. It is so wonderful to be in such good company, and the food is marvellous! I feel like I'm at Court."

Sidney laughed. "Have you never been invited to Court?"

"Never!" I exclaim loudly, to the great annoyance of Chiswick. "We've just never ever been invited!"

"Hush." My husband hit me in the thigh. I pursed my lips, restraining myself.

"It is much more grand than this, with much better

company. We were invited to Hampton Court this evening, but we felt we owed Lord Edwards our attendance. So few said yes to the invitation!" She was lying, but I smiled at her, nodding.

"Indeed!" boomed the large Lord Sidney. He thwacked Chiswick jovially on the back. "That's probably why you scored an invite, Chis! All the good options are with the King!"

The love of my life sneered as he gnawed at loin of veal. I patted him sensually on his back. He tensed.

I, despite my husband, was having a lot of fun. I had spoken merely to those at our table but it was exhilarating to convince them, and it was even more fun tormenting Chiswick. I reminded myself he was paying me, and decided to make more of an effort. The sugar plums and pomegranates came out, the wine continued flowing and the guests got even more boisterous.

"Do you know despite the fact Chiswick can't eat plums without getting the juice all over his face," I wiped the dribble of fruit from his chin and wondered if I should have been paid more, "that he really is the most wonderful lover!"

The very elderly Lady Smith went into a fit of giggles, Lord Smith clapped his hands together and exclaimed a loud and public congratulations to Chiswick. Sidney, in an unexpected move, bent forwards in an apparent bid for advice. I glanced at my husband: it could have gone one or two ways. But I think … I think … I saw him smile. He was certainly more than happy to give tupping advice to Sidney.

We were encouraged to dance, though not everyone could be persuaded (the main culprit being my faux husband). I was convinced to play a part in the galliard, a quick, whirling dance with lots of flicking of the feet; one switched partners frequently, and so I did not need Chiswick to participate. I started off with a young man who refused to make eye contact. His hand, meant to be resting under my own, determinedly hovered an inch or so away from my touch. But I minded not and I enjoyed the feeling of dancing, the movements coming back from some long-lost place in my past.

A new partner.

An elderly man managed to tell me a detailed story about his granddaughter in our short time together.

Another.

A lord who had sat at the high table; I kept my wits about me here, but he was uninterested, and did not say a word.

Another.

"Elisa?" My feet stopped flicking.

I had worried about seeing someone I knew. A family acquaintance, someone who knew the Knolly family — one of the Burbages perhaps. But I had not even dared to think about this.

Sam reached his hand to his hat, and pulled it off. Dancers let out exclamations of annoyance as we blocked the way.

He was staring at me. I saw the crinkles in his brow that I used to know so well.

"Elisa?" he said again, and it was still a question.

"Aye, Samuel."

He exhaled, and ran his hands through his hair as he so often did.

"Well met."

"Aye."

A stout man grabbed my hand, and some wench stole Sam away. We were whisked away into the never ending circle of half drunk, self important, want-to-be courtiers. I craned my neck to keep an eye on him as we circled one another. He was smiling at me. That irresistible crooked smile. I felt a laugh rising up in my belly. This was unbelievable. Samuel. My tutor. Here. I let myself laugh. He mirrored me, shaking his head.

"I agree, My Lady," boomed my dance partner over the noise. "This dance is quite absurd!"

I counted the dancing couples and wondered if the jig would last long enough for us to be re-partnered. With every swapping of hands I begged the song to continue. Please keep going. Just a moment longer. It was only one more swap. But I could feel the music coming to its end. My partner bowed to me, I curtseyed. Sam was just an arms length away from me. I made to move towards him but Chiswick had sleuthed his way into the middle of the hall. Sam returned to his seat.

"Can you tell John," Chiswick gestured to a man only two seats down from Sam, "what you told Lord Smith?" I tore my eyes off Sam and looked at tonight's husband, confused. "I'm referring to my matchless tupping." He clarified, blushing. I didn't know how to extricate myself from the situation. "Well?" He pressed, aggressively.

"Yes, my Lord."

"Use the word *matchless*," he specified, stomping over to the unwitting John.

My mind couldn't solve this social conundrum. Sam watched as I followed the turd of a man walk towards him. It was so hard to tear my eyes away from his face.

"John," Chiswick snapped. I dragged my attention to the man. "This is my wife." He didn't even bother to name me. Sam was listening. I cringed, desperate but simultaneously terrified to explain myself.

"It is an honour to meet you Lord John." My mind grasped for a sensible segue to my husband's matchless fucking.

"She's a beauty. How on earth did you manage it, Chis?"

Chiswick's repugnant head turned violently towards me, signalling my queue.

"His matchless tupping my Lord," I said it as quietly as I could but Lord John burst into raucous laughter. My eyes went to Sam. He had heard, his eyebrows were comically raised, his smile now incredulous.

"How much have you paid her, Chis?" Lord John thundered.

Chiswick, the shade of pomegranate, grabbed my wrist and wrenched me away.

"You didn't sell it," he hissed, dragging me out into the entrance hall.

"I don't think he was ever in the market for such a story my Lord." I wondered if Sam would follow us out here. "You should return to Lord and Lady Sidney. They are in awe of your cock!" Chiswick exhaled aggressively but then considered what I had said. I continued, desperate to be rid of him. "I am sure Lord Sidney in particular would be eager for some more advice."

"He does seem ignorant."

"It would be a great service to Lady Sidney to speak to him." Chiswick nodded and turned back inside. I waited in the entrance hall. Surely he would come to find me. Surely. The doors opened again.

It was the elderly Lady Smith. She smiled at me and I tried to disguise my disappointment.

"Point me to the piss pot my love!" I gestured down the corridor to my left. "Much good do it to ye." She pottered off down the hall.

I heard the door then hands were at my waist. I recognised his touch immediately. I leant back against him. I felt his breath on my neck.

My whole body erupted with goosebumps. I turned into him, looking at his face. My desire had not changed, if anything it was stronger.

"Sam," I whispered.

"I have a lot of questions to put to you, Elisa."

"We need to go somewhere alone."

CHAPTER TWENTY-NINE

We went outside. He led me by the hand to the huge knot garden. We were shielded from anyone's view by the tall hedges. He found a corner of the mazed garden that gave us respite from the wind and then he released my hand. He was in a large, billowing black cloak with a fur trim, not unlike my own, and held it tight to his body.

"Samuel?" I moved closer to him. I watched his eyes turn to my lips. I wanted to kiss him. I moved in to do so, putting my hand to his face.

He made a groaning noise. "Elisa. Wait." I noticed a shift in his mood. He moved away from my touch and kicked some of the gravel in the little maze.

"I thought you dead." I had not expected anger. "Did you even think about your parents when you ran away from that cursed Nunnery? I know it was not what you wanted, Elisa, but I never expected you to forget about those who loved you. You can forget about me, but to forget about your Livia, Agnes and Eddie?"

"I have not forgotten about them!"

"They do not know what hath happened to you! They

know not where you are! You left the Abbey and the Abbess wrote to them and said you were gone! Disappeared!" He was almost shouting at me. "I thought you *dead*!" He kicked the gravel again.

"I am not dead," I said, trying to take an even breath.

"Your family think you are."

My father didn't. "Sam. You do not know the full story." He looked up at me pitifully. "I am not dead, Sam. I am here, with you." His face softened.

"And what about this fool you are here with..." He half smiled.

I momentarily forgot his name. "Um ... Sir Chiswick."

"So have you run off and married one of the greatest laughingstocks in London?"

I managed a laugh. "He is not my husband."

"I thought not. But did you come here as his wife?"

"Yes."

He looked at me, wanting me to explain.

I had sometimes imagined what I would say to my sisters if I saw them again, about what I had been doing, what had happened after the Nunnery. It included a wishy-washy story about getting a job at a tavern. I had decided I would lie. The Stew did have a bar, and sometimes I did serve drinks. But I did not want to tell Samuel that story.

"Let us go further into the garden." He gestured for me to follow.

I felt an echo of the past, a fluttering in my tummy. I felt my body concaving inwards with modesty and shyness. But then I remembered who I was. I was not Lady Elisa anymore. The woman who had looked at her naked body in a mirror and felt revolted. I straightened up. We walked deeper into the maze.

"What happened, Elisa?" he asked, sitting down on a stone bench. "What part of your history am I missing?"

"All of the history, Samuel," I said. "You know not of what you speak, so you must not make any more accusations."

"I will not," he conceded.

"First, tell me why *you* are here."

"It is not an interesting tale: I am acquainted with Lord Edwards. I knew him at Oxford. I got leave from your parents."

"And how is Eddie?"

"He is very well, maybe three inches taller than you left him and just as naughty."

"And my sisters?"

"Your sisters, as far as I can tell, are well. Livia is happily married and talks obscenely about her poor husband whenever she visits. Your parents are as they ever were. And Mary misses you terribly and speaks of you frequently. We tried to write to you."

I winced. "I received your letter." I swallowed. "It drove me nearly mad that I could not reply."

He looked at his feet as though only just remembering what he had written on my treasured letter.

"I still have it. I kept it."

He didn't look up. His feet were shuffling, kicking stones on the floor.

"What is't, Samuel?"

He looked to me, his eyes watery, his smile, hard.

My temper simmered.

"I am well in health, but the house has not been the same. I have missed you." He sniffed, and blinked repeatedly.

His hand lay next to him on the stone chair. I sat by him and covered it with my own.

"I have missed you too, Sam." He looked down at my hand, surprised. "You did not hear of anything happening at the Nunnery? You did not hear from my parents about a letter written to them before the report of my leaving?"

He shook his head. The servants nearly always knew the

family gossip. It surprised me that he did not know. My parents must have read the letter and burnt it; they wanted to take its contents to the grave. "What happened?"

I took as deep a breath as I ever had. "The chaplain of Lacock raped me."

He stood up as quick as if he had just sat on something spiky. But he did not say anything. The words rang in the air.

"He attacked me in one of the sheds on the grounds, amongst the pitchforks and the cobwebs." I saw his jaw clench and unclench. "He raped many of the Sisters, I believe."

His eyes glanced over my body as if he was looking for physical signs of my pain, or perhaps signs that I had proceeded to hurt myself after the incident.

"Lord Sherrington wrote to Mother and Father and told them of the fact. And, I presume, of his purchase of the Abbey. Even if I had wanted to stay there, there is no home for the Nuns there now."

"I never heard a word. Not of any of this," he said through his teeth.

"And I heard no word from my parents. I was not fetched. I was not sent words of comfort. For all they knew, I was left homeless and unprotected for the Chaplain and his ilk to have their ways again and again and again."

"He didn't though … he did not?"

"He did not." I wanted to talk of something else.

"Elisa." I saw his lip quiver. He looked up at the cloudy sky, trying not to blink. His cheeks were red with cold.

"I need not your pity, Samuel. I healed myself. I helped myself. I did not need my family."

"You left? Immediately after this, you left?"

"No. Until I learned of the Abbey's purchase I stayed. I was working in the Infirmary. I worked with the sick." I saw a twitch of a smile. I knew he would like that part of my story. "And I had an … intimate friend."

"What? Was he a man in the hospice?" He sat back down, his face close to mine.

"No, no sickly man. Her name was Constance."

His eyes flicked between my lips and my eyes. A true smile on his face now. "You did not."

"She was beautiful, Samuel, you wouldst love her. Entirely naughty. She kept a wooden phallus behind St Thomas Aquinas's books in the library, and she kissed better than you." He laughed, and threw his hands in the air, accepting his defeat.

"But she was taken from Lacock by her family." I wrapped my cloak tighter around me, nuzzling my nose into the fur, warming my nose. "Do you know whether the Abbey has closed yet?"

"Not that I've heard."

"It will be soon. Have you heard of this Sherrington?"

"I have heard his name."

"I locked him in the bakery and then I left. There was naught left for me. It was more of an early exit than a running away."

Samuel had been shaking his head incredulously for most of the story. I wanted him. After all this time, and all these things. It was still there. My mind wondered back to the time in his room.

"Then you came to London?" he asked.

My tummy was really turning now. I did not want him to change his opinion of me, I did not know if there was a limit to Sam's grace.

"Yes."

"And he is not your husband."

"No."

He stood and moved towards me. "Did he pay you to be his wife?"

I was so glad that Sam was no idiot.

"Just for the evening. Yes."

I put my hand on his chest.

"And this is a common occurrence."

"I am rarely asked to be a wife." He was still staring at my lips as I spoke. He did not seem revolted or even shocked. "But yes, it is a very common occurrence of late."

"Do you work at a stew?"

"The Bishop of Winchester's own."

"Are you well?"

"I am very well. I do not need rescuing."

"I can see that."

"I even met the Bishop of Winchester in person."

"He visits the stew?"

"He does, and so does my father."

"What?"

"Lord Grey. My father. Your master."

"Ah." Samuel's face was unreadable.

"I think he will not visit again."

"He saw you?"

I nodded.

"He has not spoken of it."

"That does not surprise me." I paused, and took a deep breath. "The words you wrote on that first letter you sent me, do you still mean them?"

He frowned, trying to remember. "I cannot recall my wording. But if it has anything to do with needing your lips upon my own, then yes. The sentiment still lingers."

A wind whipped around the tall hedge. I looked up to the heavens. A flurry of snowflakes was making its way to earth.

"Keep me warm?" He made to put an arm around me, but instead I saddled him, just as in his cottage. "Do you want me because th'art curious? Do you want to see what I hath learnt?" I brushed my lips against his.

"I can scarce believe it is you." This thrilled me.

"Is there nothing left of Lady Elisa?" I asked, brushing off a snowflake that had landed on his lashes.

"There is everything left. You are Elisa, I see you, you are the woman I have missed."

I think Sam had always seen me the way I saw myself today. Not a whore, of course. But he had seen me as a woman, as someone who owned herself, owned her choices.

"But you are more. The way you hold yourself ..." He put a hand on the back of my head, pulling me towards him. I melted into his touch, and my whole body reacted to the feeling of his lips upon my own. But then he pulled away. "The way you kiss." He shuffled me closer on his lap. "Is this Constance's teaching?"

"She helped, of a certs."

"I like this Constance." His hand went to the back of my head again, but this time he started kissing my neck. It began to feel frantic, urgent. I let out a moan.

I bit my lip and hiked up my skirts, so my thighs were on display. His hands went straight to them, reaching higher and higher. He found my hips and pulled me closer to him, almost thrusting himself against me. Damn all these winter fineries.

"I need you, Elisa." I began tearing at my corset ties. Samuel helped with my cause, and having conquered it, put his mouth to my breast. I yelled out. Turned my head and ... I saw them.

Lord Chiswick and Lady bloody Sidney. I'll be damned. He'd conned his way into a romp in the bushes with another man's wife.

"Oh my, is that not your wife Lord Chiswick!" Lady Sidney squealed. Samuel, realising what had happened, took me by the hand and we ran.

"There is another exit this way!" Sam said, dragging me around corners, expertly avoiding all the dead ends. "Lady

Sidney's in for a disappointment!" He laughed over my panting.

We found ourselves on the far side of Holdsworth Manor, gasping for breath.

"Running with one's breasts out is quite the experience," I wheezed.

"A spectacle too," Sam confirmed. "I am staying on Sheep Street not far from here. Would you accompany me there?"

"Sam, I don't know if you know this, but I have never ever been to an inn on Sheep Street, and truth be told it hath always been a dream of mine to stay at an Inn on Sheep."

Sam laughed. "What about your husband?"

"He seems adequately entertained."

We walked quickly and quietly off the property, the fresh snow stifling our footsteps.

We kissed on our walk, we kissed at the door, we kissed all the way up the stairs and fell into his room, kissing. We took a small break from kissing to regroup once we were on the bed. I tried to remember who I was, what I had done, but I knew I was blushing and my hands tingled with nerves. He took me straight back. Straight back to before all of this had happened.

"You must get undressed first," I instructed.

He nodded; we got off the bed and stood an inch from each other. Sensibly, he took his top off first. He had a trail of blond hair that trickled into the top of his breeches. I battled desperately to stop looking at it, but then I remembered I did not have to battle. I looked, and I looked further when he was fully free of his breeches. I touched the light line of hairs. Tracking them downwards lower and lower. He grabbed my wrist.

"Do not make me wait much longer Elisa," he whispered "I have thought about this moment for quite some time."

I raised an eyebrow. "Undress me then."

He did so. Aptly. His fingers running all over my body. I was shivering by the time he was finished—from the cold, nerves or pleasure, it was undecided. He tried to move me to the bed, but I put a hand on his chest.

"Wait. I have spent the evening with a man whose odour is not unlike Eddie's after he's rolled in the orchard. Will you wash me?" I looked to the cloth and water that had been left by the inn staff.

"With pleasure." Sam wetted the cloth and gently dabbed it along my chest, my breasts, my neck. "I doubt, or at least I pray that his scent has not reached your thighs Elisa, but I shall do my duty." He got down onto his knees and began washing my calves, my knees, my thighs. He reached higher and higher. "Would you take a seat for a moment?" he asked, spreading my legs, and pressing the cloth against the inside of my leg. He looked me in the eye and very intentionally put the cloth on the floor, replacing it with his lips and his tongue, moving higher and higher until he met me. No one had done this to me before. It was exceptional. I felt drunk with need. The heat within me was rising higher and higher and I put my hands in his curls as he worked me, and melted me and ruined me until I yelled out, louder than I had with Constance, but I was allowed to make sound in a cheap roadside inn. I caught my breath and then I lifted him up and moved him to the bed.

"Your turn Samuel." Slowly, inch by inch I straddled him. I delighted at his expression. I had been with thirty-two different men. I counted. But I felt almost virginal as I sat astride him. He was looking up at me, breathing heavy, his curls messy, his eyes glassed over. I felt I was owed this moment. By God. Samuel should've been the one to take my virtuous chastity. This moment was stolen from me, by Godly shame. I looked down at my body, and wished there had been glass to witness myself. I looked divine.

Sam groaned loudly, pulling at my hips, quickening my pace.

"Do you know how much I dreamed of this?" he managed, his face almost pained with pleasure. I slowed down.

"Oh?" I leant down to his ear, nibbled at it and then whispered, "I desireth as much to be yours as you do to have me." He flipped me over, taking control. I was glad of it. The heat had already returned and was pulsing within me. I wanted it to consume me whole.

It was very early in the morning. I must have only slept a few hours.

I rolled over, resting my chin on the tutor's chest. I could hear the world beginning to wake outside our window, in the non-existent winter light. The sound of trundling cart wheels crumpling over fresh snow, the baker and the fishmonger exchanging morning pleasantries woke him.

Samuel's eyes half opened. "Th'art an early riser," he murmured. We stared at each other for a long time.

"You know, back before I was a whore, and before I was a Nun," I whispered, "I used to imagine you were a lord, hiding from your responsibilities, and we would marry and we would lie together."

"I used to just lust after the lying." He yawned.

"Verily, no, Samuel: you asked me to run away with you."

"Ah." He nodded. "That is true, I did dream about waking up to you day after day." I played with his hair. "Can I ask you a few more questions?" he asked hesitantly.

I nodded.

"Why work in a stew? Why not somewhere else? Doing something else?"

I frowned, and sat up in bed. "I looked for work in London, but the city reminded me of the Chaplain, the hands, the looks. I was assaulted by urchin boys, and then the people at St Albans threw tomatoes at me, and I felt like my body belonged to London and all the stinking men who make the city vile. But when I am at the stew, with the women, my body is my own, I make my own choices, I make my own money."

"So you made the decision? No one found you or … made you."

"No one made me."

"Do you regret it?"

I smiled. "Do you see this ring?" I straddled him again, showing him the emerald on my left hand.

"I do."

"I bought this for myself, because I wanted it."

He smiled. "Didst thou buy that one for yourself as well?"

"This one?" The depth of the garnet caught in the dawn light. "No; a cully gave me this, I remember not his name."

"Will you ever come back to your home?"

I dismounted him, irritated. I had been trying to be patient. "Why would I do that, Samuel? My parents spent their lives humiliating me for sins that are also their own. I have seen my father naked in a whorehouse. My whorehouse. But, worse than that, neither Mother nor Father cared enough to rescue me from my earthly hell at the Nunnery. I deserve better."

"But what about your brother?"

"Samuel!" I began violently untying my plaits, letting my curls spring loose. Medusa's snakes unleashed. "They lost me. They deserve me not."

Silence. My curls transformed him to stone.

"By my troth, I am sorry," he said eventually. He touched my naked back. "I just want not to leave you." There was another long pause. "What will you do after your work at the stew? When th'art … finished."

I rolled my eyes. Lord Jesus I was irritable. "Do you want me to say I will stop my whoring?"

"Sweet, do not put the world's expectations of you upon me. Do not treat me as if I were Nicholas, or you parents. I want to hear your honest answer."

Honestly, I had not thought about it much. I gathered the sheets around me, and ran them through my fingers. "I have not seen a woman above forty in Southwark, and I don't fancy fucking with grey hair and no teeth."

"Would you continue practising the healing you did in the Infirmary?"

"I do still practise — I look after the girls in the stew every day. I am their apothecary and healer."

He smiled. "If thou needst anything, Elisa — if thou ever needst anything at all — come and find me."

"And you can always find me at the stews in Southwark. Mistress Hibbens's house. I cost a pretty penny, but I think for you we might be able to arrange something."

He had got up. I watched him walk naked to the bowl of water. He did not find me funny.

"Will you not come back with me?" he asked, gripping the basin with two hands.

"Nay." How exasperating: I had just explained this. I could not go back. To do what? To be sent away again? Or to lie about my doings since Lacock only then to be married off to anyone, anyone who wouldst take me. Sam still had not turned around. He was just staring into the basin.

The sun was rising; the room was filling with pink light. It really was time to go. I got out of bed and walked to him. I placed my hand in the small of his back.

"I have to leave."

He was unblinking. If he had succumbed, I think tears would have fallen. His hair was dishevelled. I smoothed it over and gently kissed the corners of his downturned lips. "I am sorry."

He shook his head, and rubbed his eyes. "I could never have imagined that you would find peace like this."

I exhaled. The eaves creaked, like they had also breathed a sigh of relief. The tension in the room dissipated. My anger at Sam left me. I kissed his cheek.

I did not say goodbye. He helped me redress and we laughed about the absurdity of layers and lace, and then we laughed about Chiswick and then we laughed because my skirts got stuck in my shift and then I simply left. We caught a glance of each other through the closing of the door, but then it was done.

CHAPTER THIRTY

I felt disheartened stepping into the stew. I should have told Sam to get more leave from tutoring Eddie. We should have gone on a journey. Overseas perhaps. A boat ride with Sam. Spending each day and each night with him. I swanned across the parlour as if I were on a boat deck on my way to France. I was halfway up the stairs before I realised someone had been watching me. Shivers erupted up my spine as I saw the figure sitting in the corner of the room.

"Good morning, Elisa."

"Mistress Hibbens!" I clutched my chest. "I did not see you."

"And Chiswick did not see you last night." I wondered what he had told her.

"My apologies, Madam. But as the dancing started I recognised someone from my," I cleared my throat, "from my past. I did not think it wise to reveal my real identity, so I left the feast."

"Indeed."

I nodded, but she had not finished. I was not out of the woods.

"Why is it then, that you float across the parlour floor just after cock's crow?"

"I stayed in an inn."

"Why?"

Why had I not troubled to think of an explanation? I stared at her. I felt young. Like a child.

"I require the truth from my girls."

I had nothing to offer her other than the truth anyway. "The man recognised me. He was a friend from my days as a lady. We spent the evening together."

Hibbens strode across the floor to me. "You will refund me the money Chiswick paid you, and you will pay me that once more again as a fine for this unprofessional fuckery." I nodded. "If you want to stay here, Elisa the whore, if you want to stay here under my good grace, you must behave as I want you to behave."

She pushed past me. I stayed still for a long time. Until everything was silent. Then I went to my room. I undid all of Sam's hard work, struggling and tearing at my gown, escaping the binds and ties, the suffocating cloth. When I was free, I put myself back to bed and I sobbed into my sheets.

I had never been good at handling a telling off. By God's toes, I can recall Agnes yelling at me for stealing one of her ribbons and I had hidden up a tree until sundown. But I do not think my tears were only for my reprimand. It was all too close. The names of my family, past wounds, past worries: they had found their ways into this life. When it was all kept the one from the other, it simmered but did not over-boil. But now Samuel was there in that room with me — I hadn't left him at the inn as I had attempted to do. And his words, his words about my parents and my sisters and my baby brother, they had all followed me to the brothel too.

There was a knocking sound on the door. I eyed it suspiciously. Perhaps Hibbens wanted her coin right away.

"Hello?"

The door creaked open a crack and then Alby tumbled in. I was relieved to see her, a distraction from my thoughts. But she was more than just a distraction. I leapt from my bed.

"Mercy God!" I ran to her. She had a head wound and she was clutching her middle. "What's afoot, Alby? What hurts? Help! Alby's been hurt!" My voice rang out around the corridors, but working girls were good sleepers so early in the morning.

Alby couldst not speak. The cut on her head was not too deep, but I worried about her middle; she was curled up in pain, clutching her stomach.

"Charles," she muttered. She groaned nonsensically.

I got her to release her belly, and saw that she had knife wounds across it.

I grabbed my parcel of bandages and herbs. She would need relief first.

"Drink, drink this!" I poured a bottle of spirit down her throat; she choked and spluttered, but most of it went down.

Hibbens appeared. "What what?" She tutted, looking down at Alby on the floor.

"She said the name Charles," I said, cleaning the wound with water and oil. She had been slashed, not stabbed, praise Jesus. Thank you, God.

"Oh." Hibbens nodded.

"You know him?"

Hibbens did not seem panicked, but sat down on the floor and stroked Alby's hair as I worked. "Oh yes. He's done this a few times before."

"Forsooth?"

"Joanna lacks one earlobe because of Charles. He bites, he punches, he gets his knife out."

I was flailing around with the pieces of sheets I had cut up; they were tangled, but I needed them right now.

"Those sheets will need replacing if you have them from my store room," said the bawd, as prim as a merchant's wife counting her silver spoons.

"Why do you send the girls to him?" I was hysterical, sorting pieces of sheet into a large soft pad and strands to keep it in place.

"I mention not his last name for a reason, Elisa. He is one of our most important clients."

"But look at what he did to Alby!"

"You think she will not make it?" She sounded surprised.

How had everything that was so wonderful stopped being wonderful within a matter of minutes?

"Why do you not tell someone about what this man does! Report him!"

Hibbens frowned. "Elisa, it's *Charles* —" She waggled her eyebrows, begging me to read her mind. "If I report him, the King will protect him. Or I bring the authorities to our house, they see that we are working on feast days and Wednesdays, they see that you have board here, they see that you are wearing the colour red. Then after they have done, all that *seeing*, they have forgotten all about Charles and I am in the stocks or maybe on a pile of hot sticks and you are on the streets with no money."

"But look at what he hath done to Alby!" I could feel the house stirring, my screaming finally rousing the asleep.

Hibbens looked at me, the way she always did. Reading me. "I'm sorry, Elisa. I know that the stew has treated you well. That these women have become your family. That you enjoy the jewels that bedeck your neck because you earned them on your own back. But we are still in a stew. You are still a whore. We are still men's playthings that they can stab or fuck depending on their mood. The world has not changed because thou hast had a few good months here. God still hates us."

She left me on the bloody floor with a stabbed whore.

· · ·

Alby did not recover quickly. She was unable to work, but bent constantly over, her stomach healing but then tearing open again as soon as she stood up. I did not know what else to do. She went and saw a physic; I even took her to see a witch. I thought of Isabella when we stood in her shoppe. No witch or man or Elisa was helping her. Hibbens took away her rooms, as she was not earning her keep.

I bought Alby rooms in an inn down the road and visited her every day, bringing her food and more medicine. I bought Alice ribbons for her hair; I payed all their bills.

A week later there was another incident, this time with Little-Elizabeth. This client had different tactics from Charles. Though he did not have a knife, he had strength. Little-Elizabeth fell and hit her head. She had seemed fine for a while, but then she died. Left us all. I held her as she passed. I had never held anyone as they died before. It was not peaceful. It was not beautiful. She vomited. She spoke strange sentences. She had fits. She was not given last rites. No priest would come into the stew to do God's work, though they did not mind visiting for a fuck.

Elizabeth was buried outside of consecrated ground and I cried and prayed for her soul. I had dream after dream of her stuck with no heaven to relieve her, her head wound oozing, her mouth asking for God to save her.

"Elisa." Hibbens was behind the bar tonight. She had her client smile on, and so I mimicked her. She had work for me.

"Good evening." I smiled, and curtseyed to Hibbens and the two people she was talking to. A man and a woman. They looked uncomfortable, sipping their drinks stiffly.

"I have instructed Master Frobashaw and his wife to go to the royal suite."

"The best rooms in the inn." I smiled broadly at the wife

and she relaxes. "You will have a very pleasant stay." I stroke the wife's arm affectionately, like we were good friends. She blushed and reached up to whisper in her husband's ear.

"Yes. We'll take it," he said to Hibbens.

I could not countenance being called "it" but I showed it not. Maybe he was just nervous.

"Wonderful!" exclaimed Hibbens. "The barmaid will show you to your room." As she ascended, the wife threw me several backwards glances; I smiled at her and she giggled. I turned to Hibbens.

"He's a merchant. Sells spices. Rolling in coin."

"Very well." I did not look at her.

"And they have not done this before, so be gentle." Hibbens passed me my share of the money.

"Why don't you give it straight to Alby?" I snapped darkly. "See that she lives still and Alice is fed." Still I did not look her in the eyes.

"I'll tell Maisy to take it to her when she gets back," she conceded.

I nodded and joined my married friends upstairs.

I knocked.

"Aye?" Men's voices get deeper and ruder when they're nervous.

"It be Elisa."

"Come in," said the woman excitedly.

They had both, adorably, got undressed. They were standing by the bed, completely starkers and shaking from nerves. My bad mood shifted a little, making space for a bit of enjoyment.

"What a wondrous sight."

I moved to the woman and touched her cheek. Her quick uneven breath smelt sweet. I moved her so we were standing either side of her husband. He looked down at us. His expression, stunned. I put my hand on her hip, and my bad mood slipped a little further still. I had missed being with a woman. Mr Frobashaw reacted instantly to my touching her: I heard his intake of breath. I kissed her, and she kissed back. This pleased him greatly.

It was, all in all, a lot of fun.

Both husband and wife warmed up quickly. Wine was brought up to us after our deed was done. The man fell asleep after a single sip. The men always did.

"Perhaps it is uncouth," began the lady timidly, "but would you tell me a little more about yourself?" The woman was lying on her front on the floor, playing with the tassels on the carpet, her bottom shamelessly exposed. I smiled at her, and joined her on the rug, two bare buttocks in conversation.

I had, of course, been asked this several times before. I had a plethora of different pasts to choose from, so I thought a moment, wondering which might suit this particular woman best.

"I don't even know your given names!" I whispered, buying time.

"My husband's name is Richard."

"And yours?"

"It is Constance. Or Con, if you prefer."

I bit my lip. I had not the energy to disguise my surprise. "'Tis a beautiful name," I said finally.

"Will you tell me some of your story now?"

"My story is very long and strange."

"Is not everyone's?"

I felt like my story had surpassed most people's by this point. But I smiled and nodded. "May I talk about something on my heart?" Seeing as I was talking to Constance, I wanted to be honest, to speak my heart, which had so much on it.

Con nodded and cupped her chin in her hands. I

mimicked her and then I told her the story of Alby's attack and of Little-Elizabeth's death and the heartbreak I have for so many of these women who had nowhere else to go. I even spoke of the Nuns, so many of whom would have no home as I had had no home on the dissolution of my Abbey.

"That lady had no last rites?" Constance asked. I shook my head. She murmured a prayer. "And you healed Alby? With your own skill?" I nodded. "Where did you learn these skills?" I bit my lip and looked at her coyly. She did not pry further. "You should open up an almshouse." She said, rolling over to lie on her back, revealing her breasts.

"A what?"

"A home for those in need." It was Richard who had spake, his head poking out from the end of the bed.

"You could use your skills to mend illnesses and wounds there, and you could care for those who need a home."

"I cannot buy property, though. I would need a house to build an almshouse."

"You would need a man —" of course "— to buy it for you, but then you could run it."

The couple assured me this had been a night they would not forget, but it was I who could not stop thinking about it.

CHAPTER THIRTY-ONE

I kept it to myself for a while, but the idea wanted air.

I set it free to several of the girls in our early-morning magic hours, when I wore my starred and mooned cloak, when we sat by the fire, when we had worn out the men.

"Like an Infirmary?" asked Maisy.

"In a way." No one looked too enthused. "But a shelter, as well, for those who need a bed, or medicine, or food. But only for women. For people like us." Murmurs of vague interest. "For example, instead of Alby staying at an inn, she would stay at the almshouse."

"You want to leave us, Elisa?" Maisy asked, brow furrowed.

"No. I don't want to leave. I ... " I tried to start my explanation again, but it faded. Anne came in with the bread and we split it four ways.

"How would you afford it?" pressed Maisy.

"I have savings, from my time here. We earn more than any common merchant who owns a house. If I run out of gold, I can come back and top it up."

"Tup it up." Marguerite corrected me. These women were erudite at sex jokes.

"Still, a property big enough for a family of sick whores, space for you to perform your remedies. And you will want land, enough for growing the right herbs and food. And more food will need purchasing. Then there will be people you might need to pay. A cook, a helping hand. You might need to pay a barber for chopping someone's oozing leg off … " Maisy was a thinker.

"How does one discover the prices of property?"

"You could ask one of my regulars, a merchant, brings in spices from the East. His name's Mr Carne, and he's rich as Croesus. He has many houses and I expect to see him this week. He's a nice enough fellow. He shall talk to you."

Rich as Croesus Carne made me wait until the following Tuesday. I stood outside the Red Room in the early hours of what was now Wednesday morning, waiting for Maisy to be done with him. I prayed Mr Carne had no stamina. There was a lot of banging and floorboard screeching going on in there.

Silence. My slumped shoulders corrected themselves. I brushed down my skirts. The banging resumed. By the time Maisy came to fetch me, I was sleeping against the door. I fell into the room as she exited the chamber.

"Maisy! You took forever!" I moaned sleepily.

"Get up, Elisa! Master Carne said he'll talk with you."

I walked bleary-eyed into the Red Room. I curtsied to the entirely naked man sitting on a wooden chair.

"Elisa, is it?" I smiled at him. "Sit down my dear; let's talk about property." He rubbed his very large belly.

I enjoyed my talk with Mr Carne very much. He did not once remind me of the fact that, no matter the price, I could not legally buy a property. He only answered my questions. Told me stories about his purchases. Discussed large figures. Important Names. All the while occasionally picking fluff from his exposed belly button. It was a unique experience. Less pleasant were the realities of his lesson. Property, I learnt, wasn't just floating around for sale at a certain price. Nearly everything was tied up in inheritance — someone somewhere would be entitled to a home that seemed available for purchase. But if you looked close enough, promised Mr Carne, there would be land for the taking. Merchants with new money wanted new homes. It was not impossible, he told me. But it was pricey. Too pricey for me.

If I spent the next six months on my back, with a steady flow of clients, providing Alby got better, and making sure to spend no money on myself — then I could look at buying an almshouse in London.

I lay on my bed. I was surrounded by dozens of pieces of parchment. Some were notes about my earnings, my expenses, things I could sell. The other papers held the insights of Mr Carne, his calculations, house prices, property sizes and household incomes. I had been too ambitious — for now at least. I wiped my eyes with my shift. I was sadder than I expected to be. I really did not like to be told no. But I must not entirely give up. I did not know what was coming around the corner. If I had learnt anything, it was that anything can happen. I could become the King's favourite and be doused in money and prestige.

I looked at the sea of parchment that surrounded me. For a tiny second, I contemplated collecting the papers neatly and removing them from my bed, but then I came to my senses and tucked myself in; I would tidy in the morning.

Someone knocked at my door.

Good God, I had not the energy to clear my bed of rubbish — I certainly had not the energy for another client, let alone for opening the door.

"Yes?"

"It's Hibbens."

"Come in."

She was in her full gown and kirtle, ready for another day's work or not yet slept, I could not tell.

"What can I do for you, Mistress Hibbens?"

She looked at the pieces of paper that surrounded me. Curse my laziness. "I hath heard rumours." Her skirts whisked threateningly on the floor as she moved towards me. She picked up a handful of parchment. "That you are looking to invest in a house?"

Her voice was measured. Even. I did not know whether she was mad or impressed.

"Only dreaming, Mistress Hibbens."

"An almshouse, I heard?"

"Mayhap one day Mistress Hibbens "

"Stop lying," she snapped. "Unbosom yourself to me."

I swallowed and sat up. "I looked into it, Mistress, but I have not the means."

"Hmmm." She moved to sit down at the trunk at the end of my bed and tapped her long nails upon the wood. "Do you remember when your father visited?"

"It had entirely slipped my mind." I said tightly, sporting a sarcastic smile. She ignored me.

"He sent word about a week after his patronage."

I sat up. "Aye?"

"Aye. A letter. And a purse, actually."

"Why did not I see it? What said it?" I crawled across to the end of the bed, tearing parchment as I went.

"Verily, it started with explicit instructions that you were the only one to read the letter and receive the purse."

"Then why didst thou read it?" My voice cracked.

"Because you, whether you like it or not, belong to me."

There was an electric spasm up the scar on my back. "I belong to no one."

"That's not true." She made eye contact. "We all belong to

someone." She tapped me on the nose. "As I was saying, I screen all letters that come to my house and this one was from your father."

"Let me have it." My mouth was dry.

"I did not want you to have it. I still do not." I took a sharp breath, but Hibbens held up her hands. "The letter says nothing of importance. It merely states that the purse is for your use, and your use only. There's a false apology, wrapped up in your precious Knolly seal. All in all it is very badly written." Another bolt of pain ran up my spine. "I could only assume that it was meant persuade you to return to your home." I sat back and stared out the window.

"My family have very little free coin. I wonder how he managed it."

Hibbens sucked her teeth. "He's desperate, I con. Perhaps he borrowed it. It seems he will do whatever it takes to keep you silent and out of this profession. Ignorant man."

"Why did not you give me the letter?"

"Because you are a Hibbens goose. I have invested in you and I feel it has been fruitful. I could not risk losing you."

"Why tell me now?"

She blushed. "Because I felt Judas's hot guilt in me as soon as I heard about your plans with the almshouse. I myself could have benefited from such an establishment when I was young and naive. I could benefit from it now, send the girls there when things go awry, have them cared for and returned." She wanted me to do it.

"Do you still have the letter and coins?"

She put both on the bed.

If I had learnt anything, it was that anything can happen. I could become the King's favourite and be doused in money and prestige, or my father could send me an emerald embroidered purse, filled with an abundance of gold coin.

CHAPTER THIRTY-TWO

I sat in Alby's room at the inn. Today was the day. Alice was sitting in the corner under the small window. Alby lay on her bed, staring up at the roof. A goose called Joy was living there too. She would be giving birth soon and there was a lot of superstition about tupping a woman-with-child. She had not been wanted at the stew.

The room was tiny, enough for two mattresses on the ground and no private place to keep the chamber pots. I picked one up and poured the piss out the window, which I left it open, hoping a fresh breeze would air out the room.

"Why won't you pour it out when you're done pissing, Alby?" Her injuries had rendered her alike a child.

"'Tis not me, 'tis Joy! She thinks because of her belly she's exempt."

Joy lay in her bed, cradling her large stomach.

I shook my head.

I had told Alby about the almshouse and she had been quick to point out over a dozen flaws. But over the last few weeks I had thought things through. I had sold nearly everything I owned. Hibben's herself was going to invest, if it meant I would take and rehabilitate the geese when they were down on their luck. I had spoken to a plethora of people and I was back with answers, counterpoints to her doubts.

"I have the funds, Alby. I spent not a penny on myself in the last four weeks and I have been on my back that whole time."

"You do not have to always do it on your back, Elisa," Alby snarked. I ignored her. I had not told her about my father's "donation". I had spent some time debating what to do with the coins. It felt like dirty money — dirtier than all my earnings. I knew not what it was. Was it a bribe? A shitty apology? A mistake? But it also felt like too timely a gift to not use it for my almshouse. It had arrived on my bed the moment I began to doubt the idea. Like a sign, but from God?

"I have written to a man recommended by Mr Carne and I have a list of properties that might be available to purchase." I passed her the list.

She had aged, her dark brown hair was sprinkled with sparkling silver. "None of these homes is in London."

"No. Well … 'tis expensive here. Besides, these are not far. Just a days ride away."

"It matters little anyway. None of this —" she jabbed her finger at the papers detailing the houses for purchase "— will solve the fact you have these." She prodded my breasts one at a time. "People with breasts buy no houses." She had become bitter. "You are not even a woman, Elisa: you are a whore."

Joy gave a horrible short laugh.

"I thought you were asleep?" I shot at her. Her eyes snapped back shut. "Well it matters not what you think Alby. I've a carriage waiting outside and it is taking me back home, to Grey's Court."

Joy's eyes were back open again; even Alice looked surprised, and I had not known she had been listening.

"I'm going to ask Samuel to buy the property for me." Still silence. "With mine own money, of course."

"You going to ask him to marry you too?" Alby said finally.

I stood up. "Do you have any other raging objections to my plan?"

She looked around the chamber, as though searching for a retort. "'Tis worth a shot, Elisa," she said, finally.

That was all I needed.

"I will be back within two or three days." I turned to Joy. "Do not dare have your baby until I return. And Alice?" The little girl looked up from her sewing. "Take care of your mother."

She nodded. She was smiling less and less these days.

All my decisions were being made quickly, because if I thought about them too long the decisions would die. They would die in the London gutters and I would never consider them again. I even made the driver swear he would not turn around, even if I begged him. And I had begged him. As soon as I started recognising the fields and the villages I asked him to take me back to London.

Dutifully, he had told me exactly what I told him to tell me. "I got one job, Lady Knolly, I'll be dropping you at Grey's Court."

I had given him my full name. I know not why. The sound of it made me feel dizzy.

He was not to deposit me at the front of the house, but about a half mile away, so I could walk straight to Samuel's cottage and wait for him until he got home.

Of course, I was not just back for my whimsical almshouse. I would move as stealthily as I could but I knew I would be secretly searching for signs of my family, to know they still lived, and existed, despite the fact that Elisa, the old Elisa, had died.

"Right," said the driver sternly. "I know this is hard. I know you do not want to go back home. But you promised yourself this morning you would go through with this. I heard you." His wild greying eyebrows bristled in the autumnal wind. "So don't be letting yourself down and walking back to London by foot. Ya here now. Do what you come to do."

Of course, he had no idea what I came to do, but his words gave me courage. I began walking the familiar, haunted roads.

If I could have tell my child self, back then, that the next time I hopped over Farmer Harry's stile I would be a lady, turned nun, turned goose, I would never have believed me. I was unrecognisable.

I saw a glimpse of the red bricks of my old home. Emotion, not sadness, not joy, but some sort of old energy was coursing through my body. I cut around the forest and started walking the long way, my ears on the alert for any one taking a walk around the garden. I thought I might have seen Livia strolling with her new husband. Though they did not live there any more, they were not far, and Livia had loved to potter around the grounds. I had also half expected to see Eddie and Samuel in the kitchen garden, but they were not there either. I had seen a whip of white near the back of the house and I thought it could have been Mary airing out some clothes. But the house was silent. The grounds were empty. I arrived at Samuel's home and let myself in and still I had seen no one.

It were as though I had left this home and the people there had stopped existing. It was almost as I expected, because how *could* they exist in their same ways when my life had deviated so much? I sat on Samuel's bed and I waited, I waited hours, until I was convinced that the way I had lived my life had meant that they had stopped being real. I laid my head on the pillow and I fell asleep.

· · ·

I woke to a loud bang. It was some time before I remembered where I was and why. Sam had walked in, and had dropped his books in surprise.

"Elisa." He breathed, bending to pick up his precious manuscripts.

"Pardon me. Pardon me." I rushed to help him. "I hope I have not ruined any of the binds."

"It is no matter," he said, looking at me as we both stood up. "Are you well? What has happened?"

"I am well. I am well, Samuel."

He exhaled. "I am glad."

"I am here to discuss something I want to do."

He was surprised. "I will put the pot on the fire."

"I want you to know this isn't about my coming back home or running away with anyone."

He stopped with his hand on his pewter pot. "I understand."

"I want you to help me to buy a house."

He didn't turn around; he stayed crouched by the hearth.

"I have money enough for some of these properties here." I put the piece of paper down on the bed. "I need you, because th'art a man." He still had not moved. "And a friend. I need you to help me purchase it, so that I can start a home. I want it to be an almshouse for women who need shelter, or healing. I want it to have an Infirmary where people pay for treatment and I can teach others how to heal. I was thinking I could see where Sister Jane is, she's the lady who taught me at the Nunnery, and I don't think she had anywhere to go when the Nunnery closed, and — and I was wondering what happened to Joan from the village. Do you know if she is well? Also Isabella —" I was rambling, filling in the silence he was creating. Did he think it a bad idea? Did he think I could not do it? Because I could do it. He was a prick if he thought I cannot do it.

"I know of a place," he said, turning. "'Tis on the road to London, halfway there perhaps. The owner came to the village the other day — he does not want it any more, and is taking a pittance for it. It was his father's home, methinks, and he died of sweating sickness not a week ago. We should go and see it."

"I have these houses here," I said, prodding the piece of paper on the bed.

He perused the parchment, then shook his head. I was about to protest, annoyed, when he said, "Half the price."

"What?"

"The one I mean is half the price and we could get it by tomorrow."

"Jesus," I breathed. Sam's face was a mile away.

"There be a very good apothecary in that village too."

"Tomorrow?" I repeated.

"He wants it gone. Will you stay for another day or two? We can get this done without fuss."

I nodded absent-mindedly, butterflies tickled my skin and insides. I had not expected this. It should not be so easy. My mind was darting this way and that. I might see one of my family if I stayed there another day or two.

Sam passed me some hot water with a bit of ginger in it. It warmed my tummy but did not stem the tingling sensation.

He was pacing, completely taken by my proposition.

"Dost thou think it a good idea, Sam?"

He turned to me, surprised, as if he had not realised I was there. "Elisa. You might have left Christ by the wayside and not even King Henry could afford the indulgence you'd be charged to escape hell, but whenever you do anything, ever since you were a child, whenever you put your mind to something, it comes good. And this idea is my favourite idea."

I grinned. "Good."

"Will you stay at the inn in the village?"

"I am staying here," I said quickly.

"'Tis a good choice." He grabbed me by my waist.

Still, the next day, we managed to leave Grey's Court without having seen my family. I did not want to see them. I especially did not want to see my father. Would he expect a refund? Would he want to know my plans? Would he put a stop to my plans? No. I wanted not to see my family. Yet I felt annoyed as we sat in the carriage, rolling away from Grey's Court. Where were they?

"Be'est thou here to buy an almshouse, Elisa? Or to see thy family? Because you could have paid someone to bring me a letter detailing everything you told me last night."

"I wanted to see you, Sam."

"I hope so," he whispered. "But you can want to see both me and your family."

I did not want to talk about it. I looked down at my lap. I had sold all my finery except for one outfit. One outfit that I had saved for today. For when I was to purchase a house. My headpiece weighed more than my own head did and my thick skirts were too hot for a spring day. For God's sake, my sleeves nearly touched the carriage floor. I could feel my cheeks burn hot as I rearranged my jewelled hood: it was too much. I was overcompensating. I was Alice playing dress ups. Fool, Elisa. I longed for the fine wool I was planning to fashion into simple but long-wearing gowns for my new life as an alms mistress. This was all so *foolish*. I started taking off my rings, I removed my necklace — maybe I could take off the gown and wear merely the kirtle and corset. Sam took my hand, stopping me completely de-robing.

. . .

The house had not been halfway to London. Sam was a liar. It was perhaps only an hour and a half away from Grey's.

"I was wrong." He shrugged, helping me out of the carriage.

"You are trying to get me to live close to you."

"What is your problem being close to me?"

"The almshouse needs to be in reach of the women who need it."

"Lacock is not far, and there is another priory being closed five minutes away by carriage. And you can bring the London women here. Give them some country air. It's only a day's ride."

"A very long days' ride." I corrected, but my anger waned as soon as I saw the building.

The door was a dark blue with white lining. The house was made of red brick and it had several peaked triangle roofs. It was squeezed in between the village baker and the village apothecary.

"You are my sister," he instructed.

"God forgive you, this relationship is not holy."

He brushed past my bust and grinned, amused.

The man let us inside. He was in a rush to get rid of it, speeding us through each room. He lived not there, he said, and had a store in London he needed to go back to, today preferably.

"God's toes, it's perfect," I mumbled to Samuel.

"Will you take it?" The man was actually dancing on his tiptoes.

Sam turned to me. "This home will take about eight women, Elisa. You can bring them here. 'Tis near several closing convents. 'Tis nearer your little brother. Constance cannot be that far away. Neither can your friend, Isabella. And 'tis near to me." He looked desperate. Almost as desperate as twinkle toes.

"But everyone in London. The women I want this for."

"You bring the women who need treatment here. 'Tis a carriage ride away."

The two stupid men were staring at me: they wanted me to make a decision now.

"This is happening too fast. Leave me for a while." I walked outside.

My almshouse. Christ. No. The house. The house was at the top of a hill. It was on the main street in the town. The smell of spring's first flowers was in the air. I missed the country. I just loved it when the air smelt not like piss. But it was too much. It was happening too quickly. I needed more time to figure out the workings of it all. Where would I purchase furniture? Where would I get my herbs? Who would cook? How would I help those with children? Lord, the list was endless.

I turned around, ready to turn back inside.

I ran into someone. I had been staring at the cobbles at my feet, declaring myself mad for even contemplating this venture.

"Forgive me, Madam," I said instinctively. I looked up into the face of the innocent who had crossed my path. I felt a glimmer of recognition. I blinked. "Joan?"

"Lady Knolly."

She had aged. I had been away for just shy of two years but surely this woman had experienced twenty.

"Call me Elisa, please."

This was very well orchestrated. I turned to look at the door of the almshouse. Sam was watching us. The puppet master.

"Are you ... well, Joan?"

Her silver-spangled hair was still long, and it still hung loosely over her shoulders.

"Well enough, my Lady. But we lost John to a bout of the sweating sickness."

"God rest his soul." I crossed myself. "I am so sorry, Joan."

"Thank you, Lady Knolly."

"Elisa." I reminded her. "What have you been doing since his passing?"

Her mouth moved but no words came out. I put a hand on her arm. "It hath been hard as a widow, with my reputation. Though John cast me not out, the town ..."

I embraced her. I held her close to me, as I had wished to do at church so long ago. When I had been forbidden to forgive her.

"Do you live in this village?" We walked back up the hill, hand in hand.

"No, my Lady. I got a letter early this morning. Samuel instructed me to be here."

Scheming man. "Didst he indeed?"

She gave me a watery smile, blushing. "He said you might have a job for me. In an almshouse for women down on their luck? I can still cook a good pie, and I am useful with herbs."

"I doubt it not." A huge rock of emotion sat painfully at the bottom of my throat. "I will certainly be in need of your skills." I tried to swallow tears. "There is a job for you, and a place to stay, if you would like it."

Her lip quivered with emotion. Again, she mouthed silent words. I squeezed her hand, and kissed her fingers. This woman had haunted my dreams, my waking thoughts, since I had seen her outside the Church on that jaded day. Since then I had walked around in a ghostly sheet of my own, but I had got used to my ghost. I had even warmed to the apparition. My nakedness shamed me no more. I looked at Joan and saw myself reflected in her watery eyes. I had completed a circle: I had tied up the frayed ends of my life.

"I do not want to interrupt your meeting, my Lady."

"Nonsense." I made her stand next to me. We faced the two men.

"You are conniving, Samuel, even if it is for the good of others."

He shrugged. "Joan needs a job. I thought you might have one for her."

"What is your decision?" asked the merchant.

I tapped my foot and wrung my hands, watching Sam and the merchant's faces reddening. This was my choice, even if Samuel had pushed his will on me. This was my home. My ambition. My little life.

"I will take it."

The merchant let out a sigh of relief.

Joan clapped her hands together. "Oh bravo. Congratulations!" she whispered under her breath.

I looked to my tutor. "Be'est thou happy, Samuel?"

"Very."

"I as well," I admitted.

"I'm *most* happy," declared the merchant.

I got out my purse.

CHAPTER THIRTY-THREE

Joy's babe was not a good sleeper. Nor was the six-month-old that had arrived with its mother last week. When one woke, it woke the other.

I rushed hurriedly to the Nursery, scooping up baby John and peering into baby Margaret's cot to see if she had been stirred. Success. Still asleep. I jiggled Joy's newborn up and down. He would want feeding, but I could give Joy a few more minutes sleep.

I greeted Joan in the kitchen; her face covered in flour, she waved a doughy hand in greeting.

Then I walked past Alby's room, still bobbing the tiny child against my chest. I could hear Alice talking. I opened the door quietly.

"Morning, Alice," I whispered. "Morning Alb—" A knock from the front of the house interrupted me.

I listened again. Silence. Then, once more, a small knock. "Will you take John?" I passed the baby to Alby and I crept outside into the hallway.

It was coming from the front door.

It must be someone in need in the village. I tiptoed quickly to open it.

No one was there. Instead, a small trunk had been left on the doorstep.

I bent down. It was an expensive chest, engraved with a Lady and a Knight. Inside was a mix of bottles, bunches of herbs, and a very generous purse of coin. I looked up and saw a figure walking quickly down the way.

I went after them. Donations such as these should be recognised.

"My Lady! My Lady?"

She was at the bottom of the hill and I was only halfway down but she turned.

I thought for a moment it was my mother. She dressed much like my mother would. But her hair. It was blonde.

"Constance?" I ran to her. She didn't move; she didn't run from me. "Constance." I was only a foot from her now. It *was* her.

"Elisa." She wasn't smiling. "I shouldn't be here. I just wanted to leave you my donation."

"Constance." Words were not coming to me.

"My husband does not know I am gone. I must return before he wakes." So, her father had finally found someone who would take her perfect hand. I hated him.

"Is your residence near here?"

"It's not too far, but I started walking when it was still dark."

"I want to see you again." I reached for her hand and she let me take it. I rubbed her knuckles gently and she shut her eyes. In pain, I think. "He does not deserve you."

I saw a twinkle of her former self. "No man does." She quipped. "But he has me. So I must return. He's a slugabed, but by the time I am home it will be late morning. I must go Elisa." Reluctantly, I let her go.

"I will be here." I reminded her.

"Nay. You will be here." She touched her heart, and brushed her lips against my cheek. Then she was gone. I watched her disappear. I should've done something else. Said something else. Kissed her. Or taken her inside. I stood staring at the place she had been for some time until I started to grow damp with the morning dew.

I paused briefly outside my front door and looked up at the new engraving, commissioned by the town mayor, who had insisted upon it.

This alms house was established by Samuel Finch for the habitation and relief of eight poore woman, who had been down on their luck.

I dusted off my skirts, picked up the box, and went inside.

ACKNOWLEDGMENTS

To my beta readers, Katy, Raechelle and Cecils, thank you for being the first to witness Elisabeth, and in turn to witness so much of who I am. I am so grateful. To my editor James Read, you held Elisabeth so gently and so intentionally. I am grateful for you seeing her worth and value. To my parents, Kath and Steve, who read this, even the sex bits, and who have never done anything but support me as I committed to my creativity. To Kate, my copyeditor, thank you for dealing with the details and finessing this story with your magic. To Lena, my cover designer, thank you for making it all feel so real. To Seth Godin, Amanda Palmer, and Julia Cameron, thank you for seeing me, despite having never laid eyes on me. To my husband and favourite author, James Winestock, thank you for celebrating me, for believing in me and for doing this journey with me. The life we have created together is filled with magic.

And finally, thank you to my community of artists. It's hard to find the words, but I wouldn't be doing this without you. You gave me space to come home to myself, and to become who I needed to be. It is the greatest gift. I am indebted. Thank you.

ABOUT THE AUTHOR

Amie McNee is an author, speaker and creative coach. Amie studied medieval history at university, focussing specifically on sex culture, sex work and pornography. Alongside her historical fiction, Amie has written several much loved books all of which discuss the realities and magic of leading a creative life.

Amie is known for speaking, teaching and coaching artists all over the world and helping them to achieve their creative dreams. She has been called to create supportive, empowered communities for writers and artists. This is a big, beautiful but oftentimes hard journey, and creatives don't need to do it without support.

You can find Amie on Instagram, Pinterest and your podcast app.